About the Author

Daniel Clarke Smith is a retired physician whose desire to reach people through words has never flagged. He is married with five children and five grandchildren. He and his wife are in the process of migrating from Minnesota to North Carolina where they plan to garden and tend to their six cats. Dan can often be found unleashing energy into striking golf balls into mostly navigable turf grass or simply enjoying the rewards of a life fully lived.

The Chronokine

Daniel Clarke Smith

The Chronokine

Olympia Publishers
London

www.olympiapublishers.com
OLYMPIA PAPERBACK EDITION

Copyright © Daniel Clarke Smith 2023

The right of Daniel Clarke Smith to be identified as author of this work has been asserted in accordance with sections 77 and 78 of the Copyright, Designs and Patents Act 1988.

All Rights Reserved

No reproduction, copy or transmission of this publication may be made without written permission. No paragraph of this publication may be reproduced, copied or transmitted save with the written permission of the publisher, or in accordance with the provisions of the Copyright Act 1956 (as amended).

Any person who commits any unauthorised act in relation to this publication may be liable to criminal prosecution and civil claims for damage.

A CIP catalogue record for this title is available from the British Library.

ISBN: 978-1-80439-085-6

This is a work of fiction.
Names, characters, places and incidents originate from the writer's imagination. Any resemblance to actual persons, living or dead, is purely coincidental.

First Published in 2023

Olympia Publishers
Tallis House
2 Tallis Street
London
EC4Y 0AB

Printed in Great Britain

Dedication

In memory of Robert Fassnacht.

Acknowledgements

For unflagging love and support, my wife, Sheila. For editing and critiquing the work and query letters, Marcia Trahan and Alyssa Matesic.

Part 1: Freshman

Beginnings

The first time I traveled back in time was the spring 1967 before I went to college.

Ever since I was small, my parents found things I could do in the house or yard during the annual ritual, be it raking piles of leaves, sweeping cobwebs in the basement, or cleaning storm windows my dad had taken down. It carried the air of make-work, none of my friends had to do it, and this year I had other things to do with my time: chiefly driving up and down Warrington Avenue looking for girls. I didn't get access to the family Chevy often but I had friends with cars.

At 10 AM on a bright Saturday morning in April my dad banged on my door and announced "Paxton, I need my future college student to help me outside," he said in the tone of voice that brooks no debate.

"I'm not sure I even want to go to college," I said.

"Sure you do. Nobody in our family ever has. I went from the Marines in 1945 to US Steel. You can do better. Besides, your mother wants you to go." He fetched an extension ladder from the garage and leaned it against the back side of the house.

"Get up on the roof," he said.

I muttered a final declaration of opposition under my breath and climbed the ladder. The pitch wasn't steep, but the roof faced north, and the shingles carried the inevitable growth of lichen that hadn't fully shed moisture from a downpour the day before. I wanted to point out that the slippery roof signaled the need for replacement. Factors like his wages as a Pittsburgh steelworker, mortgage payments, and the cost of living meant little to me, full of wisdom gained in after school bull sessions with my peers. No generation had ever been in the position held by ours: on the verge of solving a host of problems facing the world. From poverty to inequality, all that was needed was the willpower. We had everything on our side, including the best music, the best sports, and the best science. Men from the USA would be going to the moon in a few years.

My dad's voice brought me down to earth in a hurry.

"Start at the far end. Get on your knees and clean out the gutter. Drop it, don't toss it. Easier to pick up that way," he said.

I took care not to slip, but my high-top sneakers weren't designed for traction on a frictionless surface. I fought the relentless pull of gravity threatening my balance. Somehow, I traversed the fifty feet to the corner. I looked into the slimy brown sludge and prepared to plunge my hands into it. I needed to get on all fours.

I squatted, prepared to pitch forward on my hands, when my right foot slipped and the rest of me followed.

"Crap!"

My fingers briefly snagged the gutter, barely slowing the descent. My dad shouted something and then my world turned blue.

I don't mean blue like my Levi's or a robin's egg or the sky or the surface of a lake on a windless day. A blue that dazzled and shimmered and pulsated until my eyes hurt. I hung suspended in the glare, longer than the time it takes for a ball hit by Roberto Clemente to climb in a graceful arc above Forbes Field before crashing into the bleacher seats in left.

I should have been on the ground, writhing in pain from a

broken limb, but instead I felt only the awe of witnessing a power greater than any natural force. A blue fog swirled before my eyes. I tried to touch it but failed. I tried to speak but uttered nothing. Was I dead?

Blackness replaced the blue but only for an instant, like a camera shutter. The transition from my rooftop fall was seamless but, in another way, abrupt as a bolt of lightning. I found myself sitting at the kitchen table, a plate of scrambled eggs and toast before me. My dad held the Saturday edition of the *Post-Gazette*. My mom poured him a cup of coffee. The usual Saturday breakfast scene, replayed from an hour before he'd summoned me. The headline read the same: *Greece Declares Martial Law*. And it hit me: I knew what would come out of his mouth, because I'd heard it before. The implication was nuts. I had shifted backwards in time. I knew what was going to happen next. The usual Saturday breakfast scene, replayed from an hour before he'd summoned me. The headline read the same: *Greece Declares Martial Law*.

He's going to talk about tornadoes in the Midwest, something he read in the paper.

"Horrible storms in Illinois. Tornadoes killed a bunch of people," he said. Check.

The Pirates finished their game against the Cubs before that.

"Looks like the Pirates got in their game anyway. They beat the Cubs six one." Check.

My mom wonders why tornadoes are always in the central part of America.

"I never understood why tornadoes always pick on those poor people in the middle of the country," she said. Check! This wasn't a fleeting sense of have lived the scene: I knew exactly what she would say as well as my Dad's reply

"It's due to the convergence of warm, humid air masses from the Gulf of Mexico with cold, dry air moving in from Canada," I said. In fact, I blurted it because I had already heard Dad spend five minutes explaining it to us.

He put down the paper and exchanged looks with Mom. She appeared close to wearing her 'My son is such a smart boy' face while I could tell my dad was startled because I'd taken words right out of his mouth.

"I didn't know you had an interest in meteorology. Just running track, baseball, and the Beatles," he said with a look of mild disapproval.

"I'm trying to widen my horizons for when I start at Blaze in the fall," I said, improvising my answer.

"Well, good for you. When you help me clean the gutters today, you can give me a lecture on the other things you know about," he said.

I couldn't go back on the roof again. Nor could I explain why without sounding crazier than a patient at Mayview State Hospital.

"I had a dizzy spell this morning," I said, looking directly at Mom. I couldn't blurt out that I'd traveled in time. And I knew I didn't want to fall off the roof for real the next time.

She reacted in predictable fashion although I knew she was puzzled. I wasn't one to ever complain of illness. She made me lie down, took my temperature, and placed a call to our family doctor. Dad grumbled about the younger generation not wanting to take chances and went out to work on the gutters alone. Dr. Harris arrived in half an hour, parked his Buick, and ambled to the front door with his black bag in hand.

Dr. Harris was an old school general practitioner. My mother thought he was a genius, but my friends and I thought otherwise.

If I'd been really sick I'd ask to be taken to the University of Pittsburgh medical center. He didn't ask me any questions, just put me through a short routine of physical tasks, blinded me with a penlight, tapped on my knees with a rubber hammer. I maintained an exterior of indifference, but my mind sorted through a limited but frightening number of outcomes, the worst being the conclusion that I was malingering to get out of my chores.

The exam complete, he and Mom stood in the kitchen out of earshot for a summary of his diagnosis and prognosis. She began to cry in the middle of his summary. I felt about her reaction but not enough that I could tell the truth. If I needed a dizzy spell to stay off the roof, so be it. Anyway, she always overreacted to bad news. I wondered sometimes how she got through World War II with my dad serving in the Marine Corps. Dr. Harris patted her on the back and crooked a finger in my direction.

"Paxton, there isn't anything to worry about, as I have tried to explain to your mother. I'm referring you to a neurologist. A nerve doctor."

"You think I'm nuts?"

He smiled and shook his head. "Not the mental part. Brains and nerves. Think of it like one of those big Univac computers and all the tubes and wires it holds. Sometimes there can be a short circuit, and funny things happen. Fixable things."

"Surgery?" said Mom, voice breaking.

Again, the avuncular head shake and smile.

"Medication."

After that my situation eased. Dad had to clean the gutters while I played the sick role for the rest of the weekend, even though it meant I couldn't see my buddies. Mom pressed Dr. Harris for a promise to push the referral as quickly as possible, meaning the following Monday, and he agreed.

The neurologist's office was in downtown Pittsburgh. I got to skip school for a whole day "just in case," according to Mom. The doctor had a thick German accent and made my mom leave the room during the exam and told me funny stories about when he was in high school in Germany, which he explained was called a gymnasium. Just like Dr. Harris, he tapped on my knees with a rubber hammer, made me watch his finger while he moved it around in front of my face, and did some other stuff. Nothing painful. He brought my mom back in the room and told her things weren't abnormal with my exam, but just to be sure, "Let's do some tests." He meant drawing blood and a brain wave test.

His office building connected to the hospital by a tunnel. On the way over, my mind performed more calisthenics on the topic of what would have happened to me if I weren't lucky enough to materialize in the kitchen. What if I had reappeared in the middle of a street in front of a passing car? The seeming randomness of it all scared me.

My mom held the requisition signed by the doctor to give to the technician at the EEG department. I looked at it after she sat down in the waiting area before the tech came out to get me.

Chief complaint: near syncope. Rule out seizure disorder.

I asked the tech what that meant.

"Oh, he thinks you might have epilepsy."

A stunner. People who fell down and twitched, foamed at the mouth, bit their tongues, wet their pants. Sometimes died where they fell. I refused to believe it. Doubt crept into my mind. What made less sense: a time jump or an illness?

The tech was a very pretty girl. Couldn't have been more than five years older than I. Long brown hair tied back in a ponytail. Green eyes that bored into me as she began attaching electrodes to my scalp. My crew cut made that easy. People told me all the time I should grow my hair out, so I'd look like a blond, blue-eyed California surfer dude. Except that I had a typical runner's physique: five-nine and 130 pounds. Girls wouldn't be impressed by what they saw with my shirt off. Still, she smiled at me the whole time, and when she leaned over me, her smock opened enough that her breasts, restrained by the sheerest of fabric, loomed inches away for a full ten seconds.

I wanted to share that part with my best friends, Tim O'Gara and Phil Petroff when I returned to school the next day but I didn't want to divulge the reason for my absence. We'd been tight since grade school, fought imaginary Indians in the woods down by the river, rode our bikes over makeshift jumps, dropped firecrackers onto semis passing underneath an overpass. Anything out of the ordinary, like being epileptic, might jeopardize our fellowship. Or so I believed then.

I just told them I went to the dentist for a toothache

I had another time incident later in the fall when I took the SAT. This time I welcomed it. Not the test, just the do-over. My parents wanted me to go to college. I had a good chance of getting a track scholarship. Nobody in the Knox family had attended college. My dad might have, but World War II got in the way. After the Marine Corps discharged him, he went to work for US Steel.

I had a bad feeling about it from the start. The questions were difficult and there were many I simply had to take a wild guess at solving. I started to breathe fast and I felt like I might faint, On the drive home I felt worse thinking about the stupid test. College didn't seem so important if I had to endure the torture of tests. My head started to hurt, and the shimmering started. Then the fog appeared and I realized I didn't even need to take a blow to the head for the time jumps to happen. When the fog cleared away, I found myself back in the EEG lab.

The same girl was there, told me the same things as before, and bent over me the exact same way. This time I was ready. I beheld the beauty of her boobs for the full ten seconds. Like a jerk, I made a sound. Groaned or sighed. Stupid.

She straightened up, a look of alarm on her face.

"Hope that didn't hurt," she said.

"Not at all. You're very skilled." I felt blood rushing into my face.

"I've been working here for a couple of years. Met some really smart doctors."

"I'm taking the SAT for college admission," I blurted, as if that would make me more attractive to her.

"Those doctors are such dreamboats," she said as she stared at her reflection in a glass case and played with her hair.

She didn't have to add: and you are such a nothing high school senior.

With the EEG behind me I had a week to prepare for the SAT; Not wanting a repeat performance, including the hyperventilation that tripped me back in time, I used every resource I could find at home and the school library to review what I knew was coming. My Mom made it clear she appreciated it with the way she started to preparing my favorite meals. My friends scoffed but left me alone. When it came time for the test, I felt confident. I finished in under the allotted time and the results weeks later made college admission a lock.

In the meantime, I had a follow-up with the neurologist.

"I have good news: it's not epilepsy, exactly."

My mom gasped. She grabbed my hand.

The neurologist continued. "Not normal, either. I don't want to alarm you. But the waves don't exhibit the classic spikes I usually see. There are some unusual excursions that I'm going to show to some specialists at the university. I'll send you a letter with their thoughts later. Paxton, I'm going to prescribe an anticonvulsant for you to take this summer. You'll need a blood test in a couple of weeks to check the level."

"How about another brain wave test?" Thinking of the EEG tech.

"No, we've got all we need to know from the first one."

The pills were big and tasted bad. Made me a little dizzy at first, then I got used to it. I continued to learn about my strange new talent as my final year in high school came to end and in the pre-college summer. I had no episodes during my runs or races, no matter how hard I pushed myself. Then one summer morning I tried to retrieve a piece of bread stuck in the toaster with a table knife. Bad idea. The blade closed a circuit and the resulting electric shock sent me reeling backwards in time to the previous evening and a deadly dull date with the daughter of my Mom's best friends. Her name was Patty and despite knowing her for most of my life I'd never spoken more than a few sentences to her. Adolescence had been unkind to her: she had braces and a poorly controlled case of acne. She played the violin and thought popular music was trash. She planned to attend Duquesne University in Pittsburgh, major in music, and live with her parents. Her younger brother was 12 and supposedly a genius. While waiting for her to get ready I played chess with him and lost in ten moves. He sneered at me, tempting me to smack him good, but didn't. I took Patty to see the Pittsburgh Symphony Orchestra. Twice.

A few weeks after that disaster I went with Tim and Phil to a carnival in a shopping center parking lot. We hoped to meet up with some girls there but they didn't show up. We gorged on corn dogs and cotton candy, then dared each other to ride the Tilt-A-Whirl, a rickety and dangerously assembled ride supervised by a pair of toothless carnies. The machine stayed intact but my stomach rebelled big time, and after a few circuits I started puking my guts out. The ride lasted five minutes but seemed like five hours. As I staggered away, my friends started laughing at me, then the shimmering started and I experienced a brief time trip backwards to the minutes we waited in line for the ride. I ducked out without explanation, earning me more ridicule but atr least I kept the food down.

By then I had come to accept my excursions through time as a normal part of life, one that I had to conceal from the rest of the world. At least until I could find someone to accept me for who I was. My parents were too uptight. I knew from experience that my friends looked at the world from a simple point of view: life should be predictable. Having a friend who tripped through time might be more than they could handle.

Blaze

Freshman orientation week. Blaze College. Rockville, Maryland. My parents drove me from Pittsburgh. Just under 300 miles over the Appalachians. They wanted to return home before nightfall. We'd been there on a gray sleeting day in November for a tour and interview. I'd been recovering from mono and felt crappy. So crappy I felt certain I'd blown the interview.

Today the campus looked amazing from the moment we drove through the gates. Ivy covered buildings of brick and limestone. Metal racks corralled special white bicycles intended for community use. Broad avenues shaded by ancient hardwood trees. In the center of campus, a large commons area crisscrossed by sidewalks and hedges. Groups of ten to twelve students sat in circles on the grass. Freshmen meeting in orientation groups, according to the handbook I'd been studying.

My Dad pulled up in front of my dorm, Carroll Hall. We unloaded and carried my belongings into the ground floor. My room was to the right inside the vestibule and practically underneath a stairwell leading up four flights. I figured I could run the stairs for workouts in bad weather.

I hadn't expected luxury and therefore wasn't surprised to see the room furnished with a double bunkbed, two dressers, two desks and two chairs. The window shades were yellow with age. Pillows and mattresses were clean, but clearly ancient. I heard my Mom gasp at the sight, but my Dad simply said, "A lot better than what I got in boot camp in 1942."

My roommate had preceded me but wasn't in the room. He had brought double the volume of my luggage. His large steamer trunk had a name stenciled in white: Andrew Barrett III. A phonograph with attached stereo speakers sat on one of the desks next to a pile of LP albums. I walked over and checked them out. On top, *Surrealistic Pillow* by Jefferson Airplane.

"I like his taste in music," I said.

"Isn't that group known for using drugs?" said my Mom.

Back then kids hadn't learned how to eye roll.

"Oh Mom, please relax. I'm a runner. Don't smoke or use drugs. Bad for performance. If I don't run, bye-bye scholarship," I said.

"Always a spot for you on the line back at US Steel," said my Dad.

"No thanks. Management, maybe. I think majoring in Economics like we talked about would be a good base."

What I thought, but didn't say, was that I could go anywhere I wanted with that major. I loved my hometown, but I needed to see more of the world than the Allegheny, Monongahela, and Ohio rivers.

"Don't lose your student deferment, whatever you do. Boys are coming back in body bags from Vietnam every week," said my Mom.

"He could do worse than serve his country," said my Dad.

That was about a big an argument as they ever had in front of me. I knew they had their private battles. My Dad had bad sleeping problems. Every night he fell asleep holding a beer bottle. Even though I slept on a different floor, the shouting from his nightmares woke me on average once a week. I know my Mom wanted him to see a counselor for them, but he wouldn't.

That ended the discussion. I promised to write every week,

take my pills on schedule, check in with the college health service, lights out by eleven, no girls in my room, and not to go into Washington unaccompanied. I walked out to the car and hugged them both. My Mom was crying, of course. My Dad had a faraway look in his eyes. I wondered, but didn't ask, if he would do anything different if he had a second chance.

They drove away in the family Ford, the spot immediately taken by a broad, black limousine. A driver in livery got out, walked to the right rear door, and opened it. I waited, expecting the passenger to be dressed in a tuxedo. Instead, out came what I would have called at home a hippie: male, unkempt brown hair hanging below the collar, bell-bottom jeans with both knees ripped open, a brown leather vest atop a blue work shirt, and sandals. He was smoking a cigarette which he proceeded to flick airborne, landing at my feet.

"Oh sorry. I didn't see you standing there," he said. He dismissed the driver with a wave and headed past me to the dorm entrance. I squashed the burning butt and followed a few feet behind, hoping against hope that my suspicions were untrue.

I found him unpacking the trunk in my room.

I offered my hand. "I'm Paxton Knox. Friends call me Pax."

"Hey, Peace. Cool name." He was taller than I, with thick, dark hair and whisker stubble. His features were broad, almost primitive compared to my narrow, birdlike face. Think of Neanderthal man and you get the idea.

"You're Andrew, I take it?" I said.

He nodded. "Nobody calls me that if they're my friend. I go by Bear."

"OK, Bear.

"Want to get high?" He held out a sandwich baggie half filled with crushed green leafy material. I knew what it was.

"Thanks, I'm OK. I need to get out for a run. Missed yesterday and we've got a practice tomorrow for freshman cross country."

"What are you running from?"

"What do you mean?"

"I'm giving you shit, man. But my Dad says people who are always running are trying to escape. They don't try to solve things."

"Where's your Dad right now?"

Bear laughed. "Probably drinking a double martini at the club."

"He wasn't in the car with you?"

"Fuck no. I'm glad he wasn't. Got to use the mini-bar in the back."

Bear rolled a joint, lit it and took a drag, holding the smoke for as long as he could before exhaling the cloud of pungent smoke toward the window.

"You don't smoke. I mean, anything, right?"

"Right."

"That's cool. No pressure." He flopped on a bed and took a few more hits before extinguishing the roach and storing it in the baggie.

I knew kids in high school who smoked pot. It was an amalgam of the newly developing counterculture and kids who were lower middle class and skating on the edge of the underworld. They fought early in life and often, flaunting their broken limbs and stitches as proof of manhood. They sold drugs to the wannabe hippies and found girls who wanted to break free of conventional morality by screwing the bad boys. Occasionally one of the hippie boys objected and found himself on the losing end of a beat down. The hippies were destined to go off to college. The bad boys were looking at jail time or being drafted to go to Vietnam.

"Running is your drug," he said at the ceiling. "Hey, put the record on. The Airplane."

I did, humming while I changed into running shorts and shoes. The song chased me out the door.

I strode across the commons area at an easy pace, letting my legs stretch out with the effort. I hadn't run in two days and I didn't want to lack anything for the first day's practice. I hurdled a hedge and found a sidewalk that passed a long row of dorms.

A voice called out, "Hey, cutie. Want to run my way?" followed by a chorus of giggles. I considered my choices. Do nothing. Say something obnoxious. Wave silently and mysteriously. Other, more raunchy ideas surfaced but I suppressed them. I went with option three. That brought a chorus of boos, convincing me I had done well. Gotten under their skin just a bit.

Four miles later I cruised back into my room. Bear barely started unpacking. The room reeked of smoke, so I opened the window. Bear sat at his desk; attention focused on something in his lap.

"Oh, hey Pax man." His eyes were bloodshot. He grinned.

I approached and he shoved whatever he'd been holding inside the drawer.

"More pot?"

"Nope."

"I don't care, really. But since we're roommates, better not be keeping secrets."

"OK, but you can't tell anyone. I mean, anyone."

"Deal," I said, wondering if I could keep my word.

He opened the drawer and took out a pistol.

"Holy shit," I said.

"I know how to use it," said Bear.

"I hope so." I'd handled .22s before in Boy Scouts. That was it.

"Here, hold it," he said.

It was the kind of handgun detectives seemed to always have in the movies. A short-barreled revolver with a walnut handle and the chrome plated metal parts.

"It's loaded," I said.

"Fucking A. It's a Colt Cobra. Same kind Jack Ruby used to kill Lee Harvey Oswald."

"Wonderful." My sarcasm emerged with a squeak.

"You aren't going to turn me in?"

The unspoken teenager code argued against ever ratting on anyone. Still, this was a huge step beyond tolerating pot, sneaking beer from parents' refrigerators, buying rubbers in hopes of having sex, or keeping a stash of Playboy Magazine under the bed. This was a tool with only one purpose. Killing.

"I recall seeing something in the student handbook about no firearms on campus."

"What of it? Lots of rules in there. It says no alcohol too. No visiting girls' dorms after ten. Keep the door open and three feet on the floor. There are going to be some changes."

"You don't really need a gun to make out with a girl, do you?"

Behind his stoned eyes flickered the steel of a deeper purpose.

"When I buy pot, I go into bad neighborhoods. I carry a lot of money. I kind of stick out like a sore thumb. A white boy. They know why I'm there. There are some who'd just as soon kill me as look at me. I'm in favor of black liberation, but that doesn't matter. It's too late. They've been oppressed so long; all whites are the enemy. So, I need this piece to protect myself."

"Ever have to use it?"

"No. Yes. I pulled it on a dealer who tried to rip me off. Took my money but he had no product. I told him to give it back or I'd shoot, and I wasn't messing around. That was in South Bronx. I never went back. Because he'd be heavy next time."

"Just a thought. Maybe don't buy pot."

"Hah. Someday it will be legal."

I didn't think that was likely, but arguing with a guy holding a loaded gun, especially one who's high, isn't smart. He placed it in my hand. On one level, it resembled nothing more than a precision-made hand tool: dense, cool to the touch, projecting power.

Bear continued, "Prepare for revolution. Black freedom fighters trained in the US military will lead the struggle."

He seemed full of cheap talk. I'd heard plenty during my senior year of high school. Some college kids from Duquesne University came on campus. Said they belonged to Students for a Democratic Society. They preached the revolutionary sermon just like Bear. But they didn't wave guns around.

"Just hide it someplace good. No games. Keep it unloaded unless you intend to shoot somebody." I couldn't believe it. First day of college and my roommate owns a handgun. I started to laugh.

Bear laughed too. When our mood stabilized, we looked for a hiding place, finally decided on a loose ceiling tile above the bunk beds. It was next to the wall and allowed him to put the gun between two wall studs. Replacing the tile concealed it perfectly.

"You're from a rural state. You know guns," said Bear.

"Not really. Pittsburgh isn't a hillbilly kind of place."

"Maybe we can practice together?"

I thought about it. We'd have to go off campus. Way off campus. It might be fun.

"By the way," I said, "where did this come from?"

"My Dad. He has a bunch of guns."

"Isn't he going to miss it?"

"No. He thinks it was stolen from his car. He already reported it to the cops and his insurance company. He's got a permit and everything. He's pretty important."

"I see."

With the gun issue settled, Bear started filling up his half of the common bookshelf. I hadn't brought any books, figuring I'd buy what I needed when classes started. He had a lot of books. Some I'd heard of, others not. The non-fiction ones caught my interest.

Das Kapital, by Karl Marx.

What is to be Done? By Vladimir Lenin

The Red Book of Thoughts of Chairman Mao.

Guerilla Warfare by Che Guevara.

"Quite a library. You actually read those?" I said.

Bear was matter of fact. "Absolutely."

"So, you're a communist, or something?"

"Not, something. Yes, a communist, as most Americans define one. But more accurately, a revolutionary. I believe in the right to establish a true people's government, smash imperialism, colonialism, capitalism, and racism."

I wanted to laugh. The text and the intensity were from a B-movie script. I nodded. He didn't stop.

"Right now, the US is engaged in a war to support a dictatorship and imperialism in Vietnam. I'm opposed to it and will do everything I can to further the revolutionary efforts of the

National Liberation Front."

"The Viet Cong?"

His face flushed. "That's the name the imperialists have made up. It's not accurate."

I looked for a graceful way out. Play dumb. Laugh. It wasn't going to be easy.

"Look Bear. I didn't mean to get into politics on day one. I'm a dumb jock. Not an intellectual. I watch some TV news, read the papers sometimes. That's where I get my information."

He shrugged. "I'll educate you," he said.

I pulled off my sweaty shirt. "I'm going to take a shower now. God, I stink." I grabbed a towel and headed down the hall to the communal bathroom. In my hurry I collided with someone leaving the room next door.

"Excuse me," I said as I bounced into the wall.

"No, excuse me."

He had a British accent and was slenderer than I. Almost tiny. His skin, ebony contrasting with ivory teeth with a midline gap in the lower half. He wore a purple bathrobe with a yellow monogram: "R."

"I'm Pax."

"David. David Rono."

We walked to the bathroom and took adjoining shower stalls. He talked over the hiss of the water about himself. Born in Kenya. In a town northwest of Nairobi. I knew that was the capital, but little else about the country. "Lots of Americans don't," he said.

He won a scholarship to study abroad and picked Blaze over Cambridge. "I hate the English," he said.

"We didn't care much for them either."

He shaved at a mirror next to me, while I examined my

complexion for pimples. "Are you a freshman?" I said.

The bathroom door opened, and Bear brushed past, heading for the urinal.

"Yes, although I've had college level work already."

"What are your plans when you return to Kenya?" I said.

"I don't plan to return."

"What about developing your country?"

"Pax. Whatever do you think would motivate me to return to a country that wants to nationalize industries, in effect throwing out the baby with the bath water? I may hate the English, but capitalism has made it possible for the ex-colonies to get out of poverty. First they must choose."

Bear zipped up and spun around. "Socialism is the solution. Capitalism is exploitation," he said.

David didn't reply. He winked at me.

"What's your major?" said Bear.

"Economics."

Bear shook his head. "Capitalist apologist. I'll lend you some of my books."

David smiled as he rinsed his razor. "Please do. But you must excuse me. I have to dress for a date."

Back in the room I said to Bear: "We've been on campus for a few hours, and he's got a date already?"

"He's a foreign student. Probably older than us. More experienced. I bet he has a huge dick. If you want to meet some chicks, come with me to the SDS orientation."

The meeting took place in the lounge of the student union, attracting the curious as well as the committed. Count me in the first group. My freshman class was the largest in school history, just under a thousand. At least a third of them attended. Students for a Democratic Society had a message for them. Revolution now, not next week.

Bear pulled me in his wake. We found a spot near the front. I tried to strike up a conversation with a dark-haired girl sitting next to me. We exchanged names. Allison from Philadelphia. She wore a cut off T-shirt and no bra above faded, threadbare bell bottoms. Pittsburgh girls didn't look like her.

"Where can I get jeans like that?" I said.

"Any Army-Navy surplus store, if you've got one in your town," she said. I might as well have asked her the difference between a knife and fork for all the distain in her voice.

I tried to lob an insult. "OK to wear military clothing but hate the military?"

"Excuse me," she said moving away.

Allison and Bear stayed after the meeting. I hung around and watched them. She had eyes for only him. Maybe his ideas appealed, but his mature body and the long hair counted for a lot. I was a skinny kid that looked too young to be on campus. The speeches hadn't made much of an impression on me. It wasn't that I thought I knew everything. The people at the meeting had already made up their minds and were ready to act. Their certitude repelled me.

The Grind

By mid-September, the rhythm of college life had settled in. First period Monday, Wednesday, Friday was Astronomy 101, traditionally known as Stars and Mars. It was all freshmen. Tuesday, Thursday, Saturday first hour was Econ 101, another frosh favorite. Nothing second hour.

Also on MWF, Third hour English, Fourth hour, European History

TThS Second hour Introduction to Politics.

Afternoons I ran with the cross-country team.

From the beginning I had problems waking up for my first hour classes. I slept through my alarm at 7:00. I'd skip breakfast and barely make it. Bear didn't help because his classes were all afternoon. My medication had to be the problem.

I stopped taking it.

That solved my oversleeping problem.

It didn't mean all problems.

I barely had contact with Bear. He was sleeping with Allison by now, splitting their time between two dorm rooms. If I was studying in the library late and returned to the dorm after 10 PM. I could expect to encounter a locked door, the smell of pot and noisy lovemaking. The second-floor lounge became my backup bedroom.

"Why don't you turn them in to the RA?" said David.

"Well?" I didn't have a good answer. Maybe I secretly wished I'd connected with Allison and I was the one banging her while Bear stood impatiently in the hall. Maybe I felt the sting of hypocrisy for helping Bear hide his handgun and wanting to bust him for breaking the rules. Rules are rules. I can't pick and choose the ones I want to follow. I sucked it up.

Until the time the library closed, and I needed to study for an Econ quiz. I got back to the dorm around nine and found my door locked. I rattled the knob until Bear answered. A pungent haze surrounded him when he opened the door. I knew what that meant.

"Come on in, man," he said.

"Um, no thanks. I don't smoke."

"You need to lighten up."

"Look, I'll just grab a book and go study in the lounge. The library is going to close, and I really need to get caught up in Econ."

"OK, suit yourself." He wore the smirk of the stoned as I entered. There were three others in the room. A couple on a couch Bear had bought at a yard sale, and Allison on his bed. At that moment envy overtook me. Allison's work shirt was unbuttoned, her left breast exposed. Her face wore the mask of disconnection from the world. Love for Bear or just high? It didn't matter.

"Move along," said Bear from behind me.

Usually I had the lounge to myself. A signup sheet existed, but never used. Parties went off campus. Pirates consumed any food placed in the mini refrigerator. Half the student body owned TVs. The need for a lounge no longer existed. Tonight, though, the place was occupied. A meeting, from the looks of it. Folding chairs arranged in ranks, a chalkboard facing the audience. The quiet hum of conversation ceased before I'd taken two steps into the room.

"Hi," I said, to no one in particular. I held up my book to

explain my purpose.

A girl brushed past me carrying a roll of posters. She and another girl started taping them to the wall. I recognized the faces as they went up. Malcolm X. Stokely Carmichael. Huey Newton. H. Rap Brown.

The seconds ticked by. A radio played in the background. "Ain't No Mountain High Enough."

"I like Marvin Gaye," I said.

Silence.

"I'm not here for the meeting. I'm just going to do a little studying. My roommate has a girlfriend over. You know. Kind of awkward to be around them."

No response.

"The library isn't going to be open much later, or I'd go there."

A voice from the assembled answered: "The student union is open all night. The white student union."

"Yeah, but this is a dorm lounge. Belongs to everyone."

"The Black Student Lounge has priority."

"From?"

"The Dean of students."

"Are you telling me the Dean sanctions a racially segregated lounge?"

"It's not segregated if that's what we want."

By now I'd looked over the room. Thirty-two black students. And me. I thought of Dr. Martin Luther King, whose picture was absent from the gallery of posters. I recalled a conversation I'd had with Mom the previous spring when I told her about a boy who quit the track team rather than run with black athletes.

"He's missing a life lesson," she said.

I braced myself for a lecture.

"We must learn to live together as brothers or perish as fools. A great man said that. Don't forget it."

I walked out of the lounge.

My passion was cross country. Blaze, although a small school, had a tradition of excelling in track and field. Track scholarships equaled those for football. I loved football and baseball but was too small for football and lacked a good arm for baseball. Put me on a track and ask me to run all out for half an hour, and I'd generally win.

I'd train for two or three hours a day. 100 miles a week was the standard because that's what my idols ran. Jim Ryun had set the world record for the mile run that summer. The rest of the time I allotted to attend classes, eat, sleep and study.

The first meet of the year was held on a local golf course. Public, of course. The golfers got banned so we could tear around the place with spiked shoes. Greens became roped off sanctuaries. It seemed like such a waste of space to maintain so many acres for a truly dingy pastime. Golf, I mean. Fifteen other colleges sent teams. In high school the races were three miles; college courses were six, closer to the international distance of ten thousand meters. I harbored a long-term plan: I wanted to run in the Olympics. Mexico City 1968 loomed too near to be realistic. 1972 seemed like a good year for it. Munich, Germany planned to host the games. The Germans were fanatic organizers. Everything would go smoothly.

My nerves didn't get up until the call to the start. A slight breeze cooled us from the north. One hundred fifty runners decked out in school colors, red and white for Blaze. Our conference rival, Sanford, wore all black and lined up next to us on the line. The starting gun cracked, and I went to work, pushing myself to the front group of ten after a quarter mile. The race remained that way for the first of two loops around the course. A pair of Sanford's runners led the way, sharing the pace in a smart show of teamwork. I decided to shake up the pattern. I surged into the lead just before a sharp turn around a small grove of trees. The runners had bunched, and the pack spread out wide just enough for me to launch an attack that propelled me in front by a few strides as we entered the turn. I planned to go on all-out sprint for a hundred yards or so, and then assess the damage I'd caused.

The Sanford guys weren't going to let me go unchallenged. They stayed on my heels and caught me a few strides away from a large oak tree that defined a ninety-degree turn. One of them cut in front of me, the other came alongside on my left. I was boxed unless I could break free from the trap. There wasn't going to be enough room for me to get past on the inside. Going wide would surrender the lead. I made space to pass with my left elbow and heard a grunt. A gap appeared ahead. I surged, only to tangle with the other runner's ankle.

The next two seconds seemed to go by in slow motion. I threw my left arm out for balance and at the same instant, my left shoe spikes snagged on a tree root hidden in the longer grass. I fell, diving headfirst at the oak. I tried and failed to get my hands in front of my face. Too late, I crashed into the tree.

The bitter taste of blood filled my mouth and nose. I fell, galaxies of stars spinning before me until the unmistakable blue cloud eclipsed them and the world as I knew it vanished. The anticipated pain didn't arrive. The air turned into liquid, but I didn't need to breathe. I thrashed in panic until peace replaced fear and my arms propelled me upward, toward a place of greater light. The speed of ascent increased with my confidence. Above me troughs of waves traveled from right to left. They broke and reformed, carrying a train of bubbles behind. I swam closer and entered a vortex that spun me higher until my head emerged into the air. I lingered there for an instant before all traces of blue vanished. I fought to focus. In front of me stood a line of runners snaking to a line of portable toilets. I cursed myself for stopping the medication. A door opened ahead of me and a teammate emerged.

"Hurry up, Pax. Race in five."

I mumbled a reply and stepped into the enclosure. I had a full bladder, even though I'd peed a few minutes before. I jogged to the starting area still reeling from the effects of the concussion. Worse feeling ever.

"Runners, to your marks. Set."

"Take your sweats off, Pax. Are you nuts?"

I'd forgotten.

The rest of the team was staring down the fairway. A yellow flag waved in the distance. I yanked off my sweats and hurled them toward the sideline.

"Set."

On my right, the starter raised his arm.

Bang! One hundred forty-nine runners took off, leaving me in their wake, dumfounded. My plan forgotten, I let the pack get ahead before an adrenaline surge lit my engines.

At the halfway mark I was still 25 yards behind the lead group. They rounded the tree where I had come to grief before and the memory stirred up anger. Bastards. Push me? Not this trip. I attacked the gap between me and the leaders. After the surge I was only ten yards down, but I needed to recover. The course turned into the wind and the leader backed off the pace, hoping to force an aggressive rival to take the lead and break the air resistance. A common tactic and it helped my effort since no one in the first group attacked. I got back five yards. Just under two miles to go. I maintained my pace, recovering with every stride. The last half mile contained the toughest segment before the final straight. A series of turns that descended steeply and then climbed for two hundred yards before breaking out into the flat fairway finish. The crowd would be on its feet, pressing into the barriers, screaming for the favorites.

I flung myself through the downhill curves, surrendering my body to gravity. Then I charged up the next grade, catching the lead Sanford runner at the crest. He was tall with a long stride that ate up distance like a Kentucky thoroughbred at the Derby. But my leg turnover was quicker. I inched past, watching him from the corner of my eye. Hearing his desperate chest heaving to squeeze a few more molecules of air into his blood. It wasn't enough. I surged a final time and broke him, then threw up my arms as I coasted through the tape.

Afterwards, I queried my teammates. "Does my head look OK?"

"What about it?"

"Well," my explanation faltered. They had no idea.

Somebody borrowed a compact mirror from a girl spectator's purse. I held it in front of my face and stared. Nothing but sweaty skin, flecked with pinpoint gobs of mud, flung there by the spikes running in front of me.

Stewart

I thought about starting the medication again. Even though my race concussion benefitted me, I hated the idea of slipping back in time. Maybe it wasn't real anyway. The doctor mentioned something called psychomotor epilepsy. I didn't like the idea of being psycho-anything. I decided to confide in the smartest person I knew: Stewart Lone.

Stewart sat next to me in Stars 101. Seating was alphabetical. Mandatory attendance checked by Astronomy majors. Stewart always arrived before me; always remained after me. He kept his black hair slicked back and wore thick, tortoise shell framed glasses. During lectures he seemed not to pay attention, instead working a slide rule, and writing in a notebook. When he raised his hand to ask a question, all eyes in the room fixed on him.

"I read the textbook last summer," he explained when I asked him about it.

He offered me a doughnut, wrapped in wax paper, and sealed with tape.

"Keeps the freshness in," he explained.

"Thanks," I said.

"My parents send me a dozen a week. I can't eat them all. I can tell you don't need to worry about calories."

He lived in Washington.

"My parents teach at Georgetown University. I could have gone there if I wanted."

"Why not?"

"Wanted to get away from home. My life has been sheltered."

Another student had already told me Stewart had scored a perfect 1600 on the SAT. Doubtless he could have gone anywhere.

"Blaze has a strong physics program without the cutthroat competition at bigger universities," he said.

If he had an opinion on my condition, I was prepared to consider it.

Before class one day I asked him: "What do you think about time travel?"

He turned slowly to look at me. I anticipated a hearty laugh. Instead, he cocked his head sideways and said, "Do you mean an Einstein-Rosen bridge or a Van Stockum cylinder?"

That made my eyes glaze over.

"I have no idea what you just said. I'll try being direct. I think I travel through time. Short trips. Backwards."

He didn't ridicule me. His expression remained deadpan.

"I need to be somewhere after class. Talk to me tonight. I'll be in the lounge of Singleton Hall at six o'clock tonight."

Singleton Hall lay on the other side of the campus. Its cornerstone read 1965, making it the newest dorm at Blaze. Furnishings and décor put Carroll Hall to shame. Except for a lucky few freshman, its inhabitants included seniors and juniors only. Part of the draw was the ability to convert its spacious lounge into a theater. This being a Friday night, the theater was open for business. I had to pay fifty cents to enter. I spotted Stewart alone in the middle of the front row. The crowd was sparse, the cause evident when the lights dimmed.

Fantastic Voyage was a science fiction work about a miniaturized submarine navigating through a stricken man's bloodstream in order to destroy a life-threatening blood clot. Raquel Welch provided the only attraction for me. I wouldn't give it high marks otherwise. I wasn't a sci-fi fan. Not the case for Stewart, whose attention focused on the screen for the entire film.

Afterwards we shared a table in the union and drank cokes.

"Stewart, you are the smartest student in our class. Do you watch science fiction just for entertainment or do you think it could turn out to be real?"

"I'm here talking to you about time travel, aren't I?"

"You don't think I have a brain disease like epilepsy?"

"It's possible. Tell me what happens."

I laid out the progression of events up to that day.

He scribbled notes as I talked. He didn't interrupt. His expression stayed impassive as a sphinx except that his tongue started to stick out of the corner of his mouth five minutes into the story.

"Hmmph," he said. Out came the slide rule. He completed a series of calculations and entered the results below his other notes. He leaned back, surveying everything he'd written, not making eye contact.

"I have epilepsy, right? I should take my medication and shut up," I said.

"Have you ever tried to make this time travel happen?"

"God no. Think I'm nuts?"

"You should."

"Why?"

"If it's merely a brain disease, nothing will happen. If indeed you can synchronize your brain waves with the pulse of the universe, eventually you will gain the skill necessary to jump forward or backward. Like a baby rolling over, then crawling, finally walking."

His acceptance astounded me. I didn't know anything about the pulse of the universe, but I could learn.

"Should I try now? I stopped taking my medication."

"By all means."

I pushed away from the table a few inches, closed my eyes, tried to visualize planets and galaxies rushing around me as I hung suspended light-years away from the earth. With nothing to guide me except Stewart's vague suggestion, I had no clue.

Five minutes later I opened my eyes. Stewart hadn't moved or changed his expression.

"Nothing happened," I said.

He shrugged. "Didn't think so. Anyway, if you had told me it did, I wouldn't have believed you. I'm used to people trying to put things over on me."

I could see that, but I didn't confirm it for Stewart. Besides his coke bottle glasses and lack of grooming, an aroma of over ripe cheese hung around him. He told me his assigned roommate had transferred to another dorm within the first week of classes.

"I didn't know that was possible," I said.

"The feeling was mutual. I like living by myself."

My watch read nine-thirty. I stood up.

"I have Econ tomorrow at eight. I need to study for an Econ quiz," I said.

Stewart didn't take my offered handshake. "Touching people is not my thing. I'm sorry," he said.

"No offense. When can I talk to you again?"

"I'll be at the computer center all day tomorrow working on a project. Drop in any time," he said.

Econ class behind me, I walked to the Math building along a

winding boulevard under the canopy of hardwoods changing to fall colors. After a cool start, the air warmed to perfect shirtsleeve weather. Nice weather meant keggers before and after the football game, girls in skimpy T shirts walking in groups trying to be noticed but not bothered, and political demonstrations.

A semi-circle of students blocked the front entrance to the Math building. A hundred or more. Most carried signs. All chanted slogans.

"Get the war off campus."

"If you believe war is good business, invest your sons."

"Boycott the war mongers."

In the forefront stood Professor Saul Stone, my Introduction to Politics teacher and my academic advisor for the year. To say he was popular was an understatement. He held rock star status. I enjoyed his class. An appointment with him was sure to be interrupted by phone calls and drop-in visits by past and present students. He had an air of mischief surrounding him, a look in his eyes that suggested he was having more fun with the process than people like Bear.

"Hi Pax," he said. Always good with names.

"Saul." He preferred to be called by his first name.

"Going to crash our picket line?" He made a move to put me in a headlock like the former wrestler he in fact was, then laughed and released me.

"Well, no. I'm meeting a friend here. Another student. He works in the computer center and he's helping me solve a problem."

"Don't mind us. This is just a little guerilla theater to get the students motivated about the war. The U.S. Army has a contract with the math department to work on the logistics of delivering groceries to their stateside bases. I guess computers can really simplify things."

"Not a project about the war?"

He laughed. "No, but nobody has to know, do they? It makes for a nice two-minute story on the six o'clock news, people then take the trouble to learn more about the war and things they can do to protest."

That relieved me. I recognized a couple of the pickets as friends of Bear. Not current students. Dropouts with self-professed revolutionary goals. Everyone else seemed to be there for a good time, an alternative to watching the football team lose to Sanford.

"I can go in?"

Saul nodded and pointed left. "Use the side entrance. There is a film crew coming and I want the picket line to be solid, not porous. You dig?"

I took the long way, keeping my distance from the group as fresh participants arrived to swell the ranks. A frosted glass door with "Computer Center" stenciled in black led to my destination. The computer filled half the room. A background hum suggested the inside of a giant beehive. Cool dry breezes straightened yarn strands tied on four window air conditioners positioned to counter the heat released by thousands of vacuum tubes. Large rolls of recording tape spun in a herky-jerky fashion behind numerous ports. A row of terminals sat at the base, each one a station with a keyboard and slots holding punch cards whose simple patterns sent instructions to the memory.

Stewart sat at one of the stations, not noticing me at first. I almost grabbed his shoulder, then recalled his aversion to touch. I leaned into his field of vision.

"Hi Pax. Is it time?"

I looked around. No clocks in an advanced computer facility.

"Time to continue our talk about my time travel."

"I've given it more thought" he said. He left the terminal and we sat at a nearby table. He scribbled on a pad. A line of circles with two-way arrows connecting each to its neighbor appeared. Next, he wrote a long equation filled with lower case Greek letters and upper-case English ones.

"Perfect. That chicken scratching reminds me why I hate math," I said.

"Don't be sarcastic. It's for me, not you. I'll explain it in simple words."

"Go."

"Each circle represents individual consciousness at a given instant in time, starting with birth, ending with death. Linear progression, one direction. Entropy dictates that."

"What's entropy?"

"I feel like I'm explaining something to a toddler," he said.

"Humor me, OK?"

"Entropy in simple terms is the amount of disorder in a system. It determines the direction of time. Takes a lot of energy to make it go backward. To make it go forward would release a lot of energy. Boom. Not so good. But in a four-dimensional universe, consciousness could shift into parallel realities and jump ahead or back in the timeline without that happening in the traveler's frame of reference."

According to Stewart the spikes in my EEG represented opportunities for the short circuit to occur. Either naturally or by manipulation.

"You mean I can learn to regulate the spikes, so I make a jump in time?"

"Or it could be done externally. Far more practical. I don't think your body can generate enough of a potential difference to move you far. You seem capable only to go retrograde, however, and I find that intriguing."

He spent a few more minutes on the equation, succeeding in increasing my confusion.

"Enough of the math. What now?" I said.

"Take your medicine, forget about it. Alternately, try to explain it to conventional scientists and they'll put you in the nuthouse. And what I'd recommend, get access to medical equipment that can spark your brain sufficiently to effect the time jump and make history."

"Spark my brain? That sounds like shock therapy?"

I had heard all I needed. English class first assignment of the semester: One Flew Over Cuckoo's Nest. The main character gets shock treatments and finally, a lobotomy.

"It's not what you think," said Stewart.

"No, it's worse."

"Worse than your brain shocking itself with no warning?"

"What are you talking about?"

"That's all epilepsy, or seizures, or whatever the doctors call them are doing. That's why they put you on drugs."

"The diphenwhatchemacallit."

"Diphenylhydantoin. Dilantin is the trade name."

"I hate it. Makes me dopey. Can't think straight."

"Fine. I'm not telling you what to do. You're old enough to go to Vietnam and kill people. You ought to be old enough to decide what medicine to take. Just be aware you're making a tradeoff. And shock therapy isn't so bad, by the way."

"I suppose you know because you read so much.,"

"I know because doctors used it on me two years ago. I was all set to kill myself. After treatment I got better."

Grounded

Monday, I didn't feel very energetic at cross country practice. No appetite for dinner. Curled up in a study carrel in the library and tried to concentrate on my English assignment: *Invisible Man* by Ralph Ellison. I hoped it might set my mind right about race relations. Gave me plenty to think about, but I had more questions than answers. After an hour I stopped reading. Sitting all scrunched up gave me a stitch in my side. Annoyed, I walked a few laps around the library and the pain got worse. I headed back to the dorm. Still not hungry but my inner Mom told me I ought to eat something. I ordered a burger and fries at the Union grill. It looked good until I got close and could smell the odor of cooked beef and ancient fry grease. Not pleasant. I ate half of it anyway until I got a strong sense of satiety, like I'd wolfed a plate of pancakes and tried to run an all-out mile.

I made it as far as the hallway in front of my room. David was returning from somewhere with his girlfriend Missy. He hadn't had a chance to say more than "Hello," when I covered my mouth and puked. Then I fell to my knees and couldn't stop. This wasn't a gentle heave-ho from my stomach. It was a vile, unrelenting river of bilious fluid, mixed with the undigested burger and fries and something from breakfast as well. My diaphragm kept cramping and I kept on puking until my stomach hit "Empty." The stitch in my side had become a shark bite, white hot and worsening. I rolled on my back and lay still. Any motion intensified the pain. Sweat trickled into my eyes.

Missy got a wet washcloth and wiped my forehead while David went to the phone. In due course a team of two white coated attendants arrived, tossed me on a gurney and rolled me outside to a waiting ambulance. I felt every bump along the way, clenching my fists to keep from screaming. We took off with sirens blaring. One part of me thought the ambulance ride was cool, the other part wished I were dead already.

They didn't keep me waiting in the emergency room. Took me right back to a cubicle where a bored-looking intern asked me a laundry list of questions and then pushed down ridiculously hard into my right lower abdomen before letting go without warning. That made me scream. And say all the swear words I knew at the time.

"Acute appendicitis," he said to the nurse standing by the bedside. Like I wasn't there. Shouldn't he be telling me the diagnosis?

"I'll call the OR and have them page the on-call surgeon," she said.

An orderly wheeled me back into a hallway and into the lab. I read his name tag upside down. Calvin. He had white hair and leathery brown skin. "Tell me what's going to happen?"

Calvin smiled and lit a cigarette. I focused on it bouncing up and down as he talked.

"Son, you don't need to worry about a thing. They going to operate on you and fix you up good."

"God, I hope so. This hurts like a mother." I started crying.

"Don't be upset," said Calvin. He patted my head. He stepped out of the room and I heard him talking. A nurse appeared and gave me a shot in the butt. In a few minutes, a pleasant haze settled over me. I could still feel the pain, but I no longer cared. The last thing I remembered was Cal's beneficent face smiling at me from above, still smoking the cigarette.

Six weeks off running. I couldn't believe it. Goodbye cross-country season. I spent two weeks back home. My professors mailed me study questions and I did my best to keep up with the assignments. My high school friends Tim and Phil stopped by a lot. They weren't in college. We took a ride one day in Phil's car.

"The draft is breathing down my neck," said Phil.

"Get married then," said Tim.

Phil's girlfriend Patty wasn't a prize. They'd been dating for two years. That amounted to being engaged in our circle. Next stage turned into marriage for most people. I didn't think Phil was ready. He liked to party. He and Patty did it in the back of his car mainly. She figured that kept him tied to her. I know he saw girls on the side. Her family was Catholic, his Methodist. Another obstacle.

"The war will be over in a year," I said, parroting what I heard on TV.

"Not what Tommy Henderson says."

"What?"

"His brother's in the Marines over there. Place called Con Tien. It's brutal. Guys get killed all the time."

"Wasn't your Dad in the Marines?" said Tim.

"Yeah. In the Pacific. He doesn't talk about it."

Tim and Phil exchanged knowing looks.

They dropped me at home where my Dad sat on the front porch. It was Indian summer, with the leaves all fallen and a clear blue sky and bright sunshine. He took long sips of beer.

"Hi Dad," I said.

He had the faraway look again.

"What kind of a car is that?" he said.

"Datsun. It's Japanese."

"I know."

"Gets good gas mileage," I said.

"I fought the Japs on Peleliu. I'll never buy anything made in Japan," he said.

I returned to Blaze feeling good but not cleared to compete. A good time to direct my energy in class. To help concentrate, I skipped my medication. Bear continued to monopolize our room. Allison moved in. She shared the closet, Bear's bed, and the dorm bathroom. My presence didn't bother her. Not much did, given the pot she smoked. I got used to seeing her next to naked.

"It's the future. Communal living," said Bear.

That attitude took a hit the day that one of the two black students on the floor stood and stared at Allison when she emerged from the shower. He may have said something as well. All I knew was that she returned to the room in tears. Next thing I knew, Bear removed the ceiling tile that concealed his Cobra.

I was moving faster now, but not enough to block him from going out the door. I ran after him, Allison screaming at my heels. He covered the fifty feet to the bathroom before I'd gotten halfway there. I flew through the door in time to hear him yelling "I'll kill you, nigger."

I tackled him, not thinking of my own safety. Bear fell over my back and I wrestled away the gun. The dorm RA, a usually jolly senior who played offensive tackle for the football team, arrived and with his help we subdued Bear.

In due course the cops arrived. First thing they did was check the Cobra.

"Not loaded," said the ranking officer.

That didn't make much difference to anyone. The cops

created a path through the angry crowd gathered in the street. Bad news always travels fast. Bear went in the police car, sparing him the challenge of running the gauntlet. Allison, the RA, and I had to pass through the crowd. The sentiments were angry and directed at us as the personification of every injustice suffered by blacks in American history. Behind the leading edge of the mob a bunch of SDS types gathered, adding their voices to the din. I don't think they realized the cops had Bear in custody. The leader of the Black Student Society recognized me from our standoff in the lounge, pointed me out, and the crowd surged to capture me.

"Motherfucking honky!"

"We'll shoot your sorry ass!"

"Klan asshole!"

They picked me up bodily. Not difficult since I weighed 130 pounds. I saw the cops watching from behind the doors, hoped that they would burst out and carry out some police brutality on the mob. To my horror, they did nothing. The crowd dragged me farther away. It was all I could do to protect my head from bouncing along the pavement.

I'm dead. Or soon will be. What an injustice. What irony. I hope my parents understand I tried to do the right thing. I hope the end doesn't hurt too much.

One desperate thought pierced my consciousness. I could escape. Not with brute force, but mental power. Stewart had made the offhand comment I could shock myself. With nothing to guide me I focused on the moment I realized my Dad was so broken, he hated the Japs years after the battle. I could see his face, drawn and life-weary, smell his beery breath, hold the hands that shook every waking minute. I needed to send the needed spark through my brain before anything worse happened.

I'm coming to you Dad. I can't cure you, but I can help.

Flashes of light arced in my peripheral vision. White hot at first, then cooling to an iridescent blue which advanced like a tide, constricting what I could see. It began to shimmer and created spiral patterns that broke up the remaining picture of the environment. The crowd noise receded, replaced by a monotone hum and the cool fog of unawareness swept through me. I felt at peace before forcing my consciousness to refocus. I wanted to reach Dad. Humming gave way to silence which in turn became a chorus of crickets and I found myself on my front porch, watching my Dad stumble into the house. I found words where none had been before.

"Dad, wait."

He stopped, slowly turned.

"What do you want to tell me?" he said.

I wanted to cross the void between us. Only a few feet of porch, but a vast chasm in terms of life experience. I held his hands. I wanted him to see what I saw. Time isn't immutable.

"What you experienced is unspeakable. No one can make it disappear. But it doesn't need to define who you are. You can beat it. Not by fighting it but by recognizing emotions can work for good and evil. Put the good side to work for you."

He didn't move. He smiled ever so faintly. Held out his arms and we hugged each other.

"God, I'll surely try, Pax," he said.

Unlike my other experiences, I didn't remain in the new frame of reference for long. Perhaps I lacked the talent to direct the time flow for long. An abrupt transition occurred, like dreaming I've stepped in a hole and woken in a panic. Alone in my room, sweating profusely. No sign of Bear. No idea what day in which I'd landed. I stumbled into the hallway, accosted the first person I saw and asked what day it was.

"What kind of acid did you take man?"

"Just tell me." I didn't care what he thought.

"Halloween. No more treats for you," he laughed.

A calm settled me. November first was the day Bear used the gun. I had time to intervene.

I thought about throwing it into the Potomac, but then he'd miss it. God only knew what he'd do then. Maybe I could talk some sense into him. I found another place to hide the Cobra. The next day I made a point to be absent from the room before Allison took her shower. The lack of a handgun only delayed his eruption by a few seconds. He lost his temper and got a swift ass-kicking for his trouble.

Two days later I showed him the ceiling tile on the other side of the room where I'd put the Cobra. If I expected gratitude, I was a bad judge of character. He cursed me as if I'd taken away a precious heirloom. As a precaution, I'd put the ammo in my desk. He pointed it at me for a second before reason at last descended into his lizard brain.

"You should thank me, Bear. If I hadn't changed the hiding place, you might have shot that kid. He might have taken it from you and used it."

"Seems weird you did that. No reason."

"Call it freshman intuition."

"Whatever."

So much for charity. A few days later he told me he wanted me out for good. Allison didn't trust me. I was a reactionary, in the terms of the Movement. Important actions by SDS could be compromised if the wrong people knew about them. I wasn't going to dispute the charge. I wanted no more late-night talks fueled with pot and focused on revolution. Bear and Allison's sex show held no interest either.

The next day I moved in with Stewart. The King of clutter. He'd cleared out space in his bookshelf, already packed with texts on quantum physics, advanced calculus, computer coding. Plus, a vast collection of paperback science fiction novels. Walls populated with posters of Einstein, Newton, Galileo, and a bunch I didn't recognize. His bed covered not by a comforter but dozens of magazines. Nothing interesting like National Geographic, Time, Life, or Playboy. Instead, Popular Electronics, Analog, and Amazing Stories.

A device resembling the college computer terminals sat on his desk. A keyboard, a small television screen perched on top and a slot for who knew what? He explained it was a prototype for a semi-portable computing device.

"Good luck with that," I said. The college computer was immense. To improve power would require a machine the size of a house.

A plastic cube rested on his desk. At first, I assumed it was a colorful paperweight. Two by two inches composed of smaller cubes of red, white, green, orange, yellow, and blue that rotated on internal axes. I picked it up and spun the cubes. My non-math brain guessed there had to be close to a million different combinations. I said it out loud.

"Three million, six-hundred seventy-four thousand, one-hundred and sixty, in fact," he said.

"What do you call it?"

"A three-dimensional puzzle."

"That's pretty boring. Who would want to play with it? Looks too complex for children."

He sighed. "I suppose you're right. Just a stupid idea."

The next day I went to the library after breakfast and stayed past lunchtime. Back in the room Stewart had left me a note. *If you're up by three, come over to the Math building. There is someone who wants to meet you.*

Indian summer had ended, replaced by seasonally cold air. I pulled a hooded sweatshirt over my shirt and jogged to meet Stewart. As I approached, the unmistakable sounds of a demonstration filled the air. A march on the Pentagon a few days before attracted many Blaze students. The organizers had predicted the mass protest would levitate the building into outer space. That didn't happen. The US Army chased off the protestors and the war dragged on. A handful of students and faculty from Blaze had gotten arrested. They were campus heroes. The campus demonstrations at the math building gained more participants. According to Stewart college employees there had requested police protection.

On my arrival the demonstration raged at full strength. I took a spot behind a barricade next to a cop. I wanted to enter but I didn't have my student ID. Only authorized people allowed inside.

The jeering and sloganeering echoed off the walls.

"One, two, three, four, we don't want your fucking war."

"Vietnam for the Vietnamese."

"Draft beer, not students!" A catchy slogan but it lacked substance. Like a lot of kids, I wished the war would just go away.

I'd been waiting fifteen minutes when Stewart walked out, flanked by a girl wearing a white nurse's uniform and cap. Blaze ran a nursing degree program. But why was she here?

Stewart kept his distance from her, as he would have with anyone, but they appeared to be leaving together. The chanting volume doubled as they approached the barricade. Still, the crowd seemed no more dangerous than spectators at a football game. Intense but mindful of boundaries. Stewart waved to me.

Everything changed in the next instant. A dark sphere arced overhead from the rear of the crowd. Someone screamed. It followed the perfect trajectory for maximum mayhem, hit the nurse flush in the face, drenching her in red liquid. Stewart didn't escape the splash either.

She dropped to her knees and I yelled. The mob reacted with a ferocious cheer. A touchdown explosion. I ran around the sawhorse, past the cop who had spun around but hadn't done anything else. The nurse sobbed. Stewart stared at the gooey red mess on his clothes, tried in vain to wipe it off. Two demonstrators squirted from near the back of the crowd, heading toward a grove of trees. Maybe I could catch them with an all-out sprint, but the crowd closed ranks and pushed me back.

"Did you see them?" I yelled at the cop.

He looked sheepish. "What could I do? There's only one of me."

Stewart was wiping his glasses.

"It's only paint," he said.

A student walked up close and took some flash photos of the three of us. The mob chanted. "Hey, hey, ho, ho. Bomber research has to go."

A strident girl rushed at us. "Fake blood on you. Real blood of Vietnamese freedom fighters."

I shoved the photographer and he bounced to the ground.

"Pure coincidence you just happened to be here for the paint balloon," I said.

"Back off, fascist. First Amendment of the Constitution. Free speech."

"What? Attacking another student is free speech?"

"Reporting about it. I work for the campus press." He whipped out a laminated card and I threw it back.

"Who tipped you off? Because you clearly were in on it. That isn't reporting. It's propaganda."

The nurse turned to me. "It's OK. I'm not hurt."

In that moment I forgot about the photographer, the shrieking harridan, the belligerent crowd, the paint throwers. Beauty transcended the vandal's attack. Somehow the random splatter of color merged with her facial structure to produce a compelling living sculpture. I'd never seen anyone that stunning.

"You sure? Because I can catch those jerks and make them feel sorry they were ever born."

"I know. Please don't leave when we've only just met. Stewart promised he'd introduce us."

Stewart finished wiping his face. "Pax Knox, Eve Calhoun. There, I did it."

"Stewart, why have you been hiding her?" I said.

"I'm teaching her about computers."

"Computers will revolutionize medical care," she said.

"For a girl, she's mighty smart," he said.

"For a geek, you have a nice personality," she said, punching his shoulder.

He adjusted her glasses and smiled. For once he didn't shy from the contact. "I've done my duty. Introduced you. Now I'll go," he said.

The demonstrators had retreated enough for him to pass through the crowd, which parted like the Red Sea for Moses.

"Can I walk you home?" I said.

"I live off campus. About half a mile."

Off campus! Only seniors were exempt from dorms.

"Must be nice," I said.

"In some ways. I'm farther from campus life."

We walked side by side, making small talk. She had long hair worn in a bun under her cap. What wasn't paint covered looked honey blonde. Her physique ran to the trim side but not frail. She made emphatic gestures when she spoke of things she cared about. When she looked in my direction her gaze found my eyes every time, never looked past me. Her accent didn't strike me as down-home southern.

"It's not. I'm from the Low Country, and we speak differently from the girls up in Columbia, for example. You wouldn't confuse us with girls from Georgia or Alabama either."

"Are you going to go back after you graduate?"

"That's hard to say. My parents, of course, would like that. Get a job, get married, have a family."

"You've got other plans?"

"No, just want maybe to break the mold. Start living a modern life."

"What's modern to you? Are you stuck in *Gone with the Wind?*" Her chuckle at my question left me embarrassed but in a good way. She wasn't putting me down. My take on the universe flowed directly from what I saw at home. Clearly her views soared beyond boundaries of my upbringing.

"Probably not any more than you. Stewart told me you're from Pittsburgh, your father is a steelworker and your mother stayed home to raise you. Doesn't have an outside job."

"She volunteers," I offered in defense.

"Nothing wrong with that. I respect her choice. I bet she gave up a lot."

"She would have gone to college, but the war changed that. Dad joined the Marines and she married him so they could be together. I'm the first in my family to go to college."

"No siblings?"

"My birth got complicated. She needed a Caesarian section and bled so badly they had to remove her womb. I became her top priority."

The houses bordering the campus belonged mainly to professors and the professionals of Rockville. Their immaculate lawns projected a sense of peace and prosperity. We meandered under a canopy of old growth trees, blue sky peeking through the gaps made by fallen leaves. A gentle breeze overhead rustled the survivors. Surrounded by so much beauty I couldn't imagine the specter of war threatening it.

"Here we are," she said.

The modest two-story brick apartment blended well with its surroundings. A creek ran behind it. One of my favorite running loops followed a trail along its banks. She checked her mail on the way in and led me up a flight of stairs to the rear apartment.

"The landlady teaches at Blaze. She's on sabbatical this semester so I've been caretaking the place."

I kept standing until she invited me to sit at the kitchen table. She told me to help myself if I was hungry. I should have been. Nothing since breakfast, but I couldn't think of anything except her beauty and how cool that she'd invited me. She lit a candle.

"Lavender," she said. The small kitchen was efficiently designed with clean lines created by a granite counter and fine-grained hardwood cabinets. A bay window with comfy cushions provided sleeping quarters for a dark gray cat. I approached and it opened its eyes for an instant, assessed my threat potential. then went back to sleep.

Eve excused herself and disappeared into her bedroom, the door decorated with Andy Warhol's Love poster. I opened the fridge, picked out a Coke to sip on while I waited for her, and explored. There was a small TV in the living area and a small but powerful stereo component system with a modern turntable. At least a hundred record albums stacked on edge next to it. The Beatles' Revolver lay on the console.

I could hear the shower running. She stood one door and a shower curtain away from me, naked and soapy in my mind's eye. Common sense told me she was over twenty-one and probably seeing somebody. She'd learned computers from my friend Stewart and to reward me for my chivalry at the demonstration, let me walk her home. That was as far as it would go. I'd finish the Coke; she'd thank me for standing up to the demonstrators and we'd head back to our respective lives.

I treated myself to a song. Something to remember the afternoon by. Couldn't go wrong with the Beatles. I put on *Revolver* and selected my favorite track: *Got to Get You into My Life*, then settled on the couch.

"Nice," she said from the doorway.

She wore a white terrycloth robe and a blue towel on her head like a turban.

"All the paint came out," she said. Was that disappointment in her voice?

"I sort of miss the red mask," I said.

"Maybe I can wear one for Halloween," she said, walking to the couch.

I started to stand but she held up a hand to halt me and sat next to me. She smelled like honey. The fragrance mixed well with the lavender. I took a tentative sniff, smiled in what I hoped signaled appreciation.

"You like it? Body wash. Clover honey."

She leaned against me and my senses began to blur. Her face was inches away. Her lips parted. We kissed, long and fully. The robe didn't conceal much as we stood, slowly rocking, while more of the Beatles provided a soundtrack.

She pushed away, gently.

"I like you a lot," she said.

"What now?" I said.

"You want the world and I want you to have it. I'm not like a lot of the girls you've been meeting. Chase me. Woo me. I'll be worth it. I don't come cheap or easy."

"I want to keep seeing you."

"How does Saturday night sound?"

"Seven?"

"Let's make it eight. I don't get off my shift until six and I want to look nice for you."

The Date

The wardrobe available to me consisted of a sweater my Mom knitted the previous winter, brown corduroy slacks that carried a sheen from cycles through the family Maytag, and brown wingtips I wore rarely, if ever. I asked Stewart to critique my fashion quotient and all I got was a blank stare.

"I wear Hush Puppies and a plaid sport coat over a T shirt everywhere," he said with a shrug. "Ask the RA. He's a senior and goes on lots of dates."

I did and got plenty of advice I couldn't afford. Robert the RA lived in the Chestnut Hill area of Philadelphia and his father was a banker. One of his casual outfits would have set me back a couple of hundred.

If I hadn't waited until Saturday morning, I might have had more time to cobble something together. Desperate, I returned to my old dorm and found David.

"You're experienced. What should I wear?"

I showed him my selection. He frowned.

"Pax, my friend, do you want to make a good impression on this girl?"

"I will die if I don't."

"Come over here." He pulled me by the arm to his closet. It had no free space for anything. He reached into it and extracted a shirt, slacks, tie, shoes, and matching Harris tweed.

"What size shoe do you wear?" he said.

"Nine."

"Excellent, so do I. We're about the same build, so everything else works. You need your own underwear and socks. Don't wear white. Black to work with the shoes. Keep them as long as you want. As you see, I don't lack for garments."

I broke into my emergency money stash: a hundred dollars in Traveler's checks my parents gave me when they brought me to college. I knew they weren't intending it for my social life.

"Easier to ask for forgiveness than permission," said Stewart.

I arrived at Eve's apartment fifteen minutes early, killed time by reviewing the list of restaurants in Washington that Robert provided. I'd never heard of any. I asked for inexpensive establishments and he gave me a withering look.

The nearest one to Rockville was called Benny's and he said it was the cheapest. Even the wine list was affordable, according to him. It lay just inside the Washington/Maryland border, not too far from the National Cathedral.

Eve opened her door at my first knock and I'm sure I looked like a blathering fool with my jaw slack, practically drooling at her beauty. Girls at my high school wore makeup but applied it clumsily and to excess. Eve used it to accentuate her exquisite facial structure and the color of her eyes. Her hair, worn long, wasn't the flaxen hippie chick look I'd seen in the SDS rally girls. The waves were added but subtle enough to look provided by nature. She wore a black dress with a neckline low enough to suggest but not reveal, and a gold choker necklace that a blue-collar kid like me recognized as coming from a background I'd not known growing up.

"You're too good for me," I said.

She stepped up and kissed me.

"Nonsense. I love your taste in clothes. It's a welcome

surprise."

I went to call a cab, but she stopped me.

"I borrowed a car from a friend. You don't mind if I drive, do you?"

Saving the cab fare meant that my parents' hundred plus my wallet's meager contents got us a fine meal plus tip. We lingered over coffee thanks to an indulgent waitress who once had been, in her words, young and foolish.

"I can tell things about people," she said as she cleared the table.

"What can you tell about us?" said Eve.

"You're meant for each other. Don't put off what your hearts are telling you."

Back in her apartment, Eve put on a record.

"Something to remember the evening by," she said.

Frankie Valli sang Can't Take My Eyes Off of You.

We slowed danced to it. As it ended, we clung together.

"You are the most beautiful girl I've ever seen," I managed to croak.

"Really?" She leaned closer. Her head tilted right. Mine left. Our lips met.

I reached behind her waist and pulled her closer. Our gazes locked. I kissed her, softly at first, then with aggression. She kissed me back, hard, then she pulled back, but only to step out of her dress. I stood still, transfixed, as she didn't stop there, but unhooked her bra and let it fall. Her breasts came free, and I closed a hand around one, felt its nipple hardening as I rubbed it.

After a long minute she stood and walked backwards, dragging me with her, opened the bedroom door and pulled us onto her bed. We kissed more. She rolled over and sat back on her haunches, then kicked off her panties and helped me out my clothes. Ripped them off, to be accurate. I lay still, frozen with amazement at the geography of her nakedness: twin alabaster peaks swaying before me, unrestrained; the flat plain of her abdomen leading to the wetlands between her thighs. She saw me staring and laughed, grabbed my hand, and held it against her crotch. I probed her and she arched her back, moaning.

My instincts took over. We rolled like a pair of feral cats, taking turns on top, aggressor, then victim. I followed her lead and she straddled me.

"I want you this way, babe," she said.

I nodded. Marveled at the dexterity of her touch and how neatly our bodies fit, gliding together to form a single entity, working but not with exertion, to a common goal, which she reached moments before me, exploding inside and crying out with the absolute joy of how what had been minutes before two separate people were now united and inseparable.

We lay side by side, spent, for a few minutes before I broke the silence.

"If this were the movies, we'd be smoking a cigarette," I said.

She plucked an imaginary smoke from my lips and flicked it away.

"You never did this before," she said. Not a question.

"Not even in my dreams. My friends back home do it in cars."

I propped myself on my elbow. She'd pulled up the sheet, saw me staring and let it drop for a second.

"The windows are open. It's chilly. But don't let it stop you from looking," she said. Twenty-four hours before, the idea of me naked with a girl was the height of absurdity.

"I have a confession to make," she said.

My heart flip flopped. Oh no. Here comes something.

"Don't worry, I'm not going to blind-side you," she said.

"Whew." I pretended to wipe sweat from my brow.

"You won't remember, because you were out cold."

"At the cross-country race? Did you see me hit my head?" I said.

"No. I know nothing about that. I helped with your appendectomy."

"Really?"

"Not with the operating part. I prepped you. When the doctor scrubs his hands and puts on his gown somebody must clean the area where he operates. Anti-bacterial soap and iodine. Then shave you all the way down to your balls. Remember waking up and looking at yourself? See any pubic hair?"

"No."

"I hope you were happy with my work. No cuts or abrasions?"

"None."

She giggled and dropped her sheet, let it stay down this time. She cupped her breasts and squeezed. I got aroused, she pulled my sheet away and raised her arms heavenward.

"My God, you have the best dick I've ever seen. I wanted you so badly that day. It was all I could do to not have an orgasm on the spot."

This was news I'd never suspected. Maybe not all girls, but some anyway, were as horny as boys. And acted on it. What a world!

She continued: "I saw Stewart visit you in the hospital. I checked and saw that he was listed as a resource to tutor about computers. A perfect way to meet you. I had to see what kind of a person you were. He talked about you all the time. You're his only friend. You're kind and respectful, even though he's a little bit different. I'd never seen that in a guy. And then I met you. Not quite in the way I'd planned. But you rose to the occasion." There was that laugh again. She reached out and we were on each other again. No preliminaries this time. All action. Same result.

I fell asleep. Only for a few minutes. Eve woke me with kisses.

"Don't worry. I know you need some time to recharge. Anyway, I'm starving, lover boy. Let's have some food and we can talk."

She put on a record, some Motown stuff, then fried bacon, put it on paper towels to drain while she fried eggs in the grease.

"Southern style," she said, serving me with a can of beer to wash it down.

We ate at a small walnut coffee table. She popped a strip of bacon in her mouth and chewed it slowly. "Sorry, I'm addicted to bacon. Although I think I'll change and make you my drug of choice."

"I accept."

She winked at me. "Tell me about the secret Stewart said you had. I don't think he meant the size of your dick."

"No. I feel like a freak. It's crazy."

I launched into the story, watched her astonished look grow with every detail. I left out nothing, even the part with the EEG technician.

"You are a naughty boy. Can you time travel at will?"

"Just the one time after the shooting."

"He's that caveman leading the chants at the SDS meetings. I wish you'd have let the mob beat him to a pulp."

"He claims to want peace."

"That'll be the day. I've been here for four years and it gets crazier all the time. Watch out for him. Someday he'll do something you won't be able to stop."

"You're going to graduate soon. What about us then?"

"We'll figure out something. Right now, I know this seems crazy. I feel a connection to you. I'm not going to lie; you're amazing to look at. All I could want in a man. Something more lies between us besides the sex. After your operation when you were in recovery I talked to your friends. Stewart and the guy next door in your dorm.

"David."

"Yes. Anyway, they went on and on about what a sweet person you were: thoughtful and generous. The perfect combination. Sounds corny, I know. But it's true."

Dusk crept around the trees and quiet lawns. A sense of fulfillment surrounded me. I never wanted the day to end. Eve put on a single by Marvin Gaye: *Precious Love.*

Tired from the alcohol and heavy sex, we fell asleep.

My eyes opened and I listened to her breathing in the dark before waking her with a back rub. She rolled over and her eyes fluttered open.

"Do you believe in marriage?" I said.

"Heavens yes, darlin'," she said. "Are you proposing?"

"Oh God no. But I'm in love with you."

She was a Southern girl from Charleston, South Carolina. Went to the 'right schools' and then rebelled by eschewing the fashionable College of Charleston in favor of Blaze. For a Yankee school, judged not the worst.

Eve's family had lived in Charleston since before what the local tradition called the War of Northern Aggression. The Civil War to us Yankees. Related to John C. Calhoun. Slaveowners.

"How did a girl like you get to be a girl like you?"

"You mean, not turn out like all the good Southern belles preparing for a life unfettered by concerns about equality, human dignity or having a good time with a man?"

"Something like that. Maybe not in that order."

"My family may have been brought up as ignorant, racist plantation owners. That's a joke by the way. My Daddy was editor of the newspaper and he took some heat for his views. But they weren't blind or deaf. They knew things weren't going to remain the same. They started shipping me North every summer when I was 10. We had relatives in Wisconsin. I got to experience a different perspective. I read books that weren't allowed back home. I swam in the same pool as black children and didn't die. It was rather fun. Subversive, you might say."

"Not like Bear."

"I have an open mind; I don't think he's considered he might be mistaken about some things. Based on what he called the black student maybe he's not as progressive as he believes. I see so few people at either end of the political spectrum who aren't flaming hypocrites. They have a prescription for the world's ills, but they won't take their own medicine."

She walked into the bathroom and ran water in the tub. I stared at her naked splendor while she worked. She turned off the faucets and climbed in.

"How's the water?" I said.

"Get in here and find out for yourself, Romeo."

Capitol Luck

My cross-country break ended in mid-November, and I was far from being competitive. I kept working out with the team, dropping to sixth overall in the rankings. Rumors of my new love life circulated with the buzz that only horny eighteen-year-old boys can generate. Thanksgiving loomed. Eve had family plans in Charleston. Her surgery rotation ended and all that awaited was a stint in pediatrics following the holiday.

"What then?" I asked.

She was uncharacteristically silent. "I've got some possibilities to consider," she said.

"You know I want to be around you."

"I want to be around you too. I love you, Pax."

"I love you more," I said. I meant it as far as it goes. I had no idea about real love except the lust part. Eighteen-year-old boys aren't capable of much else. Looking at my parents as a model, I saw plenty of day-to-day affection and loyalty. What went on in their bedroom wasn't for me to know about. The rest of the time my dad was attentive to my mother. She reciprocated, more so when he disappeared from family life for days.

"Are you going to tell your parents about us?" she said.

"Are you?"

"Probably not. Bad enough that I should speak of not living in Charleston the rest of my life. They have a squadron of boys they think I should date. All from well-heeled and reputable families of course."

"But they let you go to college here."

"A compromise, my dear. They were afraid to lose me. I'm afraid I made life quite difficult for them. The payback is that they expect me to settle in a proper life. They're thrilled about my being a nurse. Perfect for part-time employment when I have children."

"You want to have kids?" The prospect scared me. That meant responsibility.

"Of course. And with you. But on our timetable, not theirs."

I accompanied her to Washington. She had a train to catch, me a bus. The weather gray and drizzling, like our mood. Union Station was jammed with travelers, many of them in the military. A lot of them as young as I. What separated us was my student draft deferment. A small number had tans acquired in Vietnam. They didn't make eye contact. The fresh-faced soldiers and Marines gave them a wide birth as well. They might as well have been carrying a fatal contagion. I tried to imagine leaving a war and returning to an environment where people weren't trying to kill me. I couldn't. A group of anti-war protestors stood with placards and tried to engage the soldiers and Marines who passed.

"Stop the killing. End war now. Vietnam for the Vietnamese," they chanted. I watched while Eve went to the restroom. Most of the uniformed boys ignored the group. One of the demonstrators, a skinny ginger with a frizzed-out Afro, grabbed the arm of the nearest passing trooper. Mistake, I knew in a milli-second. The guy had three stripes on his sleeve, crewcut hair half an inch long and fists like burls on an oak tree. Probably as solid too, because he laid that boy out cold with one punch and continued walking without a second glance. The rest of the military bunch stepped over the unconscious protestor without missing a beat.

Eve returned, asked me what happened.

"A hippie messed with a Marine," I said. The fallen boy's friends knelt in a circle around him. Another marine slowed long enough to grab a protest sign and deposit it into a trash can. No one else interfered or spoke. Nobody cheered for the guys in uniform, either.

I hugged Eve goodbye. People had to move around us, and we didn't care. She gave me her home phone number. "Don't call after 7 at night," she said.

I should have told her no way did it matter; instead, nodded and watched her join the queue of travelers. She boarded a shiny Pullman car and waved for a final time before the train started inching forward, picked up speed and vanished into the night. My watch read 5:50. The Pittsburgh bus left at 10.

I wandered aimlessly around Washington. Found my way to the Capitol and strolled the Mall. The place had shut down for the holiday, but the buildings were brilliantly lit by spotlights. The drizzle had changed to fog, and visibility was crap, A flicker of movement in the distance alerted me to three figures coming out of the shrubbery. They walked abreast toward me, silhouetted by a distant streetlight. No hurry in their gait. The middle one broke rank and strode ahead, boot heels scuffing the pavement, hands in his coat pockets. He had swagger. Authority. He was the boss. He wore a dark beret cocked to one side. The flankers were hatless. They wore featureless canvas jackets.

We stopped ten yards apart, their faces masked by the dark. The flankers moved out and then cut towards me, cutting off retreat. Something they practiced, not a coincidence. Beret guy shook his right arm, and something dropped into his hand. I couldn't see what.

"Hey man. C'mere." Softer than I'd imagined, if meant to scare me.

"I can hear you fine," I said.

"Got a cigarette?"

"Don't smoke."

"A light?"

"What's in your hand?" I said.

He pointed it at me and pressed his thumb down, snapping open a blade.

I took a step back. They took two forward.

"I don't have any money," I said. A lie I didn't expect them to believe.

"Be cool, man. Just want to talk. We're hungry. Thought someone like you would be into sharing. Your brothers at the demonstration last month were cool. Money, food, weed. Whatever. We got well. Now it's same old shit as before. We can't get a break, you know. I got a cousin over in Nam. He's doing as good as he can. Keep his head down when the shit starts flying. Then waste any motherfucker that gets close. I'd go, but on account of my record, they won't take me. I'm ready to kill whoever."

"Hold on," I said. I started to walk backwards and ran into a bench. The two flankers pressed forward. I took out my wallet. It contained fifty dollars, my driver's license, student ID and pictures of my parents. I tossed it at the feet of beret guy.

He snatched it up and had the cash in his pocket in a flash. "You lied to us, boy. You do have money. What else? What's in the backpack? Dope?"

"That's it."

"No man, I don't believe you." He nodded to his soldiers and they darted at me, but half a second after I made my own move, juking left, then right and just out of the grasp of the beret guy.

"You're dead, motherfucker," he yelled.

I didn't look back. If they'd been into sports in high school, it hadn't lasted. I kicked for all I was worth, backpack notwithstanding. Their footsteps fell away. They cursed in vain.

I welcomed the halogen streetlights. A few cars whizzed past, oblivious to my frantic gestures to stop. I kept going, away from the Capitol dome. Saw a cop car and flagged it down. The officers were unexcited by my story. They'd heard it all before.

"Lucky you ran," one of them said.

They took down my information. Asked me how I planned to get back.

"They took my money," I said.

"Any friends here? That you could call?"

Not in Washington. Back at Blaze the dorms were empty. I could reach my home, but I felt ashamed to tell them.

"I'll hitchhike," I said.

The cops exchanged amused smirks. They gave me a lift to the most likely spot to catch a ride and not get mugged. I only had 240 miles to travel, but it took an hour before a citizen brave enough to pick up a skinny college student stopped. A rusted Ford pickup with West Virginia plates. The driver was going all the way to Morgantown. Hunting with his family for Thanksgiving, he said. I gave him a short version of my sojourn in the capital.

"Mel. Mel Little," he said.

"Paxton Knox. Friends call me Pax."

Mel wore a gray jumpsuit. A shoulder patch identified him as a government employee, custodial services, US Capitol. I couldn't judge his height, but he had a wrestler's build. Something wasn't right though. Then it hit me. He used his right hand to drive. He kept the left one concealed below his seat. I saw why in time. A metal hook. He noticed me staring.

"Booby trap last year in Nam."

"I'm sorry," I said.

His voice was matter of fact. "Shit happens. At least I came home and not in a box."

"How long were you there?"

"Two tours. Landed in Danang in '65. Didn't quite finish the second one."

Twenty minutes passed before he spoke again. "I suppose you're out there with your college friends, demonstrating against the war?"

"No sir."

He laughed. "Don't call me sir. I was just a lowly E-6. That's a sergeant to you civilians."

"I know. My Dad was in the Marine Corps."

He totally brightened at that. Flooded me with questions, some of which I could answer. Many I couldn't.

"Yeah, doesn't surprise me he doesn't talk about it. Sounds like he survived a meatgrinder, from the little I know. What are you gonna tell the families of dead Marines? Sorry about that. Your old man probably felt guilty as hell about leaving that place alive. I know I did."

"You're saying the war is a mistake?"

"You don't follow me. All wars are mistakes. The men doing all the killing. They aren't there to save the world from Communism. Or Nazism. Or the Japs or whoever. When you're in a fire fight, all you think about is not letting down your brothers beside you. Then get the hell home if you can. I'd go back if I had two good hands. I have a decent job cleaning hallways and shit in the Capitol building. I see Senators and Congressmen all the time. I don't think any of them knows jack shit about my service. I'm not saying we never go to war. Just that if we're in one, that we fight to win."

The miles rolled on. Little opposing traffic. No deer in the headlights. Mel put the radio on a DC station that played country music. I liked it, to my surprise. He sang softly, tapped out the beat on the steering wheel. At one point he turned to me. "Tell you what. It's not that much farther to Pittsburgh from Morgantown. If you want, you can crash at my parents', they have room. We'll get fed, get some sleep and I'll take you home in the morning. Save your folks the drive. Deal?"

"Deal."

Mel's parents lived outside the city of Morgantown, on a dead-end road that terminated a stone's throw from the Monongahela River. The house was salt box style, clapboard painted white. The landscaping was professional grade, and I told Mel so.

"Better be. My Dad is superintendent of grounds at West Virginia University. I'll tell him you noticed, and he'll be happy. He says mostly people don't comment unless they see something they don't like. Then they bitch."

We entered quietly. Mel's parents weren't night owls. He showed me to the guest room. From the looks of it, more like his childhood bedroom. Walls covered with pennants, photos, mainly of him.

"Just so you know, blame my Mom for turning it into a Melvin shrine. I didn't learn to get neat until I joined the Corps."

I called my folks before retiring. They weren't crazy about my hitch-hiking. I didn't mention the mugging attempt.

"Who's Eve?" my Mom asked.

"A girl I know from school."

"Well, obviously."

"I've been, um, seeing her for most of the semester."

I wasn't much good at writing to them. Sex and romance were sensitive topics to begin with. When they'd last seen me, I was post-op and still a virgin. How does one explain the sudden and explosive romance I'd experienced?

"I'm glad you're involved in a social life besides all the running you do. Your father and I agree on that. You could become too focused on activity."

My Dad entered the conversation from the bedroom extension. "You need to keep that scholarship alive and get an education. Don't forget you're the first in the family to go to college. We're proud of you, son."

"Eve is very anxious to meet you." That was wishful thinking. I omitted the age difference, my marriage proposal, her family's wishes. The more thought I gave it, the less likely it could ever work. But it had to.

"If she's around when we pick you up for Christmas, maybe you can introduce her. Where does she live?"

"South Carolina."

"Really?" An amber caution light, I knew from her tone.

"I like that state," said my Dad. "Parris Island where I went to boot camp."

"Well, she's not as backward as a lot of people in the South. I mean, regarding the race question," I said.

"I certainly hope not," said Mom.

Instead I focused on positive news. "The man who gave me a lift served in the Marines, Dad. Lost his left hand in Vietnam. Works as a janitor at the US Capitol. Great guy."

"I'm glad to hear that, son. Too bad about his injury. Even more reason for you to stay in college, keep that deferment." He didn't have to say, let some other poor bastard get killed in

Vietnam. He didn't have to say: *or come back alive with psychological scars.*

"Don't worry," I said.

I got ready for bed. The stillness broken only by the tick of a grandfather clock in the front hall. I opened my backpack seeking toothpaste, toothbrush, and medication. First two in a plastic bag. I had stopped taking the pills because they made me tired. But I had to bring them along in case my parents checked. Because my Mom would ask me. I remembered putting in an outside pocket. Not there. I checked the other pockets. Not there. I suppressed my panic and dumped the contents on the bed. Not there.

Stupid me, in a hurry to meet Eve, had forgotten to zip the pockets. Probably my frantic escape from the muggers had thrown the bottle clear. I told myself things to reassure me. None of which succeeded. Stress did not help my state of mind. I needed to relax and sleep. I filled a glass of water in the bathroom, drank it in one gulp, pretending it washed down the pills.

Returning down the dark hallway presented no problem until my toe snagged a corner of carpet and pitched forward. I extended my arms too late to catch myself and face planted, impact sounding like a melon hitting concrete. I rolled onto my back, suppressing the urge to scream a stream of obscenities. I reached to check for blood, found that impossible. I felt nothing, heard nothing and all I could see was the now familiar blue fog leaving everything it touched with a shimmering layer of fluorescence that swirled and pulsed and thickened. A baritone hum wavered in synch with fog's activity. I felt pin pricks of cold on my skin, like I'd been caught in an autumn sleet storm.

The interval ended with me back on the platform chasing

Eve's train, waving to her as it pulled away. Her sad eyes tugged my heart strings. Later I could tell her how close I'd been to a second goodbye.

"Holy shit," I yelled in frustration.

I approached a porter taking a smoke break. I had to be sure.

"Excuse me," I said

"Yes, sir?"

"What day is it?"

"Excuse me?" He stared hard. Perhaps thinking I'd smoked too much pot. Then a sympathetic look. "You feeling OK?" he said.

"Just tell me. Please. What is the date?" I tried to slow down my breathing.

He ground out his cigarette. "November the 27th," he said, grabbing my elbow. Maybe he thought I would pitch onto the track.

"1967?"

"Yes."

I nodded and pulled away, stumbling toward the waiting area. I found an empty bench and sat there. Minutes passed and nothing else happened. I didn't wake up somewhere else. I looked at my watch. Just past six. Eve had departed at 5:52. I had no idea what to do, as if the fracture in time had broken my ability to execute simple acts.

I was a fragile egg waiting to crack. Missed my dose by a few minutes and spun backwards. The stress or the fall, maybe the combination had done it. I checked the pack and found the bottle in its place, the pocket unsecured. I dry swallowed the pill to be safe.

I could avoid the muggers by taking a cab to the bus station and waiting. Mel would drive home alone or maybe pick up a different hitchhiker. My gift of time travel enabled historical changes of a small order. I would embrace it, rein it in, put it to use. Not for frivolous ends, either. My conscience loomed large. The punks who had attacked me would simply find someone else to rob. Could I live with that? I had to do something.

Arming myself was out of the question. Three on one odds against. I didn't have fighting skills. What about the police? Assuming I could locate a squad car, how would they feel about a crime that hadn't been committed? Lock me up for suspicion of drug use. No way would they believe a story about time travel. Time to man up, as my Dad would say, and do the right thing. At least I had the luxury of surprise.

I slipped through the night like an assassin. Avoiding lights and gravel paths, hugging the cover of trees and shrubbery, wet with evening dew. On my left, the towers of the Smithsonian castle rose like a medieval fortress. I knew the gang was close, but I saw nothing. Taking cover behind a tree, I waited. Prey or predator?

The crunch of footsteps came from the direction of the castle. Someone taking a shortcut, perhaps hurrying to catch a bus. A woman with arms encumbered by an umbrella and a purse. A secretary, I guessed, working late. Behind her, moving a shade faster, the pack of three. Time to act. A nearby trash barrel provided a bottle. Ripple, drink of choice for bums. I shook out the vinegar residue and walked toward the showdown.

"Hi," I said as I stepped out of the darkness.

"Oh, my God,"

"You're in danger."

"What's in your hand? Oh please, no." She started to scream.

"Look behind you," I blurted.

"No, you don't, creep." She dropped her umbrella and dug

in her bag, pulled out something and aimed it at me. I stood frozen long enough for a liquid to hit my chest. Tear gas. I knew the smell from the clothes of Blaze students gassed at the war protest.

I back-pedaled, choking, half-blinded, and fearful she might have another weapon.

"Get away, you motherfucker," said the woman, charging me.

"I'm just trying to help," I pleaded.

The muggers attacked, knocking her down. She dropped like a felled tree and I swung the bottle, smashing it hard against the skull of the leader. the muggers surged past me, carrying away her purse. I pivoted and hurled the bottle after them. It crashed harmlessly in the darkness.

The woman escaped serious injury, suffering only a black eye. She calmed down, even apologized for spraying me with tear gas. I told her I'd seen the muggers approaching. Absolutely true, but inaccurate. I flagged down the patrol car I'd seen before, and they gave her a lift.

At a coffeeshop near Ford's Theater I ordered a coke and a cookie. It had a pay phone in back, and I called my parents and tell them about my change in plans. I hadn't met Mel, but they didn't know that. I avoided an uncomfortable bus ride and let them go to bed on time.

I walked back to Constitution Avenue and waited for Mel, secure in the belief that the replay would happen as predicted. Mel stopped his truck and off we drove. We had the same conversation. Not word for word, but darn close. It felt, well, scripted. All the while I felt self-conscious, while he acted as though nothing was amiss. I thought I'd try something clever.

"Ever experience déjà vu?" I said.

Mel thought it over. "Somebody asked me that once before." I thought I'd die laughing. We had broken the ice already, but that capped it.

"Is that a negative?" I said, smothering my giggles.

"I know what you mean, and of course I have. In Nam if happened all the time. Probably because we were doing the same crap, over and over."

"And expecting different results?"

He frowned. "The definition of insanity. That about sums it up. Poor bastards who never got the chance to profit from their mistakes. I should say, our mistakes. We all made them. But whether it got you killed was a matter of inches. And dumb luck, sometimes. My hand came off. Somebody else triggered the booby trap and got killed. I was only maimed. Could have been my head. In a firefight the squad leader popped up quick to check the enemy and took a bullet in the forehead. All a grunt could say was: It don't mean nothing. A way to put death in a compartment without dealing with it."

"You think that's good?"

"Hell, no, my friend. But it's human."

Later, I almost stumbled on the same stretch of hall. Gave me the sense that time resisted changes. This time I woke up in the same bed.

Catastrophe

Hanging out in my hometown produced equal quantities of relief and anxiety. Relief because everything looked familiar. I understood where I belonged. I could navigate physically and psychologically. Anxiety because I recognized the façade of familiarity lacked substance. Time traveling undermined a trust I took for granted. Worse, only two other people in the world knew the truth. I couldn't take a course in the metaphysics of time travel. I had to figure it out for myself.

I called Tim and Phil the day after Thanksgiving. We cruised for hours. in Tim's Chevy Nova II convertible. He was a motorhead from the word go. The ink on his driver's license wasn't dry when he bought the car. In high school he was the absolute envy of everyone. After graduation, he worked as a mechanic, naturally. He had a lot on his mind this year. No one envied him now.

"Fucking Vietnam," he said.

"You going?" I said.

"Got my draft card after my birthday." Me too, but I had a student deferment.

"Class I-A? The top of the list?" I said. Didn't take a rocket scientist to figure that out. Tim was six feet, 180 pounds, rock solid and healthy. How could he not be?

"Fucking A."

"You could go to college," I said without conviction.

Phil, riding shotgun, piped up. "Cut one of your fingers off.

Pinkie left hand. You don't need it for work. You can grab snatch with it. But Uncle Sam won't take you."

"I'm no draft card burning pussy. I'll go if they call. Just don't like the idea. You read the shit that just happened over there?"

I hadn't looked at a paper since I started seeing Eve. My life was running, studying, and Eve.

"No," I said.

"Fucking place called Hill 875. Jesus Christ, they don't even have fucking normal names over there for places. Anyway, a lot of our guys got killed taking it from the gooks. Including when one of our own planes bombed our troops. So, we win, say the generals. Then we leave, give it right back. What the fuck?"

Phil had wall eyes so bad even thick glasses didn't correct them. "If you go there, bring me back a Viet Cong flag, OK?"

Tim punched him hard in the shoulder. "The fuck, you say, Mister Four F. I'm keeping my head down." Then he shot me a glance in the rear-view mirror. "Mr. Joe College back there. You ain't going to no Vietnam. You're just sweet talking those college girls to get them to put out for you. Am I right?"

"Well, I..." and let my voice trail off.

Tim and Phil teased me without mercy for five minutes. Maybe if I'd told them about the EEG girl.

"You had a crush on Ellen Comstock, Tim said

"Never got started. Thrown out running to first base." That brought a huge laugh.

"Come on," Phil wheedled. "It's different now. I seen those news stories about the hippies and protestors. Those girls are different. Hell, they don't even wear bras. They burn 'em. They got birth control. It's an orgy every weekend."

He stared at me. For confirmation, I supposed.

"It's not that way. All the time, anyway."

"Aha," Phil chortled, giving Tim a payback punch. "What'd I tell ya? Pax is fucking like a bunny now that he's a big shot college guy. We oughta take him out, have him show us how to pick up a girl."

Black Friday didn't hold attraction for boys like us. We talked about sports and girls. Our beloved Steelers had lost to an equally anemic New York Giant squad the Sunday before. Next up were the Minnesota Vikings.

"I like our chances," said Tim. "I don't see the Vikings ever being able to do much with the team they've got."

"Hey, listen up," said Phil. "Wouldn't it be cool to be able to see into the future and learn who wins games? Like the Super Bowl?"

"Just bet on the Packers if they're playing. And if they're not, then the National Conference. The American is full of has-beens and wannabes."

I didn't say a word, but my mind traced the possibilities. Not football. Gambling was illegal most places outside Las Vegas. But the stock market. Food for thought. If only I could go forward in time and return.

Tim took us to a bar where he knew the bouncer. We slipped in through the rear entrance, walked past the kitchen, and found a table for three far away from the front door in case a cop should peer through the window. Not too likely, but Chris, the bouncer, insisted. He brought us three Budweisers and three shots of rye. Boilermakers, just like the big boys drank. I watched Phil and Tim for guidance, tossed down the rye with as much bravado as I could muster. It burned all the way down, forcing me to suppress the world's biggest cough.

"That was fantastic," I managed to squeak through my

burning larynx.

Tim flashed a fifty and winked, waved to Chris for another round. "Got paid yesterday," he said.

The shots arrived and we three gulped in unison. "Aren't we supposed to do one shot per beer?" I asked.

Got dumb looks in response. I finished my beer in a hurry. The boys were already starting their second. I'd gone to a kegger at college, but always stopped short of getting drunk. In high school I'd adhered to the athletic league code of neither smoking nor drinking, unlike most everyone else on every team at Brashear High School. Tonight, I had some catching up to do. Our boyish voices grew louder with each succeeding round. Phil attempted to shoot pool with a hatchet-faced man who was taking on all comers at nine ball, five bucks a game. He won the first game.

"This oughta be good," said Tim.

I didn't know if he meant good pool or good entertainment. After Phil lost four straight games, including double or nothing at the end, I figured he meant entertainment. Phil shuffled/staggered over to the victor and attempted a sloppy embrace, which was rejected with a stiff arm to the sternum.

"Hey, asshole," said Phil as he straightened up and took a step in the direction of the hustler.

Just in time, Chris intervened, pulling Phil away from a certain beating.

"You guys need to get the hell out of here," he snarled.

Tim eluded him for a second and somehow climbed on a table. "Just want you turd-birds to know I'm I-A for the draft and I'm ready to go serve my country so the rest of you motherfuckers can stay home and work your sorry-ass jobs, screw your sorry-ass girlfriends, kiss your boss's sorry ass." He found his speech hilarious and roared with laughter, hands on his knees. Until Chris hauled him away and kicked us out the back.

"Don't come back till you're 21," he yelled.

We piled into the car and Tim laid rubber getting way. Stopping for red lights was optional, as was staying in the proper lane. The Pittsburgh police were elsewhere that evening, at least for a while.

I don't recall much else, nor about how I found my way into my house. I heaved what remained of the boilermakers onto the floor of the bathroom and fell asleep in the tub.

Apparently, I had locked the door, because I awoke to the sound of my Dad pounding on it. I hadn't realized a person could still be drunk the morning after. I staggered across the door and pinballed into the hamper and sink on the way. My head throbbed, my guts wanted to puke air, and I had the foulest taste in my mouth.

"Paxton, are you there?"

"Minute, Dad," I said, pulling on my jeans as I lay turtled on the rug. First name meant trouble.

I opened the door and saw he had the special look reserved by parents for when they are equal parts terrified, grateful, and angry. He waved something in front of my face. My wallet. Easily recognizable by the faux alligator skin.

"Hey, where did...?" and my voice trailed off as I realized his concern lay elsewhere. Dwarfing loss of a wallet.

"Come downstairs, son."

I followed, sheepishly, imagining that the Good Samaritan who'd found it was probably waiting to witness my humiliation. Well, things could be worse, I told myself. At least I wasn't going to Vietnam.

There was no Good Samaritan. Instead, a uniformed cop

stood in the vestibule, hat in hand, rocking back and forth on his heels. My Mom sat on the bench under the coatrack, leaning against the wall with her hands across her chest, streaks of tears glistening on her face. She burst out crying when she saw me, and I stumbled over to embrace her. Dad and the cop waited for her anxious bleats to calm before addressing me.

"We found the wallet in a car wreck early this morning," said the cop. "Total of three wallets, two victims. They'd been ejected from the car after it hit a tree. Identification is going to be difficult, but since we had three wallets and two bodies, we could eliminate one right away."

His words filtered through the fuzzy wall of my hangover. Mom kept on crying, hugging me. I did my best to comfort her, and that seemed to pull into real time. I wanted so badly to hit a time travel speed bump. Not to be.

"What next?" I said.

"Nothing more for anyone to do," said the cop. He replaced his hat, made to leave. I couldn't imagine dealing with life and death in such a casual manner. I glanced at my Dad. He had a similar dissociated look on his face. He shook the cop's hand and went out on the porch with him for a few minutes. They talked. The cop left and Dad came back, stood in the door, beckoning me.

"Come along, son," he said.

I had a sense of what he wanted, and at that moment I wanted to run as fast and as far away as I could. But he was master of the household, and I couldn't defy him. I grabbed a jacket and followed. The cop drove us, with Dad next to him and me in the back seat behind the metal screen used to confine prisoners. I felt like one. The dreary post-holiday weather didn't help matters. He drove to Mercy Hospital. Just over the river into uptown

Pittsburgh. Nobody talked on the way.

The cop parked and led us through the emergency entrance to an elevator parked "Private". He had a key for it. It only travelled one way: down. The doors opened to a cave-like corridor populated by pipes and electrical conduits. The floor was green finished concrete. We came to a T intersection and turned left. In fifty paces we arrived at a windowless door marked NECROPSY LAB. The cop opened the door. Dad pushed me behind the cop. A musty, chemical odor greeted us. The smell of the paste we used in elementary school. Before now, it linked a pleasant memory. Carefree, innocent times. But no longer.

We continued past doors with eye level portholes. The first dark but not the second. I stopped to look despite my fear. The cop waited. Behind the glass I beheld a tableau of horror. A stainless table canted toward a floor drain. Two doctors in scrubs on opposite sides. Between them, a dead body. Naked. The doctor facing me raised a flap of skin with large tweezers and a scalpel, exposing a rib cage. He put down the scalpel and took a drag from a cigarette.

The cop hustled me into a room marked STORAGE and opened a walk-in cooler. I shivered even before I entered. Twelve filing cabinet doors on the opposite wall. Pittsburgh is a big city. The cop pulled the handle of drawer number three. It made a soft whirring sound and then clicked open. The cop circled behind and marched me.

I did not want to look, but I had to. No escape.

A body lay stretched out and motionless. Naked. Its head lacked a face. The features smashed flat as if by a giant hammer. Just a jumble of cartilage, muscle, nerve, and bone sitting in the bowl of its skull. Ghoulish Frankenstein-style stitches marked a Y shape running from shoulders to midline and down to the crotch.

An unrelenting pressure circled my chest and threatened to crush me. I prayed for something to take me away. Back in time. I didn't care how far. The death smell crawled into my nose, penetrated my mouth until it overwhelmed my senses. I could rinse for a week and never be free.

"He's in better shape than his buddy," said the cop, sliding the drawer back.

"I don't want to look," I said.

But he made me.

Afterwards, I sat in the squad car and cried. Dad sat in back and held me. "I was your age when I saw my buddies in the Marines dead like those boys. I prayed then I would never let any of my kids end up that way, for any reason. That's why you had to see it."

The funerals were held simultaneously, on Monday. It made me think of JFK's funeral, four years before. A weekend burned into my memory, capable of rearing up like a ghost in a haunted house. At least the martyred President had accomplished a lot. Stared down the Russians over Cuba. Sent advisors to Vietnam. He created an American dynasty. Bobby Kennedy was a shoo-in to succeed LBJ. And JFK Jr. seemed destined to ascend to the White House. Phil and Tim had been cut down without time to leave anything but the briefest of memories. In fifty years, what would we know about them? That they had been young and foolish, but no more than their fellows, just unluckier.

At the beginning of the service, Father Frederick asked us all to pray for the souls of all who had gone before, and to pay special mind to the young men serving their country over in Southeast Asia. He said a prayer for God to keep them from harm and to return safely home. But if they died, carry their souls to the most holy and special of places in heaven to await the arrival of their families in eternity. Maybe that was overdoing it, but nobody said a word against it. The only sounds for a minute were the quiet sobs of the mothers.

I walked out of the church with my parents, heart pounding because I knew what I had to do. My parents said comforting words, but I cannot recall them. I was stewing over what lay in front of me. Emotion surged until I saw the faces of my friends in life, not half-frozen in the morgue.

St. Joseph's Church had a magnificent marble staircase leading from the entry down to the street, a good twenty feet below. The continual drizzle left slick spots that from time to time caught a parishioner off guard. I stepped on one of them, and not by accident. I didn't slip. I pushed off into space, focusing on bending the curve of space-time to sling me backward. Gravity ripped my hand from the grasp of my father and freed me. I pitched forward and watched the white marble closing in.

Resurrection

My eyes opened. Just as before. No cinematic fade in from black. My head didn't hurt. Nothing did. I stood in front of my bathroom mirror, can of Right Guard in my left hand. No bruising or stitches. Elation swept over me. I'd gone back with intent and landed on target. What would Stewart have to say about that?

I played a record.

Almost immediately my Dad shouted, "Turn that damn thing down."

For a steel worker ex-Marine my Dad heard very well. Maybe he didn't like the content. Bob Dylan singing Blowing in the Wind. I stepped into the hall to challenge him.

"I thought you'd agree with the anti-war message. Didn't you tell me that World War II was the biggest disaster ever to strike the planet?"

"They should have stopped Hitler when they had the chance. Send a team to assassinate him. I don't think it's the place for some hippie to lecture me."

"OK, Dad,". Time to get a set of headphones. The audiophiles at Blaze all swore by them. Could hear all kinds of things inaudible with regular speakers. Secret messages. Stuff that people on acid trips loved. Reality seemed tough enough. My trips were literally that, not synaptic symphonies.

I began the do over in fear. The other times stacked against this were ripples in a mill pond compared to a hurricane. Saving two lives rivalled a Biblical miracle. Resurrection of the dead.

Holy Roller territory. I didn't know if I could function knowing the stakes. A few hours ago, they'd been in the morgue, bodies smashed beyond recognition. The difficulty of erasing the memory taxed my emotional fitness, but I had to try. I had to reverse the course of the previous evening. Just how to do that hadn't jelled as a plan yet. No excuses allowed.

I had an hour to kill before Tim and Phil's arrival. I played records at a lower volume. Changed gears from anti-war to something less tense. Simon and Garfunkel. Sounds of Silence. I made that my goal for the evening. Tim pulled up after dark, leaning on his horn. Another source of parental irritation, judging by the look on Mom's face.

"I can't control what they do," I said, thinking: but I want to control if they die.

Noisy and alive were a good combination. We drove to the same bar, said and did the same things. I could hardly talk, struck dumb by the self-imposed gravity of altering history. Especially when they started on the boilermakers. Feeling panic, I excused myself and found a payphone in the back. I dialed Eve's number, made brave by alcohol. Brave until a male voice answered.

Oh shit, not supposed to call after seven.

"Hello?"

Eve had a brother, Rhett David. She called him David. Army officer, graduate of the Citadel in Charleston. West Point of the South.

I stuttered, "Hello. Is this David? May I speak to Eve?" God, this was hard.

"To whom do I have the pleasure of speaking, sir?"

I had trouble spitting out my name.

"Pax Knox? I don't believe we've had the pleasure."

"No. Sir," I said, bucking the stammer. "I go to college at

Blaze. With Eve."

His chuckle reassured me. "Oh, so you're her beau?"

I took a chance. "She has mentioned me?"

"In great detail."

That couldn't be good. Yet, he was laughing.

"Good. Can she come on the phone?"

"I'm afraid not. She's gone out for the evening with some of her classmates from Ashley Hall. No doubt to compare notes on boys."

"It will certainly be boring when they get around to me. Would you please tell her I called," I took a deep breath, "and tell her I love her very much?"

"I most certainly will, Pax."

"Thank you, and goodnight," I said.

Back in the bar, the shots were falling like autumn leaves. The pool hustle hadn't started. I avoided the alcohol, feigned drinking while surreptitiously spitting it on the floor. Under no circumstance was I getting drunk or close to it. I planned to wrest control somehow from Tim, knowing full well he never let anyone else drive his baby. I brought along a six-inch-long Phillips head screwdriver. Two stabs, two flat tires would defeat any attempt to drive. We'd have to call a cab. I'd pay. He could have one of his motor head friends with a tow truck help him the next day.

I waited until the start of the pool game. I told Tim I had to pee in the worst way. He didn't hear me. Instead of going into the Gent's room in back, I exited and circled around to the street. I cursed the luck. Tim had parked directly underneath a streetlight. Anyone could see me. A couple of cars passed before I made my move. I prayed that there would be no sound save some hissing air. I knelt and got the screwdriver in position, left front tire for maximum effect.

"Hey you."

I turned my head into a harsh beam of light. Saw a pair of black Wellingtons and blue trousers with side piping. Christ, now what?

A powerful hand gripped my collar and jerked me upright.

"What the Sam Hill do you think you're doing?" The cop from my morgue nightmare held me tight. Marks, my Dad called him. He wasn't any friendlier than before.

I struggled for a believable lie.

"Just playing a prank on my friends inside."

"A flat tire is a prank? More like malicious mischief. Aren't you Ernie Knox's kid? College boy. Ought to know better."

He circled behind me and pushed me toward the door. At the entrance he stopped and spun me around. Stuck his face inches from mine. I could smell his aftershave. "Your friends better be over 21 or I'll close this place down, you hear?"

"Yessir. I'm sorry."

"Don't make me regret I took pity on you."

I stumbled inside and grabbed Tim before he could make his top of the table Vietnam speech.

"We've got to get out of here," I said.

Tim and Phil, in their alcoholic daze, stared back, slack jawed.

"There's a cop outside. He knows my Dad. He knows you're in here drinking, and if we don't get out of here, we'll get arrested, or worse."

"What's worse than getting arrested?" Tim asked. "Then maybe I won't have to go to fucking Vietnam,"

The specter of my buddies in the morgue, smashed like a couple of squirrels and laid out like field dressed deer pushed me into uncharted territory. "Shut up and let me drive, asshole," I said.

I manhandled them out the door, snagging Tim's keys in the process. Sober Tim would have grabbed them back but drunken Tim merely batted harmlessly at me. The cop watched the production. He nodded, neither helping nor interfering.

"I'm good to go?" I asked him as I shoehorned my friends into the back seat.

"I don't want to see you again."

I couldn't have agreed more. I started the Nova and, unfamiliar with its idiosyncrasies, stalled it when I let in the clutch. That brought a yelp from Tim.

"Sorry," I yelled. The second try succeeded, and the Nova lurched ahead into the night. I only lived a mile or so from Tim. No problem for me to jog back to my house after depositing them at their homes. Phil lived farthest from the bar, north of the city a few miles. I found the way to Carson Street and drove north along the river. I didn't know what kind of engine Tim had under the hood, only that it seemed the land equivalent of a Saturn rocket.

"Hey, quit lugging the engine. Downshift or speed up," slurred Tim.

Not wanting to be a wimp, I chose the latter. My family's car was a 1962 Ford Falcon with three speeds on the tree. No comparison to this machine. In seconds I was doing 60. I stole a glance at the rear-view mirror. My friends were already comatose from the alcohol. I kept the window rolled down to maintain a steady flow of cold air in my face. No point in getting drowsy. It seemed so easy. I relaxed, having negotiated the hard part of the task. The road was empty and the pavement dry.

In the distance I saw a left curve arrow, so I tried to copy the way Tim drove, dropped into third with a smooth double-clutch. The car slowed through the turn, then I hit the gas at the apex. We passed a gravel pit, empty at this hour, but one of many lovers' lane locations. On the straightaway, I pushed the tachometer back to 3500 RPM and prepared to shift back to fourth gear, at the exact moment a pair of headlights loomed, closing fast. In my lane.

Stewart the human computer told me afterward from the facts I shared that the two cars were closing at 120 MPH, or 176 feet per second. They traveled 35 feet closer before my body began to react if I had the reaction time of an Olympic sprinter. Since I didn't, I lost another second. People surviving emergencies describe a sensation of time slowing down in the brief interval between recognition of the situation and the event, in this case a collision. It seemed that way to me. The closing distance was down to 200 feet. Insurance adjusters assume reaction time to be on the order of one and a half seconds after gaining awareness of the emergency. Your results might vary. By that measure, the other car and the Nova had closed to about fifty feet before I or the other driver could take any action, be it steering or braking, to avoid the collision that now seemed inevitable. A rational driver might try to avoid locking his brakes and steer for the appropriate shoulder. I didn't feel particularly rational. Never had the chance to ask the other driver. Jamming on my brakes changed my velocity a trifle. It takes 172 feet to stop from 60 MPH. Each car had 25 feet of braking time before the collision. At which time, each vehicle's velocity was about 45 MPH. A closing speed of 90. People wonder why so few drivers avoid collisions with wrong-way drivers. "Physics is why," said Stewart.

My arms were starting to make a hard right when the cars

passed. I didn't hear tire squeals despite standing on the brakes. A surreal calm surrounded me. My seat belt embraced me but wouldn't stop the engine from crushing the dashboard and turning the steering wheel into a lethal spear.

A white streak passed inches from my window simultaneous with a metallic screech, and then the Nova bounced and fishtailed before halting in a field. A loud bang from behind made me look in the rearview mirror in time to see an orange fireball. I kicked open my door and checked Tim and Phil, who were on the floor but alive, if incoherent. I ran to the other car, its hood standing vertical, front end crushed by a tree. An inferno engulfed the vehicle, keeping me from approaching closer than fifty feet. It looked like a Rambler sedan. Burning rubber--and something else-- assaulted my nose. No one could escape the fire, even if he survived the impact.

A couple of other cars stopped. The passengers, like me, stood stunned by the horror. A girl started crying and her boyfriend tried to comfort her. "Please do something," she pleaded.

"Nothing we can do," I said, my voice cracking. My hands hurt from squeezing the steering wheel. I rubbed them to ease the cramps.

"Jesus Fucking Christ," said Tim from behind me. And then, "Is my car OK?"

The crying girl started caterwauling louder. Her boyfriend glared but said nothing.

I walked with Tim back to the Nova. Sure enough, the Rambler had left a scar of paint along the entire driver's side, the miss so close that the door opened and closed fine. Phil staggered out and vomited in the weeds. I had stopped believing in God my senior year. Now I wasn't so sure.

"It wasn't our time," I said.

A state trooper arrived, lights flashing, siren howling. Within minutes three more official vehicles pulled over, including the unnecessary ambulance. Firefighters used a lot of chemicals to extinguish the blaze. Ruptured fuel line, they said. I gave a statement to the first trooper; he took it all down. I didn't want to drive. My friends were too drunk to make the attempt. The trooper was stern but sympathetic. He called us a cab.

Delivered home, I woke my parents. We sat around the kitchen table, waiting for the shock to abate. My Dad brewed himself some coffee and lit a cigarette. He coughed deeply and excused himself to go spit in the toilet.

"You're all we have," said my mother.

"It could have been so much worse," I said.

"How could it be any worse?"

She had me there. The secret of my time travel trumped any possibility of telling my parents. I still rode the fence of worrying that I had a mental illness. Why jeopardize the present by confessing to a phenomenon that might convince my parents I needed to go to an institution? Stewart's casual remarks about shock treatment lived in the shadows of my fears.

"I promise not to drink anymore," I said.

Redemption Denied

I opened my eyes and smelled bacon. My alarm clock read 12:30. I'd slept through my usual morning run and I didn't care. Maybe I'd run later in the day. The next day, Sunday, my parents would drive me back to Blaze.

Mom made my eggs when I came downstairs. I had no appetite but forced down the meal for the sake of appearance. A late morning edition of the newspaper lay on the table, headlines glaring.

FIERY CRASH CONSUMES TWO PITTSBURGH VETERANS

Johnnie Sims, 20, and Otis Prentiss, 21, both of Pittsburgh, were killed last night in a one car crash on Robinson Blvd. in Coraopolis. Witnesses stated to police that their car crossed the centerline and hit a tree. Both men had recently returned from Army service in South Vietnam and were said to be celebrating on the eve of PFC Prentiss's wedding.

A double funeral is planned for Sunday, at the Ebenezer Baptist Church on Wylie Avenue, where PFC Prentiss had planned to marry.

"Those boys who died. It was so sad," said Mom.

Turned out that Tim and Phil had literally traded places with two young men of the about the same age. But of course, who else would be out driving late at night, probably as drunk as my friends? Maybe God existed after all, but he had a bookkeeper's mentality.

"They had just gotten home from serving a year in Vietnam."

Oh God, that must have really sent his family into a dark place. Waiting all that time, praying for their safe return, and bang, killed in a car wreck.

"Do we know them?"

She said no, they had been from across town. Not in my school, but just a little older.

"The worst thing, and I heard this from my friend Liz, who must know everybody or at least has a friend who knows anyone she doesn't, was that when they came back home just before Thanksgiving, there were a bunch of demonstrators at the airport, holding signs and yelling at them. Called them baby killers and worse. Spit on them, threw things, chased them back home practically."

That squared with the scene I witnessed in Washington.

"There's a lot of anti-war talk at school," I said. I recounted the attack on Eve, of course leaving out what happened later.

"She sounds like a smart girl. I hope you find some other nice coeds in your class to take on dates."

"There's a war going on. People are growing up in a hurry," I said.

A look of disapproval flashed across her face.

"That shouldn't be an excuse for anything goes. When your Dad went overseas the world was in a lot more trouble than it is now. A lot of his buddies didn't make it back. You've seen how it changed him."

"I didn't know him before the war."

She stared at the ceiling, her breaths coming faster. She had never come this close to opening the can of worms that was my Dad's mental health.

"He didn't have a care in the world. Laughed all the time.

Planned to go to college and then maybe law school."

"Why didn't he? The GI Bill paid for college. I know that from History class last year."

Her face became a mask of doubt and conflict. In the silence that followed I heard him coughing upstairs.

"Maybe we should check on him," I said.

She shook her head. "I have to finish what I started to say first or else I may never try."

Dad's footsteps passed in the hall overhead, heading to the bedroom.

Mom resumed her narrative. "He had a breakdown when he got back. He drank heavily. Little things set him off, like cars backfiring. He'd strike out during the night. I got more black eyes than a boxer. One day he locked himself in the bathroom and wouldn't come out. The police broke down the door and took him away. After a year he came home. A shell of happiness that I feared would shatter under too much pressure. He knew people at US Steel and got a job there. The bad times are never far away for me."

She stood and turned her back. I knew it was her way of wiping away tears. Never cry in front of me, even when a sensible person would do exactly that. It didn't take her long to finish. She turned back.

"I know a little of the pain the loved ones of those boys feel. My Ernie came back from war alive, but forever changed, and not for the best. So, we are going to the funeral tomorrow."

"But Mom, you're supposed to drive me back to school."

"I checked and there is a bus leaving at 2. Plenty of seats available. Your Dad and I can't do the round trip this late in the year."

I spent the rest of the day moping about, playing records on low volume, fantasizing about Eve. The last thing I wanted to do was alert my already paranoid Mom about our relationship. A senior. With her own apartment. That reeked of trouble. I picked out the clothes to wear to the funeral. A Robert Hall plaid sport coat, last seen at the alternate reality funeral for Tim and Phil. The mothball smell clung to the fabric. I never wanted to see the damned thing again. Dad had a similarly ancient jacket he'd worn to my graduation. A steelworker had little use for dress-up clothing.

Mom had a black dress with long sleeves and a severely high cut collar. Strictly for funerals. She cooked breakfast wearing it, ever the perfectionist. I wasn't hungry but forced myself to eat to avoid a scolding. Tim and Phil had gone out drinking on Saturday night, to my horror, but I knew I couldn't get permission to join them. I called them to see if they would come to the funeral. I wanted to tell them I'd exchanged their lives for the two dead soldiers. Nobody answered.

It was more sorrowful than I could have imagined. Two lives lost instead of five, but the guilt I felt for selfishly taking back Phil and Tim disturbed me. We had done nothing close to what the two dead soldiers risked. Their heroism turned moot seeing what fruits the sacrifice of the war dead provided. I stared at Dad during the service. He wore the blank stare familiar to me from the times he confronted his own demons. He'd never lose it.

Amorous Interlude

Eve greeted me with a kiss that sucked the air out of me. She pulled me into bed. "I thought you'd never get around to that," I said, fumbling with my pants.

She pulled off her dress and let me finish off the job. I'd perfected the art of unsnapping her bra one-handed, hooking the front to release her breasts with a bounce. She had skimpier panties than I remembered. I flung them across the room. "Bought myself a present," she laughed.

We dispensed with a lot of the preliminaries. As horny as we were it made no sense to adhere to a ritual. I could see and feel how ready she was. I wanted to hold back, but an eighteen-year-old only has so much ability to delay. She came at the same moment. Not a fake, she insisted as we lay still in the afterglow.

"Would you even tell me if you did?"

"I think you know me well enough to tell."

"I was a virgin before we met."

She laughed. "Keep reminding me how I corrupted you."

"Took advantage while I was under anesthesia."

"I only looked, darling."

I told her about the accident. Rather, the two accidents and the outcome.

"Couldn't you try to leap back in time and fix it once and for all?"

I'd asked myself the same question, over and over. If there were an infinite number of parallel timelines. Could I land perfectly on the one where my friends and the two soldiers from the Hill district survived?

"Maybe the next time I wouldn't survive," I said.

"True. I couldn't live another minute if death took you from me. I'd fight to get you back."

"I don't know what would happen to my body. Maybe that would be it."

"Can't Stewart tell you?"

"No. He isn't positive. He's working on computer models. But like he says, it all depends on the assumptions he puts into the program. He calls it confirmation bias. Says that's why nobody could build a computer model to predict the stock market. Too many variables involved and way too likely that he would inadvertently introduce his own bias. He would want me to survive, so he'd subconsciously include that outcome, whether it was likely or not. He says it's quite common in scientific papers."

"If I died, wouldn't you do everything you could to get me back?"

"Of course, baby. I'd never stop trying."

"My brother is headed over there after Christmas," she said.

"Vietnam?" I knew the answer was yes.

"I can't believe it."

"You're not happy."

"He thinks I should be. What is it about men? They think they have to fight and destroy things to prove a point."

"I don't disagree. The world has gone crazy. I had a roommate who thinks he's Che Guevara."

"I'm glad you found a home with Stewart. He's kind and gentle. I think he has a crush on me."

"He never lets anyone touch him except you."

"I like having you as my real roommate."

"So that's it? I'm being used." She pretended to pout. I knew better.

"But of course. I'll get laid as much as I can, then spend every night with my geeky new roommate, staring at the moon."

"Howling at the moon, more likely. Don't tell him I said that Pax. He's teaching me to program. I need him."

"Great. Then the two of you can blabber on about Fortran and whatever else computer nerds talk about."

She stood up and walked over to the turntable. Staring at her ass sedated me. She selected a record and turned up the amp. Jefferson Airplane. White Rabbit.

"Are you going to chase me down the rabbit hole?" I said.

She sauntered back to me, planted a long kiss on my mouth and forehead and rubbed my back. I started to get aroused again.

"You can run like a jack rabbit and I'm Alice, so I should be chasing you," she said between kisses.

We played the last song on the album. Plastic Fantastic Lover. A future filled with synthetic replacements ruled by technology and a priesthood of scientists. I wanted nothing to do with it.

"Pax, please don't go back again."

"Because why?"

"Because you are messing around with the fabric of the universe, and maybe something really bad will happen. Some arch will fracture, and you'll get displaced far away and we'll never meet. Promise you'll do what you can to avoid those time dislocations. Start taking your pills again."

"But three times now I've gotten back. I saved Tim and Phil. Maybe the soldiers' dying cancels that part out. But we, the two of us, who are destined to be together, are linked stronger than before."

"Don't ever keep things from me, Pax."

"I won't." She'd always know anyway.

"I won't start any barroom brawls."

"Seriously."

"OK, I'll start."

The phonograph needle clicked over and over. Broken changer. Technology was great when it worked.

Revolution Redux

My association with Bear wasn't quite finished. The RA had to meet with us and complete a checklist to document room damage. Our word wasn't sufficient. We signed off the agreement and I stayed around. Call it fence mending. When he wasn't stoned, ranting about politics or screwing Allison I enjoyed being around him. From the stories he told about his parents I realized being rich left a lot to be desired. We shared stories about Thanksgiving vacation. I omitted mention of the time travel. He bragged about the cool Movement people he'd met in New York.

"Big things are going to happen," he said.

"Another demonstration? It's winter. Who's motivated to march in a snowstorm?"

Bear raged. "That's what the war mongers count on: apathy amongst the population. The leadership needs to shock them out of their complacency. The average protestor wants to march for three hours, then go home to enjoy the good life. The freedom fighters in Vietnam don't have that luxury. Imperialist troops attack them day and night. What if that happened here?"

"Bear, I don't know about that. What are you saying?"

"I'm saying the mass of students need consciousness raising. The solution follows directly from that. You should come to a meeting and learn more about the struggle. It might change your life."

"OK, I'll be there. When and where?"

Bear could hardly hide his surprise. "Tonight. Seven at the

student union. There will be signs."

I talked Eve and Stewart into going with me. Stewart was even less politically motivated than I, although he seemed to know more facts than anyone.

"We've been getting drawn further and further into this thing since the early Sixties," he said.

"Is that good?"

"All depends on the definition of good."

"Let's see. How about people living in harmony and not blowing each other up all the time?" said Eve.

"Probably it's not good," said Stewart. "On the other hand, the people described as hawks on the war point out that if things keep sliding for our side, and we leave Vietnam, there will follow a bloodbath that will eliminate everyone who opposed the communists."

We arrived at the meeting a few minutes late and took seats in the rear. Saul Stone stood on the podium. The atmosphere buzzed with anticipation. Flanking him were two flags. One a large yellow letter on a red field. Stewart the explained, "It's the Greek letter Ohm, unit of electrical resistance. I imagine it means resist the war."

The other flag contained a yellow star resting on a split red/blue field. Stewart shrugged. Eve elbowed me and whispered, "That's a Viet Cong flag. My brother's classmate brought a captured one home. We should leave."

"Let's wait and see what they have to say," I said.

It didn't take long.

Stone raised his right arm, fist clenched. About half the audience copied the gesture. "We are here to register our solidarity with our brothers and sisters in Vietnam and all over the world where liberation wars are being fought. We resist the ranks of the colonialists, the reactionaries, the oppressors and the puppets of the American war machine."

The house lights dimmed, and a projector whirred in the rear. The film opened with an overhead shot of a jet plane skimming over a landscape of flooded rice paddies, separated by spiny hedgerows and villages of thatched roof huts. The jet climbed, dropping half a dozen cigar-shaped silvery objects that tumbled end over end as they fell. They landed in an open field and blossomed into a rolling ball of fire, capped by a swirling tower of black smoke. The soundtrack of classical music inspired a sense of dread and mourning.

Over the music a narrator recited the history of Indochina from the 1940s onward. He had nothing good to say about the French, the US or any Vietnamese associated with the Western powers. The full panoply of Vietnamese resistance paraded before the camera in grainy, poorly lit black and white film stock. The heroes were all there: Ho Chi Minh, General Giap, Le Duc Tho and other nameless freedom fighters of the Viet Minh.

More war scenes. American advisors towering over the Vietnamese. Half-starved villagers wearing traditional black pajamas and conical hats. Mothers carrying stoic infants around amid the wreckage of small hamlets caught up in a firefight or artillery strike. The Americans seemed like visitors from another planet. Invaders, rather, much like science fiction thrived on depiction of intergalactic travelers as being hell-bent on destroying or subjugating Earth.

Scenes with the aftermath of combat spared no sensitivity. A pile of Viet Cong bodies machine-gunned in combat as they attempted to cross a barb wire barrier. A dead Vietnamese woman with a baby still trying to nurse. A corpse being pulled behind an armored personnel carrier. A rice paddy with enormous bomb craters and a sprinkling of body parts here and there in the water. Finally, the ultimate: torture of a prisoner. A young man, shirtless, wrists tied behind, squatted on the ground. A South Vietnamese soldier carrying a carbine approached and began questioning. He spoke rapidly, fear clouding his voice. Even without translation, the meaning was clear. The interrogator wanted a confession. Resistance was futile. Denial unacceptable. The escalation was rapid and brutal. A series of open-handed slaps. A punch to the gut. Kick in the groin. Rifle butt to the chin. The boy fell and even with the lousy film quality I could see the defiance in his eyes. Two soldiers in camouflage uniforms and berets stood him up. The interrogator grabbed a carbine and pressed the muzzle into the prisoner's midsection. The bullet's impact was unmistakable. He fell and writhed on the ground. The interrogator-turned-executioner wasn't in a hurry. He fired single shots into non-vital structures. He must have gotten tired, or bored, so he shot the rest of the magazine into the boy's head. The final cut of the sequence closed in on the battered cranium of the dead VC. His brains fell out in a mangled stream as the two soldiers dragged him away.

More horror followed. A Buddhist monk sat in a lotus position and burned in the street. A US Marine used a Zippo lighter to light a fire in the thatch of a hut while an old peasant woman watched and cried. The scene cut between dispossessed villagers receiving food from a truck and the US government brain trust: McNamara, Bundy, Lodge, and last of all, LBJ. The audience exploded in outrage. For a moment I thought some might charge the screen and rip it down.

Stone returned as the lights came up and, in a moment, he had quieted the students with a calming hand gesture and a look of extreme beneficence.

"How many of you got arrested at the Pentagon in October?" he began.

Half the room raised their hands.

"How many did jail time?"

Two or three.

Stone wagged a finger. "You're not committed to the cause if you aren't willing to risk your personal freedom." He walked to the front row and pointed. "How about you, Allison?"

Allison stood up and Stone turned her around for the audience to see. He whispered in her ear.

"I had to go home to see my family for Thanksgiving, so I paid my fine."

Stone possessed a voice that rivaled the minister at Ebenezer Baptist church. He raised the decibels to 90. "Are you, Allison, and those who made that choice, telling me that being with your family for a holiday sit down, is more important than the liberation of Vietnamese people, who probably had a single serving of rice and maybe a fish head to eat while you were stuffing your face with turkey, gravy, and dressing?"

"No." It was a squeak, but the room had gone silent.

"Let's hear it." Stone waved his arms, fists clenched over his head.

"No."

"Louder."

"No!"

"LOUDER."

"NO! NO! NO!"

Bear was jumping up and down. I knew he'd gotten arrested but not if he'd stayed in jail. I wanted to ask him, but he rushed to the front and put his face next to Stone's, sharing the microphone.

"Who's with me? I say we show the folks at home what war looks like. No more napalm bombs on the five o'clock news. Mr. and Mrs. America ought to experience it first-hand."

In the instant before acclamation could begin, a voice rang out.

"What if you're wrong?"

Heads swiveled toward the rear of the auditorium. A solitary figure stepped from the shadows. A spotlight lit him from behind, shading his face like a film noire character. The room, which had been full of excited babble a minute before, fell silent.

"Get out of here, you fascist," said a voice from near the front. I thought Bear, but I couldn't be sure. Other voices started murmuring their agreement.

Stone raised a hand. He still had command of the audience. A smile broke across his features as the room became quiet again. "What if I'm not, Ralph?" he said.

Eve whispered, "It's Ralph Adams. Chairman of the Political Science Department. I took a class of his as a sophomore. Brilliant guy. He and Stone are at odds a lot, to put it mildly."

Adams took two steps forward, and his features emerged. He was of medium height, clean shaven with crewcut hair that bristled white. A right sided limp and a lacquered cane implied a physical frailty not evident in his voice. He ignored the students, walking to about fifteen feet from the stage, where he addressed Stone.

"I just want them to understand the government that prevails in Vietnam will bear little to no resemblance to what we enjoy in our country. Do you think there is a peace movement afoot in North Vietnam that holds vigils and sit-ins? Do newspaper editors write anti-war screeds that are critical of the assassinations and torture carried out by your precious NLF cadres in the south?"

Stone drew himself up to his full five feet, five inches. "All I can tell you is that the South Vietnamese and their American puppeteers are on the wrong side of history. The arc of the moral universe is long, but it bends towards justice."

"I wish we had a time machine, Saul. Then we could strap ourselves in and turn the dials to take us ahead twenty-five years. What do you think we would find?"

Stone was quick, I give him full credit. Of course, he'd no doubt had this debate before.

"That the capitalist societies would have spent themselves into oblivion with their colonial wars and need to oppress workers and minorities, while the collectivist world would be reaping the benefits of true economic equality and the brilliance of central planning over the hit-or-miss strategies of the market."

I had a time machine, sort of. I looked over at Stewart with an arch expression. He nodded like a sage. Eve watched the exchange and elbowed me softly. "What on earth are you two loons up to?"

"I'll tell you later," I said.

"I'll bet you a thousand dollars, assuming we haven't blown our planet apart in a nuclear war, that the collectivist countries will have scrapped the teachings of Marx and Lenin and will have fully embraced capitalist economic values."

Stone looked like he'd been smacked with a two by four. He employed his final weapon. He started to laugh. "Right Ralph. And all of us will be carrying around small electronic devices that will allow us to communicate with people all over the world."

The audience treated it like wolves given red meat. The roar of laughter signalled a small tactical victory for Stone. Adams stood his ground, smiling and shaking his head. Like he knew things we didn't.

One of the AV people turned on the speakers and played a record. The vinyl was well-worn, emitting much hissing and popping as the needle tracked around the disc. After the opening bars, the audience joined in.

Arise, you prisoners of starvation!
Arise, you wretched of the earth!
For justice thunders condemnation: a better world's in birth!

Revelations

Eve let her face get close enough for me to kiss her, so I did. We stopped in the middle of the quad and swayed, not conscious of much else besides our own passion. Holding her gave me a feeling I'd never experienced. Security wrapped in a blanket of animal lust. A treasure buried in an otherwise pedestrian scholastic experience. I couldn't think of a single reason why she was so perfect. My gut told me in a language far removed from rational thought or even the musings of a poet.

"I love you, Pax," she said.

"I love you more."

We hurried to her apartment, pulled our clothes off as soon as we entered and jumped into bed. We were a couple of animals rutting around. She had opened my eyes to the finer points of sex from the first day. We made noises throughout the act. Kept the lights on. Talked about everything we did and were going to do. Role-played wild scenarios. Student and teacher. Athlete and cheerleader. Salesman and farmer's daughter. I'd once seen a few minutes of a cheesy porn movie shown by some frat boys. We improved on the dialogue and the action, in my opinion. Eve wanted us to get ahold of a porn movie so we could watch it while having sex. Stewart could have obtained a projector, but he would have asked to watch the movie too, and that wasn't going to happen.

Spent, but full of loving emotion, we lay together on the mattress and listened to music. Eve spun some fantasies for me to think about.

"You must have been a holy terror in high school," I said.

"Oh my God, you won't believe it. I was a virgin until my 19th birthday. In high school I was known as the Ice Queen. Never even French kissed a boy. Certainly, never let one paw my boobs."

I propped myself up on an elbow, partly to show I was paying attention but mainly so my eyes could drink more of her beauty and sex appeal. Flawless skin, hair only slightly ruffled and smelling of lilac pollen, perfectly symmetrical breasts with broad, dark nipples. She saw me watching and smiled. "You are such a boob man, Pax."

"Tell me more," I said.

"You promise not to get jealous?"

"Scout's honor."

She laughed. "Well, that surely disappeared a while back, but I'll continue. I spent my freshman year learning a little more about boys. Then I met a man."

"A man?" Deep down I didn't want to know how she'd acquired her sexual sophistication. But if I didn't find out, the uncertainty would kill me. I sensed she needed not to confess but share with me, her lover. A slight distinction, but one that reassured me. No secrets between us. Like she'd said.

"Not a student. A professor here. He's gone now. Taught anthropology, which I took for distribution requirements. He specialized in sexual practices of other cultures. That should have told me something, but I was too blinded by his charm to notice. I suppose he felt that his youth was about to leave him at age forty, so to prove he still had it he embarked on a conquest. His wife was plain. Not ugly, just unadorned. She taught English literature. The poetry of Elizabeth Barrett Browning."

I didn't recognize the name. Literature wasn't my thing.

"How do I love thee? Let me count the ways."

"Oh yeah, that sounds familiar."

"She was famous in her day. A precocious child of a wealthy family. She had mysterious ailments and took opiates for pain relief. Some speculate that's where she acquired her vivid imagery. She married for love and was disinherited for her trouble."

"What was his name?"

"Who? My professor or her husband?" The twinkle in her eye gave away her jest. "Thomas. Thomas Jackson. Later, after it was over, it occurred to me that perhaps I fell in love with his name. Same as the Confederate General Stonewall Jackson. A naïve Southern belle, seduced and abandoned by the namesake of a regional icon."

I knew she was messing with me there, but I let it pass. Not wishing me to think there was anything ever going to come of it, she made it a joke.

"Dashing, articulate, powerful?" I said.

"Exactly. Mix with impressionable female looking for love and finding lust."

"So, you were an item?"

"Not at all. Very secretive. Later I learned about his past paramours. One was willing to talk about it. File under sadder but wiser. We started in his office, after hours. He had a floor size oriental rug. Must have had a thick pad underneath because I wasn't uncomfortable. Except for the fact that I was a virgin. But he helped me get over that. He was, shall I say, very skilled."

"A regular Don Juan."

"He steered me to a friendly doctor in DC who prescribed birth control pills. I didn't have to pay a cent. Later I learned why.

The second girl he was involved with got pregnant. She had an abortion, which he arranged. She had a breakdown after. Mental hospital, shock treatments."

"Didn't she?"

"Rat him out? Not in the slightest. That's how good he was. Made her feel responsible."

"Ugh. I'd like to punch him out."

"Get in line."

"Where is he now?"

"Europe, I think. He still writes to me. I read the first one, burned the rest unopened."

"And his wife?"

"She's still with him. She found out about us and it didn't seem to change things, except that he stopped fucking me. They had a big fight at the faculty club. Heard from a friend who heard from a friend that she threw a drink in his face and all the rest. Then he told her that it didn't mean anything. That woke me up. I didn't mean anything. He tracked me down and tried to keep me on his list of playthings. Promised he was going to leave his wife as soon as the opportunity occurred. But I was over him by then. If he hadn't denied me, maybe I would have fallen for it."

"I'm so sorry, Eve."

She caressed my cheek with the back of her hand. "Have you heard enough, baby? Your slut girlfriend's confession?"

"You're not a slut."

"Even though I picked you out when you were unconscious and naked?"

"Did you mean it about Stewart and David talking me up?"

"Of course, silly boy."

"Then I don't care about the other part."

"Thank God!" She rolled on top and smothered me with

kisses. She'd had plenty of educated, calculating men. Or was there just Professor Jackson?

"No. I have had a rich fantasy life the past couple of years. Don't have the equivalent of Playboy magazine. I suppose you just read the articles."

"I didn't realize it had more than pictures. I believe you, Eve. It wouldn't matter anyway. We're together now."

"You're unreal. From another planet. Maybe you've been doing more than time traveling." She raised an eyebrow.

"Swear to God, no. I hope that stops happening. Don't like the re-wind."

"I'd love a way to do things over. No Stonewall Jackson. Just wait for you to come along."

"Then we'd be both be virgins."

She rolled on her back and assumed what seemed to me the bawdiest Playmate pose I could imagine.

"You prefer the pre-owned model?" she deadpanned.

"Absolutely," I said, kissing her and closing my hand over her breast.

On the Brink

Christmas loomed around the corner. Eve and I studied our schedules, determined to minimize our separation. The 25th fell on a Monday, and the college calendar rolled until the Friday before. My last exam was at 8 AM and my parents had promised to pick me up at noon for the trip home. Eve was splitting her time between a surgery rotation with insane hours and her computer project for what little time remained.

"You can work as hard as you want, just so we can catch the New Year together," I said.

She looked over the vast pile of printout paper and smiled. "I have a surprise to tell you about."

Her family took religious holidays more seriously than mine. She'd be on a flight home on the 23rd in order to meet their expectations. Her brother would be home on leave from the Army then, her last chance to see him before he and his unit went overseas. It was understood that meant Vietnam, but we hardly spoke of it. I could tell she feared she'd never see him again. From what I could tell in my sporadic study of newspapers, that fear had some merit. As a platoon leader in the infantry, he'd be a target the minute the shooting started. Stewart performed a statistical analysis based on the limited information I passed along and tried to make it sound no more dangerous than other crazy stuff pulled by young men ages nineteen to twenty-five. She wasn't buying it.

"What is it?" I said.

"I've got an airline reservation to New York on December 31st. A hotel reservation at the Plaza the same night. Can you be there?"

I pushed her papers to the side. "The two of us, no school stuff. Romance in the Big Apple?"

"Ever been there?"

"A few times. But the only time I remember was my Dad taking me to see the Pirates play the Yankees in the 1960 World Series."

Eve rolled her eyes. I knew she wasn't a sports fan. Her brother had been a linebacker in high school and at The Citadel, where he achieved All-American status. Eve felt, rightly, pushed aside. I couldn't help myself. She asked why two Pirates fans would venture into enemy territory to watch a World Series game, the answer was simple: it was on a Saturday. No game was more important than me attending every minute of a school day at school, learning. So said my Dad. None of my relatives had ever gone to college, and Dad was going to see that streak ended.

"Let's talk about us and New York," I said.

We made a list. Empire State building, Statue of Liberty, Rockefeller Center and its ice rink under the giant Christmas tree, Central Park carriage ride, Radio City Music Hall if we could get in to see the Rockettes. Ambitious? Sure. But we were crazy with love and lust and saving it for another time seemed pointless. With all the crap afflicting the world, might as well live for the moment.

"I'm paying for this, Mr. Scholarship student," said Eve.

"What? No can do."

"Absolutely. I have a rich grandma who spoils me. Thank God she doesn't know about what I do in bed. I've got this covered. Later, you can invent something magnificent, and we can retire at 30 and live rich and pampered lives."

"Assuming the war is over with when I graduate, and I don't get drafted. Not that there's anything wrong with military service. I don't think I'd make a good soldier."

"Your father was a Marine."

"And he doesn't talk about it, either. My Mom told me why."

"My brother is in a big hurry to get over there. He says the war is going as expected and probably will be done sometime next year. That's what all the generals and political leaders are saying."

"It's a pity that Bear and his radical friends won't have anything to protest. I almost feel sorry for him. He'll have to get a real life."

We laughed at that idea. Then made love again, as if it were for the last time.

Heaven Must Have Sent You

December 22nd dawned clear and promising. Up early, I read the paper and noted the forecast for a high of 60. It was a slow news day. President Johnson was in Australia for a funeral, had met with the President of South Vietnam and rumors flew he would stop in that country to visit American troops. Nobody had hopes for peace talks with the Viet Cong. In Wisconsin, the Green Bay Packers prepared to play Saturday against the Los Angeles Rams. The Packers would win the game and go on to win the NFL championship against the Dallas Cowboys on New Year's Eve, the infamous Ice Bowl. I knew I'd be with Eve, so forget about football. I had a better alternative.

Speaking of Eve, she was pulling a marathon shift at the hospital in order to be able to leave for Charleston on time. I planned to surprise her if I could. But first I had an exam to get through and a final attempt to bury the hatchet with Bear. I didn't dislike him, although I had plenty of reasons. I found him overbearing and arrogant. His politics too extreme. He was more often stoned than not. Maybe that sounds like I really didn't like him, but I looked for the good in people. He was smart. Treated his girlfriend nice. He came from a wealthy and pampered background. His parents spoiled him. I blamed them for how he turned out.

I took the exam, thought I'd done well, so I headed over to the Union for a celebratory soda. Many students had been luckier and were already gone. The resident bridge players were there, a couple of guys were shooting pool, and not much else. Until I spotted Bear sitting alone in the corner, reading. A perfect time to approach him.

He closed his book and flipped it upside down. Up close it resembled a loose-leaf folder. He frowned when I approached. Ignoring the lack of invitation, I sat down in the easy chair opposite.

"How's it going, Bear?"

"Nothing much." He looked at the wall.

"Last minute studying?"

"What? Oh, yeah, well, never too late to cram before the big one."

"What subject?" It could only have been Freshman Psych, but I asked just to start the flow.

"Um, well, independent study."

A new concept. I didn't know freshman could take independent studies, much less that there would be an exam.

"It's not an exam. I'm supposed to complete a project I started. It's a big job."

"Who's your advisor?"

"Saul."

He meant Professor Stone, who preferred students use his first name. I might as well have been a cop interrogating a suspect for the Bear's response. A test from Stone had to be one of the easiest chores on campus, anyway. An A was about has hard to achieve as having a temperature of 98.6. What was he sweating? Strangely, he was dripping with perspiration.

"Can I do anything?"

"Yeah, leave me alone."

Still pissed about something, but I couldn't tell what. "Bear, I'm sorry if I haven't been the kind of roommate you wanted. All the politics, well, it doesn't do anything for me. I don't mind the pot smoking. I don't indulge because it would fuck up my running. But that's as far as it goes."

"Politics isn't supposed to do anything for you. You are supposed to do things, be active, inquire about your environment, agitate for change, make waves. My parents, our parents, they're buried under a sedimentary layer of conformity. Tell the black people to wait for laws to evolve that will give them the equality guaranteed under the Constitution. Tell the colonial peoples not to behave harshly towards the nations that ripped off natural resources and oppressed them."

He had me feeling guilty. I paid lip service to the things of which he spoke, but like the sheepish demonstrators who avoided jail time by paying a fine for demonstrating, I was on the outside, staring in.

He continued in that vein. "You're like Emerson visiting Thoreau, imprisoned for refusing to pay a poll tax," he said "Emerson wanted to know what Thoreau was doing in jail. Thoreau countered by asking Emerson what he was doing out of jail."

"Let me help you. For old times' sake," I said.

A long pause.

"OK, I do need some assistance this afternoon. Allison is on her way home so I've asked someone from the Collective to help, but it may be a three man—person, I mean--job."

"What kind of help? Envelope stuffing? Phone calls? Delivering food to hungry people?"

"No, not this time. Kind of physical. Loading, unloading a van. It will be helping people in need, for sure."

His answer cheered me. I offered him a high five and he smacked my palm without much energy. The Collective he mentioned was a campus alternative to the Greek system of fraternities. They socialized with pot parties instead of keggers, posted political flyers on every empty wall and fiercely debated with the Young Republicans chapter. People believed, without proof, that the Collective also engaged in after-hours vandalism. The ROTC office had been torched with Molotov cocktails a month before. They supplied animal blood obtained from a Baltimore slaughterhouse to throw at Dow Chemical recruiters and other corporate entities believed to be in league with war-making industries. Of course, the ongoing picketing of the Math building computer center where I'd met Eve.

"Just tell me where and when," I said.

"Right here, at five."

That gave me time to change and go for a run, then grab some food at the dining hall before it shut down for the Christmas break. In my sweats I ran across campus at a steady but low-key pace. My path took me past the Math building, where the pickets still stood, even on the final day of the term. They waved V for peace, which I returned. Maybe I should do more overtly political stuff after break. My parents might object, but only if they found out. I didn't plan on getting arrested but adding my body to the swelling crowds at anti-war protests was nothing radical.

Leaving campus, I cut through a playground and ducked under the fence surrounding the golf course. I dodged a foursome of diehard golfers without raising their ire and ran the periphery. Soon others would be copying me. My coach predicted a major surge in popularity of running.

"No American has won the Boston Marathon since 1957, but there's a kid from Connecticut who might pull it off next year."

I wished he had been talking about me. With enough training and injury avoidance, maybe he would be. I ran surges down the next four fairways in response to my fantasy. The turf felt elastic, carrying me faster than my usual race pace. I was in command of my body and felt invincible.

Five o'clock rolled around and I bounded up the stairs of the union. Bear stood next to a slender, almost skeletal guy dressed head to toe in black. Pasty complexion with a few wisps of dark beard struggled to be seen under his nose and chin. Bear introduced him as Henry. If he were a Blaze student, I'd never crossed paths with him.

"I dropped out of NYU last year," he said when I asked.

"Money problem?"

He looked annoyed. Disdainful, almost. "No. School is irrelevant, as long as the capitalists are running things. I'm getting ready for the revolution."

Bear whispered something to him.

Henry nodded and cracked a brief smile. "In a manner of speaking," he said.

Bear took us to a white panel truck parked in front of the Union, the kind a plumber might own. At one time that had been the case. "McClain & Son" had been painted over. Bumper stickers reading "Impeach LBJ" and "War is not healthy for children and other things," proclaimed new ownership.

Bear drove with Henry at shotgun. We took a circuitous route through the city. Several times he stopped for no reason and stared long and hard behind us and at side streets. He traversed several alleys, only going ten miles an hour or so.

"This will take all day at the speed you're driving," I said, trying to inject some humor into what appeared a serious project. Bear grunted something inaudible and ignored my teasing.

He turned onto Highway 190 and drove parallel to the Potomac River for half an hour, then made a tire-squealing right turn onto an unmarked county road past a succession of harvested fields and the occasional farmhouse. After crossing a waterway marked Oblivion Creek he turned left into a driveway, or the remains of one: two parallel tire tracks traversing a weed infested plain and interrupted at intervals by dry creek beds. Ten more minutes brought us to a two-story frame house needing a paint job. A thin curl of white smoke drifted up from the chimney, otherwise it seemed uninhabited.

Bear pulled the van around to the rear and parked in front of a pole barn that looked a generation younger than the farmhouse. He backed as close as he could to the doors, got out and unlocked them. Four cats dashed out and disappeared in the grass.

"Fucking animals," he said.

The doors swing open slowly as if pulled by unseen hands. He finished backing in and produced a flashlight.

He alighted from the van and pointed the light at me.

"Haven't got all day," he said, sweeping the beam across the rear of the barn. I caught a glimpse of stacks of plastic bags piled on pallets. I walked to the nearest one. Black stenciled lettering read Milorganite. I transferred it inside the van. Heavy material, forty pounds at least.

"What is this stuff?" I said.

Bear said, "Milwaukee sewage sludge. Been around for sixty years or so. Alternative to inorganic fertilizers. More sustainable. Better for the planet."

That explained the faint but obviously unpleasant odor. More hippie-dippy propaganda, I thought, but harmless. "Well. this farm has seen better days. What are you going to do with it?"

Bear answered without hesitation. "The Collective is selling it to a commune in New Mexico called the Hog Farm. We got it from a distributor who had an oversupply."

"For a good price?" I said, thinking of my Economics class

Henry worked slowly and had trouble lifting a sack by himself. If he represented the future of my generation, we were in trouble. We piled fifty in the van. Then twenty-five-gallon jerrycans.

Bear said the Hog Farm used diesel generators for electric power.

"Another bargain?" I said. We drove back to town, taking the back roads and employing the same queer looping strategy as before.

"Are the Hog Farm people meeting us?" I said.

"No, tomorrow. We're just going to park it and they will pick up the keys to the van and drive back to New Mexico."

I sniffed. "I'm glad it doesn't smell like shit. I kind of thought it might. It's got a more, well, chemical odor. Like regular fertilizer at a garden store."

"It's 100 percent organic Milwaukee shit," said Bear.

They dropped me off in front of the Union. No "thanks-for-your-help" farewell. Maybe I expected too much. I felt good about helping Bear and making a peace offering. I hoped things didn't have to be hard-edged in the future.

It was pitch dark on campus, interrupted by a sprinkling of holiday decorations. I hoped for a white Christmas. A better chance existed at home. Here in the Beltway area, a snowstorm would produce highway chaos. I'd be ready to go when my parents drove up in the morning. Not just with my luggage. I decided I needed to tell them about me and Eve. All of it if I could blur the details about sex. I had to. I was going to be spending the night in a hotel with her. My debate with my Mom hadn't gone very well. If pressed, I'd do what I wanted. Better to ask forgiveness than permission.

I lay down, surprised at how tired I felt. Fell asleep at once and had the weirdest dream. I was in New York, supposed to meet Eve at the Rockefeller Center ice rink. A few dozen couples ice-danced and in general showed off their pairs skills. I skated around the perimeter, holding onto the railing, unsure of myself and anxious that Eve hadn't showed. I waited until the lights went out and the skaters had departed. I started shivering and awoke in a cold sweat.

I looked at my watch. Nearly eleven. Eve would be getting off soon. She had to finish her computer project before leaving campus. She told me to wait in her apartment, but I couldn't resist the urge to spend more time with her. Fully rested and feeling lusty, I wanted to be with her. It was not too cold. Maybe we could snuggle like bunnies in the hedge around the building and make love in a pile of leaves. A crazy scheme but one she might accept. Beds were for boring middle-aged parents. I removed a paisley pattern sheet we'd used as a wall hanging. It would protect us from pebbles and sticks. We'd generate enough heat to stay warm.

I ran across campus with the sheet tucked under my arm like a football. Seeing my breath in the chill made me reconsider, but novelty won over reason. I reached the Math building dodging an orange VW bug with "AAA Janitor Service" painted on its doors. For once, no demonstrators blocked entry. I could use the front.

Somewhere inside a portable radio started to play a Marvin Gaye tune. A duet with Tammi Terrell. Crazy popular. *Heaven Must Have Sent You from Above*.

My heart fell when I reached Eve's desk and found it abandoned. Her notebooks and printouts predicted a return, but I couldn't sit still and wait. I found the janitor with his radio.

"She was here, and she left."

"When?"

"She's coming back. She left her purse at the hospital. You just missed her."

Marvin and Tammi belted out the chorus as I pondered my options.

Sensible to wait, but I wanted to surprise her. My frustration threatened to tear me open.

Two ways to the hospital. The longer by road, the shorter, unlit, zig zagged between academic buildings and dormitories. I rushed into the darkness, trailing the paisley shroud behind me like a contrail. I ran a half mile in two minutes.

The hospital appeared as I crossed the road, slowed to a jog, catching my breath. Vacant ambulances hugged the curb next to the emergency entrance, the only entry at night. Other than a few interior lights, and a solo security guard, no sign of life.

"Oh, you just missed her," he said, not lifting his eyes from the sports page.

"Damn it all. Which way? Never mind."

I took the street. A minute's rest gave me the strength to run another two-minute half. With a hundred yards left, I still hadn't caught up. Most odd. Then I made the final turn and the truth hit me. I spotted the white bike she'd used parked at the foot of the marble staircase.

She paused and turned at the top, her head visible behind a vehicle that had parked after my departure. I yelled her name and she waved. I spotted the panel truck I'd taken with Bear parked behind the VW. It seemed odd but my joy at seeing Eve brooked no distractions.

Stewart told me later only luck saved me.

In my headlong rush I failed to see a trench by a junction box. Learned later a utility crew dug it. I tripped, fell flat in the shallow hole which shielded me from the supersonic shock wave that arrived 50 milliseconds behind the explosive flash.

Last came the sound, echoing off every surface within a mile, a torrential crackling symphony that squeezed me like a python. The December chill had vanished, replaced by an unreal bubble of near tropical air. I pulled myself into a kneeling position behind the junction box, fearful to rise higher lest a second wave decapitate me. The vehicles had disappeared. The staircase and portico no longer existed, replaced by a crater in which lay the front of the building. The lawn burned like a prairie fire. Debris began to land. Wood fragments, glass shards, bricks, and dirt. And other things. Things I won't try to describe because I can't bear to. She was all I wanted from the world, and now even hope abandoned me.

Part 2: Vietnam

Fixing to Die

Fucking hot today. Vietnam meant fucking hot. Especially mid-July. In the northern part of South Vietnam, known as I Corps in the American military, the heat alone could take out an ill-prepared grunt. Worse in the Mekong Delta 400 miles, or 600 klicks south, according to those who'd served there. My platoon and several others from Golf Company, Seventh Battalion, Seventh Marines, got rotated out of the thick of the fighting around Go Noi Island and put in Danang to await replacements for those we'd lost in Operation Allenbrook, plus guard the air base and other facilities. The brass believed the NVA divisions opposing us planned an all-out assault on the city. Mini-Tet, they called it. The battalion had been fighting since mid-May to prevent it. Casualties mounted every time we went out. Our company commander and his radioman (RTO) had been killed by a mortar on our last patrol. Every platoon's effectiveness lay below fifty percent.

What made today different was a letter from Stewart.

Hi Pax:

Hope you are safe and well, keeping your head down. The TV news has been bad, so I never watch it. Besides, in order to get time on the computer I stay awake all night, so I sleep during the day. Cal Tech is a great place for a summer internship. I might try to transfer here or at least apply to graduate school if I end up staying at Blaze. The people here are engrossed in what they are doing, we spend little time discussing the outside world.

Probably like you in the Marines, although no one is trying to kill us.

To answer your questions: I found a researcher with an interest in time travel. According to her models, the reason you only jump short time gaps relates to the energy required. An outside force could increase the length, like I suspected. Also, and I think this is big, if you traveled fifty years forward, you would enter your body having aged fifty years. You can't travel to the twenty-second century. Likewise, you couldn't travel backwards before you were born. She did the math, but I doubt you would understand.

I'm so sorry to hear your Dad has lung cancer. You should take that as a sign you ought to quit smoking. So what if everyone does it?

The FBI and ATF regarded me as a person of interest in the bombing. After all, I helped transport the ammonium nitrate and fuel oil from the farm to the campus. The Milorganite story suckered me completely. It existed but Bear used high grade synthetic fertilizer in the van. The Hog Farm commune had never heard of Bear. The janitor survived by a complete miracle in the basement and vouched for my story. Henry slipped up and the cops in New York caught him bordering a bus for Canada. He confirmed my alibi. But Bear had made good his escape a day before.

Most of the month after Christmas remains a blur. Stewart told me I made a few attempts to time travel, to no avail. The college doctor put me on a ton of tranquilizers and started me back on the anticonvulsant drugs too. I said a lot of pretty crazy stuff, including my wish to go back in time. By the time I got off them, the window of opportunity had closed. I did my best. Nothing worked. I even persuaded a guy on the football team to knock me out. He refused until I bribed him by convincing Stewart to tutor him in math. The intended concussion succeeded only in giving me a bad headache for a week.

My Dad had started coughing blood, leading to a doctor and x-rays. My Mom occupied her time caring for him after his lung cancer surgery. When I announced I had quit college in order to join the Marines, I thought she might need a month in the psych ward too.

"Why on God's Green Earth do that?"

My logic didn't impress her.

"This boy you call Bear. You say he's a revolutionary?"

"Yes. He killed Eve."

"Let the police or FBI catch him."

"They won't. He'll be in Canada or someplace they can't find him."

"The Marines can do the job then?"

"Right now, they're killing the revolutionaries Bear supports. His comrades, he calls them. I want to kill them too, one at a time, until someday I catch up to him and send him to hell."

"Knox." Sgt Sender stood glaring at me from the bunker entry, so I tucked the letter away and stood up.

"Sergeant?" I squinted into the mid-morning sun rising over the guard tower behind him.

"College boy, right?"

"One semester." It wasn't an admission I enjoyed. Intellectuals weren't well-liked in the Corps.

"Close enough. Listen up. Battalion is sending a news crew over to interview grunts. I need somebody who can talk without being a complete moron. You've been here what, two months?"

"Give or take. My DEROS is 6/9/69."

He snickered without cracking a smile. "If you live long enough. Anyway, you aren't a fucking new guy (FNG) anymore. And you know by now these reporters want to push negative stories about Marines. We kill babies, rape women, burn villages. How we don't like being here. And a thousand piddly, shitty things that might be true, but aren't their fucking business. Don't give them any shit like that to report. Keep your answers brief. No barracks language. Don't call the gooks the gooks. In particular, the ARVN. Am I clear?"

"Yes, Sergeant." I trusted him more than I liked him. Sgt Sender was the man in charge of the platoon when a fire fight started. Paying attention to him had saved me from harm more than once already.

"Lt Burke will be there. Him not being West Point will help. The Pointers sound too gung ho. Never send a bullet when you can send a grunt. The reporters sense it, keep throwing red meat. End of the day, Mister and Missus America get the idea the Marines want to kill their son."

I met with the reporting crew and producer just off the tarmac where they'd gotten off a Huey. I didn't see the Lieutenant. Lots of reasons why he might not be there. Better start without him. Like Sender said, being a non-Pointer meant less likely he'd care.

I picked out the guy most likely to be in charge, a balding scarecrow of a man wearing the typical correspondent combat vest, khaki with an abundance of pockets, and a floppy bush hat like an Aussie. He gave orders to the others, didn't lift a finger to help the setup. Patch on his pocket read Mark Edwards.

"PFC Knox here. My sergeant said you wanted an interview," I said.

"I asked for an officer. Somebody with knowledge."

"Sir, Lt Burke is securing a perimeter because he heard NVA snipers were setting up over the wire to shoot reporters."

Taylor flinched and looked over my shoulder in the direction of the base boundary. I knew without looking that the fence lay 800 meters away, all trees and vegetation within 200 meters of it received regular defoliant treatment, and the open ground seeded with anti-personnel mines. After dark, the local VC might lob some harassing mortar fire, generally without effect.

"Damn it then, take me to better cover and we'll start without him."

I knew Sender would get the story later and give me an appropriate reward, like not having to hump a mortar tube on our next patrol.

"Cigarette, sir?" I offered him a Lucky Strike.

He accepted and showed a small amount of grace. "If you have some to spare, my crew would appreciate that."

I led the way to a sand bagged bunker we used for cover during real attacks. The crew could set up using it as background. See how safe your boy is in Vietnam? The other members of the technical crew started setting up their equipment and I passed out cigarettes. One member of the crew declined: the cameraman was not a man at all. Her baggy fatigues concealed a good figure. She wore her red hair short and pushed under a field cap. A few Marines standing nearby caught on, and the wolf whistles began. Non-Vietnamese women were a rarity in a combat zone except for the ones on USO tours, and nurses, who kept their distance off duty.

"Do all the boys out here smoke?" she said.

I nodded. "Gives them something to do with their hands besides jacking off. I started after I joined the Marines."

"What? Jacking off?"

I suppressed a laugh. Even the girls were different in a war zone.

"No ma'am," I said.

"Drop the ma'am, marine. I'm 23 and single. Don't ask if I have a boyfriend and I won't include your masturbation confession that I just got on tape."

She burst out laughing and her face lit up.

"Sorry Private," she said. "That was a dirty trick."

"Maybe I should quit smoking and just choke the chicken. When I was in college last year I didn't smoke. I ran cross country for my school in fact."

"What's your name?" she said. I thought I detected a little more than polite formality, but horny Marines can be forgiven for not being able to tell the difference.

"Pax Knox. I'm from Pittsburgh."

"You're not the typical grunt I've seen over here."

"How long have you been in Vietnam?"

"Eighteen months. Obviously, mostly not in the field. But I've talked with quite a few of the boys. You're different."

I wanted to ask: different good or different bad? Before I could, a sharp whistle grabbed her attention.

"Got to run. It's show time," she said, stroking my cheek with the back of her fingers.

She carried her minicam over to the whistler, a man dressed identically to the producer. The girl talked to him for a minute, looking in my direction every so often and pointing at me. He rocked on his heels, stroked his chin while he listened. Finally, he nodded and walked over.

"Brent Taylor," he said, offering a handshake. He looked like famous people always did. I hadn't seen many but the distant, haughty expression never varied.

"Knox, Paxton, PFC, USMC." Trying to keep it simple like the sarge wanted.

"How long have you been in Vietnam?"

I smiled at the girl with the camera. I wondered if I could get her name.

"Cut," said Taylor. He waved. "Look at me, not at the camera."

"Sorry, it's my first interview. Two months."

"What are you doing here?"

"Trying to stay alive."

I'll give him credit. Taylor knew how to interview. He got me to talk about my parents, my hometown, college life, and the love affair with Eve. It didn't take much more to launch me into my hatred of Bear.

"So, I want to kill him. And as many of his Viet Cong friends as possible. Then I can rest."

"Do you think the United States should be in Vietnam?"

"It's not for me to say. I mean, our government has put us there. They say to fight for freedom. My job is to obey the orders of my superiors and do my best to carry them out."

"You're saying that you are only obeying orders. Is that right?"

"I guess so."

"And because you want to kill Viet Cong, you agree with those orders?"

Didn't seem like a tough question. "That sounds about right."

"What about the protestors? Do you want to kill them as well?"

"The ones that made the bomb, sure."

"Their friends and families?"

"What's that got to do with it?"

"I'll ask the questions, Private Knox."

"When there's a war, people take sides, whether they want to or not."

Taylor stopped the interview and waved me off. No handshake now that he'd gotten what he wanted. He stood close to the lens for a closeup.

"There you have it. No opinion about many of the key issues of the war. A shallow, impressionable youth inflamed by the accidental death of a girl working at a controversial US Army program. He's now signed on to continue the internationally criticized policies of the US government in Vietnam. The war grinds on, and a generation of Americans, willingly at times, have signed on to continue a scorched earth policy down a road with no return. For some, it will be the ultimate dead end. But for Private Knox, he's just obeying orders."

Taylor tossed the mike to the sound guy and left, followed by the producer. Not a backward glance. Seeing my chance, I approached the camera girl.

"Is he that much of an asshole every day?" I said.

"Depends on who he's talking to. If you're somebody he likes, then you get velvet gloves on your ass."

"Didn't take a rocket scientist to figure out where he stands on the war. I didn't start it, you know."

"It's real big in the news world. Careers are exploding, reputations made over it. If you want to be somebody, you cover the war, like it or not."

She busied herself writing ID numbers on cassettes and then in a black notebook.

"Would you go on a date with me?" I blurted.

"What?" She was laughing. Not sure if she was flattered or disgusted.

"Most of the Marines here use their free time to bang any fox that they sniff, if you'll pardon my French."

"They're horny," she translated.

"What 19-year-old guy isn't?"

"So, you are propositioning me?"

"Where I was raised, a date was a social encounter in which persons of the opposite sex met in a public place for the purpose of getting to know one another. It's not a code word for sex. I just want to feel human again. Maybe get some respect. Your reporter boss didn't seem to have any to spare. In a few days, I'll be back in the bush. Humping with the rest of the grunts, trying to kill NVA before they kill us. I don't want a roll in the sack. But maybe I can impress you that I'm decent, with real feelings and intelligence, and there will be one person besides my family and a couple of buddies who will remember me as I was before." I paused. Didn't want to act like I wasn't coming back, but the reality was a lot of Marines weren't. Or we'd be like my Dad, with ghosts who haunted their dreams every night, who didn't want to make a simple peace with their enemies by buying a foreign car.

She grabbed my hand and squeezed it. "I'm sorry. I didn't expect that from you, and that was my mistake." She ripped a page out of her notebook and scribbled on it, handed it to me. "I can't go out with you. Not because I don't want to or think I might not enjoy it. We're in a big rush to get this story out so we're flying back to Saigon in a few minutes."

"Making a deadline?"

"Every day. Brent is pushing hard."

"Hitch your star to the right wagon and you could make it

big," I said.

She made a self-deprecating wave. "I don't know. I'm a small-town girl. Just want to make sure I don't end up doing dishes and pushing out babies." She laughed. "I didn't mean that to be harsh. Plenty of good women pushed out babies, including my mother. There are lots of career opportunities for women now, you know?"

"Well good luck to you. I hope your dreams come true, and I hope I live to hear about them."

Two minutes later I was back with the squad, getting all manner of ridicule for my audacity.

"Pax wants to pop some cherry."

"Marry me baby, and I'll be your Semper Fi fuck."

It continued until Lt Burke sent Sgt Sender over to give us the bad news. We were going on the next Huey or Sea Knight to the An Hoa combat base.

"Get your gear together. The war called. It wants you back," he said.

It was only then that I looked at the paper from the camera girl. Her handwriting was full of curves, like her chest. Lauren Dufresne. An address in New York City and a phone number.

Phony War

The next two weeks were quiet. No attacks, no shooting. Our patrols didn't make contact with VC or NVA. A few optimists in the ranks started speculating maybe the politicians were having peace talks. The other team had taken horrendous casualties during Tet. Maybe they'd had enough of war. Grunts were like ball players: any mention of good luck was considered harmful. Busting up a no-hitter by talking to the pitcher. The optimists shut up.

Ironically, our corpsman, Doc Steinberg, committed the sin of inviting a jinx. In the middle of one afternoon while we enjoyed a couple of cans of warm beer each, he said, "I can't remember when the last time I've had to treat any gunshots or shrapnel. Maybe my morphine syrettes are going to outdate."

"Oh fuck, no," moaned Philly, whose real name was Mertz but hailed from Philadelphia, naturally. We couldn't subject the Doc to any physical punishment. Being a corpsman made him untouchable. But he caught a lot of verbal abuse. Londell Davis, known as the Black Pearl on account of his shaved head, threw a boonie hat at him. Doc caught it and flung it back.

The Pearl's best friend, Damon Washington, AKA Cherry Tree, started in on Doc as well. "You motherfucker. You know I'm short. Don't bring down any shit on top of us. I'll use you as a shield if I have to. I'm tired of fighting this motherfucking white man's war. Any cracker motherfucker that messes with me is gonna get a taste of my Kabar. I'll slice his balls right off. I'll start with the guy that killed Dr. King and work backwards."

Bad news, of course, always made its way to the front lines. We knew all about the shit storm that exploded after Martin Luther King died in Memphis. Rumors flew that members of the Black Panther Party had enlisted in the Army and Marines and were preparing an outright race war. In the front lines we still considered the VC to be our prime enemy. But in the rear, such a threat carried more substance.

"Hey easy, Tree," I said. "You know Bobby Kennedy got shot too. Enough misery going around for all of us."

"Sheeit. It don't mean nothing. We be brothers here because we kill gooks. But back home, different story. Back home, you don't know me. I don't know you."

Doc got to his feet and played peacemaker as much as he could. But he'd put everyone on edge. Karma was going to fuck us over good now. The next day the gooks sent a barrage of mortars and 122mm rockets our way. It was the first attack in a while. I'd been mortared before, but the dread never left.

It started after dark. The grunts with experience got the jump on the new guys when they heard the plopping sound of a mortar tube expelling its contents from back in the hills. The gooks would have measured the coordinates for firing. They had plenty of help. Any Vietnamese who worked in the combat base was a potential spy. We'd dig new foxholes and reinforce our bunkers all the time, but we all knew someone, some time, was going to get killed. We'd shoot back, but during patrols the following day never find evidence that it had been effective.

Capt West assembled Golf Company the next day. He said that the PAVN company which had mauled the patrol was the tip of the iceberg. The gooks were out in strength and this was a chance for us to take them on and knock the crap out of them.

Operation Meatgrinder, he called it.

"What other companies are going out?" said Philly after Capt West left.

"We're it," said Lt Burke.

"Whose fucking idea is that? One understrength company against maybe two battalions of gooks? Probably been resting up and re-fitting over in Laos where we can't go."

"Philly, shut the fuck up," said Sender.

"Charlie and Fox Companies will be in blocking positions between the gooks and their bases. You are the hammer, and they are the anvil. Between us we smash them into protoplasm," said Burke.

"Proto- what?" said Philly.

"Like when you tie an M-80 to a frog and blow it up," I said.

"I don't do that shit."

"Like that LURP we body bagged today," I said.

"Body counts," said the Stretch in a quiet voice.

"What?"

"I heard the Old Man on the radio with Col Schiffer. Shit flows downhill. MACV wants higher body counts. Tet wasn't good enough for them. With LBJ bailing, there could be a major power shift in Washington. Kill enough gooks, maybe the other side will wave a white flag. So the Colonel leans on his Company commanders to put more grunts in the field and fight the NVA."

"And more of us go home tagged and bagged. Wonder if MACV ever worries that our side may get tired of dying first?"

We stopped bitching and got ready. As many magazines as I could carry, some belts of .30 caliber ammunition for our M-60 machine guns, frags with white phosphorus and high explosive, M79 grenade rounds. Each grunt was going to be carrying 60 pounds of gear.

Sgt Sender watched me field strip my M16 and reassemble it, as well as remove each .223 cartridge from my mags in order to wipe them clean. "College boy. You take this killing business seriously."

"It's what I'm here to do."

"You could've gotten a rear echelon post, no sweat. Logistics, intelligence, supply. You name it. Instead, you're on the frontline with the grunts. Most of them are barely able to write their names. If they don't get killed, they'll go back to the world and work in construction or as mechanics. Paycheck to paycheck. You could be a doctor or lawyer. What gives?"

"Weren't you listening to me talk to the TV reporter?"

"I thought you made that shit up."

"My girlfriend got vaporized. Like she'd been hit by a 122mm mortar."

"Fuck. They catch the guy?"

"No. He split, maybe to Canada. He had been my roommate. I helped him bring the bomb to campus. I thought I was hauling fertilizer to give to some hippies in New Mexico."

"Revenge. You waste a lot of gooks. Think that's bringing her back?"

"No, Sarge. I need to kill until a voice inside me says I've killed enough."

"How many so far?"

I shrugged. "We've had maybe fifteen firefights. Killed five or six for sure. Can't always tell."

"Feel any better?"

"Maybe some?"

"This girl was that important, you have to keep on killing? That's seriously fucked up. You're not even 21. Got a life in front of you. She didn't ask you to do this. She'd want you to live. Not go out like this."

"Sorry Sarge. I don't see any other way. Not unless I get that fucker in front of me. Kill him and this is over. I've learned every way to kill. The next time I see Bear I'll make sure it happens."

Sgt Sender shook his head and patted me on the shoulder. "You can walk point tomorrow, killer."

A Walk in the Sun

Next morning Huey helicopters ferried us out on another mission.

The landing zone wasn't hot, but the weather was. I'd taken on as much water as I could. Supposedly the slicks would return to another LZ and supply us with food, water, and ammo. That was the part the NVA had a hand in deciding.

I was supposed to walk point, but Lt Burke overruled Sender.

"Pax, let Grub take the point."

Grub was a good old boy from Alabama. There had been friction between him and the two black platoon members, Black Pearl and Cherry Tree. It wasn't enough that we were fighting the heat, insects, and NVA. We had to import our domestic problems as well.

"Yes sir," I said, stepping aside so Grub could take the lead. Philly and a grunt named Jackson followed in his wake, then me, then the two black Marines. Somewhere behind were the other members of the platoon. Lt Burke was roughly in the middle with Stretch, carrying the radio, and the Doc.

Black Pearl grinned and gave me a Black power clenched fist sign.

"No fucking fragging on this patrol," I hissed at him.

"Relax, boy. We're just chilling today." He pantomimed smoking weed, and I waved him off. He was just fucking with me. Marines would have to be crazy to smoke weed where we were. I did my share when not on patrol. I hoped it kept me from slipping back in time. I didn't need to give the gooks a second chance to kill me.

The line of men advanced slowly through the dense foliage. Our rule commanded keeping enough space between individuals that an ambush would be less effective, and a booby trap would take out one grunt. We avoided trails at all costs, fearing ambush. We might set up one of our own after dark.

I couldn't see Grub on point. I knew he was not only watching for signs of the enemy, but also blazing our path with a machete. It was tiring work, and he was perhaps the best suited of us all for the task. He was an absolute backwoods boy from Talladega, in the heart of a state forest. He knew the woods, knew how to track, and shoot. I asked myself: Why the fuck can't we all get along? I answered my own question. Grub wore a Confederate flag on his sleeve and wasn't shy about declaring his support of Governor George Wallace. Sender had told the platoon if Grub ever got killed, he'd check if the corpse had a bullet hole in its back.

Besides the point man, a pair of flankers moved lateral to the column and circled back to beat off any attempts to flank us. Operating in the blind made it difficult for all the parties to function in a coordinated fashion. We were not supposed to talk or smoke, but there was invariably chatter between the flankers and the main body of the platoon. After four hours of this we were tired and hot. Focusing on the task at hand became increasingly difficult. The column halted. At least Philly did, because he held up his hand to signal me to stop. He turned and staged whispered:

"Have the lieutenant get up here. There's a trail."

I passed the word and leaned against a tree while I sucked down the last of my water, wishing I could smoke but knowing that was out of the question. In a few minutes, Lt Burke edged past me.

"How's it going sir?" I asked.

Burke said nothing but Stretch whispered as he passed, "We're going to loop back real soon." I took that as a good sign, but it meant that any trailing NVA would find it a good opportunity to set up an ambush, if that's what they wanted.

I sat still, listening to the sounds of the jungle. The constant hum of mosquitoes was a given background noise. Birds flew around, mostly out of sight, but making themselves known with their calling. I hadn't heard any monkeys today, but they sometimes called one another from high in the trees, out of sight. Larger animals, including tigers, also patrolled, but I'd never seen one.

The jungle smelled as well, a fecund, earthy odor that some grunts complained about, but I found refreshing for reasons I didn't understand. Maybe it was the absence of aviation fuel smell and the stench of the shit fires we used to dispose of human waste in camp. If there had been a firefight recently, the smell of death was a reminder of the business of killing. Today, none of those things interfered.

I could almost have fallen asleep, it felt so good, when my nose alerted me. A sharp, fishy odor replaced the jungle scent that wafted through the triple canopy. It was almost below the threshold of detection, but I had a good nose for fragrances. This was no perfume. I waved a hand and got Philly's attention. He was fifteen meters ahead of me. I pantomimed my concerns. I pointed to my nose, then out into the jungle. Walked two fingers across my palm and then used them to indicate weapons. I mouthed the word "gooks."

I started looking into the dim green light for signs of movement. I still heard nothing, but that didn't reassure. The

NVA were as silent as Indians. In contrast, a column of Marines sounded like a parade of elephants, according to prisoners we'd taken. They could hear us clearly. Every belch, fart, and spit. I shut my eyes, which weren't helping. Focused on sounds. Then it hit me. There weren't any. The birds had grown silent or simply flown away. The gooks were right in front of us.

The shooting started. A single shot from an M-16, answered by a burst of AK fire. Shouting and screaming followed. I hit the ground seconds before a machine gun raked overhead, dropping a carpet of leaves on me. I crawled toward the sounds of the fighting, using Philly's boots as a guide.

Something exploded behind me. Grenade or RPG. More screaming. They wanted Doc. No way, I thought, then he hurdled me on his way back to the rear.

I still hadn't fired a shot. No point since I couldn't see the enemy and I didn't want to shoot a fellow Marine in the back. Ahead of me I heard Philly blasting away.

Something moved off to my right. The NVA regulars wore helmets that looked like Jungle Jim pith helmets, and that's what I saw, no body or weapon. Just a helmet with a few sprigs of foliage for camouflage. My fire selector was on full auto. I aimed below the helmet and fired a burst. The helmet vanished. No scream. I crawled on, waiting for return fire, but there was none. I pushed aside a fern and exposed the fallen NVA. His neck was laid open and his mouth made little gasping movements. I switched to single shot and put one through his helmet, just to be sure.

Grazing fire from a machine gun forced me to drop and kept me pinned. It cracked and hissed inches above my head. I hadn't been face-to-face with any of the soldiers I'd killed. Not like this. I stared into the swiftly clouding eyes of the dead man. His pigmentation faded as I watched. The dead, especially if their hearts beat down to empty, had no blood left to pink up their skin. Pale and motionless as a wax museum mannequin. Even black American Marines had the pallor. A fly landed on his face, then crawled into his nose. Before long he'd be covered with insects. Then inflate like an inner tube as decomposition got underway. He couldn't be any older than 19. My age. Probably had a girlfriend back home. Parents who would mourn him. He hadn't killed my girlfriend. It didn't matter, I told myself. A friend of my enemy is my enemy. My job was to kill him. His was to kill me. Probably not for the reasons his commanding officers believed. He wanted to go home, and the way home led directly through me.

The shooting had stopped. An eerie quiet returned to the jungle. Eddies of smoke drifted between the trees. I searched the body, stuffed some papers out of his knapsack into mine, then quickly field stripped his AK and removed the receiver, rendering it harmless. I stuck the barrel of the weapon in the dirt next to the body and placed the pith helmet on top. Perhaps his buddies would be able to retrieve his body and send word home that he had fallen in combat. I couldn't do more than that. In ten minutes, I found the rest of the patrol gathered around Doc as he worked to try to save Grub.

I could tell Grub was not going to make it because he was making the same kind of useless breathing movements as the gook I'd shot.

"Got one," I announced, waving the papers at Lt Burke. He was on the radio, calling in a chopper to meet us at the LZ. Philly brought me up to speed.

"Grub saw the gooks first. They were in ambush position but hadn't seen us. He lit them up but one of them got off a lucky shot."

"Where are they?"

He pointed to an area in deep shade. Two sets of sandals marked the bodies' positions. "The rest got away. You say you greased one too?"

"Affirmative. Came across him and he didn't see me. Found some papers on him."

Philly looked them over and grinned. "Fucking-A. It's map, see?"

I looked but didn't understand until he patiently pointed out the trail, the LZ and some squiggly lines he believed were bunkers where the NVA had been waiting. We'd been shadowed by the squad of soldiers and as they were about to spring their ambush, Grub had gotten the drop on them. At the cost of his life, unfortunately. Philly wanted to search for the bunkers and try to kill the rest of the force.

"Negative," said Burke. "Chances are we wouldn't see it until we were on top of it. Then I'd have five or six KIA to fly out of here. We'll call in coordinates as best we can estimate and let the flyboys napalm them after we've scooted."

Grub was dead now. We wrapped him in his poncho and took turns carrying him. We moved as fast as we dared to the LZ, another half a klick away. The NVA had left to fight another day unless the airstrikes got them. As it turned out something entirely different happened.

The LZ turned out to be a little smaller than we needed for the slick to land. I went with Philly to blow up a large tree. He was as close to a combat engineer as we were likely to possess. We used C-4 explosive and lots of detonating cord wrapped around the tree. Then we retreated what we thought would be a safe distance and lit the fuse. The blast was enormous and when

I looked back the tree was completely blown. So much so that chunks of it started landing around our position. I got up to run, screaming at Philly to do the same, looked up and saw what looked like a telephone pole descending.

Blackness ensued.

Déjà Vu All Over Again

I woke up and looked around. Philly was nowhere around. I wasn't in the new LZ. The sun was high in the sky. It was still stinking hot. I couldn't believe it. Shit. Time travel again. Now what? I leaned against a tree, squatting, like I had learned to do on patrol when I wanted thirty seconds of rest. Not sleep. Just a few moments of self-hypnosis that nobody seemed to notice or care about. At 110 degrees and 100% humidity I wasn't going to really sleep. But the little refreshers, as I called them, restored something. This time the displacement had shot me back to the morning of the patrol. I looked around at the rest of the platoon on our break. They were all there, including Grub.

My watch read 13:14 Thursday. The explosion had pushed me back about two hours. Soon I'd get to re-live the ambush. Could I save Grub? That would mean walking point myself. Maybe I'd catch the bullet meant for him. I could hang back, let the shit fly, and focus on survival. Then there was the dead NVA soldier. Do I try to bag him again? What if he sees me first? War was played on the edges, all the time. I had a do-over at my disposal if I made the right decisions.

"Hey, Pax. Get your ass off the deck. You daydreaming again?" Philly appeared from behind a large anthill.

I shuffled over to the bush where Stretch and the Lt were hanging out. "Um, Lieutenant, sir?" I had no idea what to say.

"What is it, Knox?" Burke was six years older than the average grunt. He looked about ten years older now. Being under pressure did that to people. He was kinder than most officers I'd met. But not stupid.

"Uh, sir, I think it's time for me to take over the point. The brothers aren't going to bother him. Put him back by Philly."

His eyes narrowed. Volunteering without pressure was unusual. He tried to finesse the reason. "Don't tell me you owe Grub money or something. Because if you do, I'm going to say no."

"No sir. I just have a feeling about something about to happen. An ambush. I think I could spot it."

Now he halfway smiled. Had to be a joke. "What, you found some gook newspaper with their battle plans?"

"With your permission, sir." I tugged at map he'd been studying and held it so both of were looking at it. In fact, I'd been outstanding at map reading at infantry training, I reminded him.

"Knox, I don't get a copy of every grunt's resume. I'll accept your saying it's true."

A small wedge I could exploit. I mentally transposed the map I'd taken off the dead gook to the topographic one from Burke. "See how we have to walk down from elevation into a dry stream bed on our present course?"

He nodded. "Hard to avoid. I admit it's not ideal."

"Well, if the gooks have been shadowing us, they'll know that. They could set up an ambush and we'd walk right into it. Despite this area being thick with NVA, we haven't sniffed any. That's unusual, don't you think?"

"They could be under orders not to engage."

"Sir, we're one platoon. They only need half a company to hurt us bad and get away before we can call in air strikes or artillery."

"Fuck it Pax. You're so smart, why didn't you go to OCS and

get your own fucking platoon?" His pride was hurting. I waited. He had to get over it. Missing a possible ambush site could be a career ending move. Literally. He could just overrule me and continue. Or take a detour around the danger zone, in which case he'd get to the LZ late and with grunts even more tired and dehydrated. No ideal solution. He snapped the map back into its case.

"OK, Pax, take the point. Don't fuck up."

"Thank you, sir."

Grub accepted the change without complaint. He patted me on the helmet. "Brother, I'll be a few steps behind. I got your back."

In a few minutes we broke formation and resumed the march. We were only half a click from where the ambush waited. The tree limbs waved in a breeze we couldn't feel but desperately needed. I took the last swig from my canteen. Water warm as a bath trickled down my throat. The normal tension of patrolling built on itself tenfold. I made every step with as much care as I'd ever used. If the grunts in line behind me didn't like it, too bad. I figured Grub wouldn't have missed seeing a trip wire, so I mainly watched for signs of the enemy. And I got it. Just like before, the fish oil smell they carried from cooking rice balls betrayed their presence. Now I was a few meters short of where I'd been standing when the battle had started. I recognized a fallen tree and its stump. Somewhere off to the right waited the NVA I'd killed. If he kept fire discipline, I was OK. Chances were, they could see, hear and smell us.

I estimated 100 meters to go. I slowed my pace. I had to be like Grub and fire first, but they would leave me open to counter fire. If I waited for them to shoot first, same result. They'd have a light machine gun, meant to hit our legs and then take off our heads once we were down. Standard ambush protocol. I had an idea. Stupid of me not to think of it already. I held up my hand to halt the column and waved up Grub, who was carrying an M79 grenade launcher. I couldn't chance throwing a frag and having it hit a tree limb and land short. But the M79 could toss a frag farther and more accurately. I whispered my plan to him.

"I can smell them. Just a little bit ahead. Go back and have someone bring up the M60. I'll drop a grenade at where I think they are and the M60 can rock and roll. I'll move to the right and try to flank them."

He gave me thumbs up and moved back down the line. I had to wait for word of the plan to reach the end of the column. I needed patience and some luck so the NVA wouldn't get trigger happy and start shooting. I watched the seconds tick off my watch and gave it a good five minutes. Grub re-appeared and waved to me.

It wasn't an easy shot. I didn't want to hit a tree limb and I couldn't lob it like a mortar. It was more like a 60-yard pass play. The grenade would arm past 30 meters. It had to hit something solid to detonate. I spotted overhanging branches at about the right range, aimed, and fired. I flung myself to the side and heard the explosion as my face dug a furrow in the jungle humus.

Immediately after, the M-60 gunner began pouring fire down the trail. From the screams, I figured he was accurate. Best of all, the reaction was delayed. Some AK fire tried to answer the M-60 and the volleys of all the M-16s, but it wasn't enough. Their machine gun must have been hit by the grenade. I scuttled through the jungle towards a point I guessed would be on their flank. Sure enough, I came upon a group of NVA that had taken cover behind a log. They didn't see me, and I fired another M79 grenade in their midst. Bodies and body parts flew in all directions. Then I used my M-16 to pick off the survivors.

That task complete, I reversed direction and headed toward the lone NVA rifleman I'd killed the first time. He was still there, disciplined to the end, but he swiveled his head like a nervous turkey as the sounds of the battle. Not what he'd expected. I stepped into his view with my M-16 ready to shoot on full auto.

"*Gio tay!*"

He didn't hesitate. Dropped his rifle and put his hands up. I got behind him and checked him for frags and knives, then tied his wrists with some cord I carried in my pocket. I slung his AK over my shoulder and shoved him forward with the barrel of my M-16. I started shouting a good distance from where the thought the platoon had stopped. Last thing I needed was to die at the hands of fellow Marines.

"Looky there," crowed Grub. "Pax boy got us a prisoner."

"Waste the fucker," said Pearl. He raised his rifle and took dead aim.

"Stow it," said Burke. When Pearl did nothing, the lieutenant raised his .45 and pointed it. Then Pearl obeyed. "We need prisoners to tell us where the NVA is hiding," finished Burke.

I pulled out the paper I knew the prisoner had in his pocket. Nobody could speak any Vietnamese to ask him what the map showed, but we had a good idea anyway. Burke began to radio in coordinates for follow-up airstrikes.

"Private Knox." Burke was smiling at me.

"Go police up the battle area. We need a body count for the colonel."

I turned to leave.

"Knox," said Burke.

"Sir?"

He had a look I'd never seen before. He removed his helmet

and scratched his head. A wry smile wrinkled his dusty cheeks.

"Never seen you pass up a kill before. You growing a conscience?"

"Not sure, sir. Maybe just hit my limit for the day."

I trotted back down the trail, my spirits soaring at having saved two lives: Grub and the scared NVA. His comrades weren't so fortunate, but I wasn't sad. I counted twelve bodies, and there were a lot of blood trails leading away. Standard practice would have been to estimate a number two or three times greater than the fallen corpses, but I was having none of the lying for the sake of a bigger body count. We'd destroyed a platoon, at least, and that made me feel good.

We made good time to the LZ, and this time I avoided the demolition detail. The tree trunk flew incredibly high, narrowly missing Philly. I'd warned him but he didn't listen.

"What the fuck. Are you clare buoyant?"

"The word is clairvoyant, and no, I'm not. Just want to stay alive."

I searched the prisoner before we put him aboard the chopper. Everyone was so elated and not having any casualties, not even a scratch, they didn't notice when I pocketed a wallet I found in his gear. I didn't want money. I wanted an ID. Found one. I wanted to keep his service number. The NVA had a bureaucracy just like we did. If I survived the war, I'd try to find out who he was. Prisoners on both sides didn't fare well. Maybe someday I could find his family and let them know.

We got drunk that night on warm beer and a bottle of scotch provided by none other than Lt Burke. He didn't join us, but his spirit inhabited the bunker where we whooped it up. Third platoon covered our guard duty that night. We were dirty, smelly, and alive. Pearl joined in with the festivities, allowing that even though the white boys were still short in the manhood division, there was at least one of them (me) who had a set of balls. He and Grub got along like long lost brothers. Being alive was good.

"How'd you know about those motherfuckers?" Pearl asked me.

"I smelled 'em."

"Yeah, that's bullshit. White people smell bad, brothers smell good and the gooks ain't got no smell unless they been dead a couple of days."

"Well, what do you think?" I said. I wasn't sure I wanted to hear his explanation.

He stared at me in his typical fearsome pose, head cocked to the side, fist supporting his chin. "My granma say some folks in this world ain't real."

"What do you mean?"

"Means they ghosts. Don't live in this world. Just visiting. They travel back and forth from one world to the next. They see the future. She told me if I ever meet a ghost, best stay on his good side."

I felt a chill despite the air being north of eighty degrees. What, exactly, did he know?

"I don't believe in ghosts. I told you. I smelled the gooks," I said.

Pearl stood up. He offered me a hand and we clasped in a black power shake. "Baby, I'm staying on your good side the next firefight we're in. No bullet going anywhere near your white ass. You're better than having two weeks short time."

Next morning, except for being hung over, things returned to normal. Pearl avoided me as usual. Nobody offered to take my turn at burning the shit from the latrines. The sun came out and I washed and hung my socks up to dry. Rumors were flying that another big operation was in the works. Based on our contact with the NVA on patrol, G-2 guessed that there were bigger fish to fry back in the hills fronting the Laotian borders. Strictly speaking, they probably were on the other side of the border, taking advantage of America's fear of expanding the war.

Lt Burke surprised me at the end of my shit shift by inviting me into his hooch for a sit down. I must have showed signs of alarm, because he offered me a warm beer to go with the best chair in the place.

"Relax, Private," he said.

I really tried. "What's up?"

"I'm still mystified but happily so at what you did on the patrol. We've got the ability to reward good soldiering with a brief vacation from the war."

I knew about R and R in Thailand, Japan, or Hawaii. It was a bit early for me to get it, that's all.

"This is in country and doesn't remove you from the R and R list. Your pay is lousy, and your hours are worse."

"Plus, I could get killed any day," I added.

"So, look at this as the equivalent of a bonus check in civilian life."

I could have reminded him that I'd never held down a real job, but it wasn't the time to be sassy. I remained mute.

"Where am I going?"

"Little place on the shore near Danang. It's called China Beach. You'll go for three days, get the smell of the jungle out of your nose, drink cold beer for a change, listen to some entertainment. Hell, if you knew how to surf, you could do that."

I was ready for a change of scenery. My war had heated up, but I had a long way to go, especially if the time displacements continued to happen. Maybe Pearl could score some good weed for me. My fellow Marines weren't helping, joking about changing my nickname from Pax to Casper the friendly ghost. When the Huey arrived to take me and a couple of other lucky Marines down to China Beach, I wasted no time climbing aboard.

Love in the Time of Revolution

A letter from my Mom caught up to me when I arrived. I found my way to an ersatz Polynesian village by the shore and bought a cold beer. That alone made the war seem far away. Watching groups of men playing football, frisbee, frolicking in the water or surfing, I opened the letter.

Dear Son,

I hope this finds you well. Any time I see a strange car driving on our street, my heart stops, fearful that it holds a team of Marines with bad news about you. Dad isn't of the same mind. For some reason he has boundless faith that the protective blanket from Heaven that kept him safe, and his father before him safe in the Great War, has room for you. He didn't suffer physical injuries, it's true, but he's not the same man that left me for the Marine Corps. He swears he will beat the cancer. Things happen for a reason. Things I don't want to know about, while at the same time the mystery of not knowing bothers me even worse.

The TV segment which featured you finally made it on the air. What a waste! If I could get my hands on that reporter, I'd wring his neck. All he did was to edit segments of you saying things about you wanting to kill Communists with footage of our troops doing things like setting villages on fire with cigarette lighters or that Vietnamese General who executed a Viet Cong prisoner on camera. Nothing about how your girlfriend was blown up by some idiot protestors, who still haven't been caught - except for one who was so dumb he tried to get out of the country carrying an ounce of marijuana. It was one big anti-war commercial. I hope you never have to see it.

We both send our love and prayers for you. Don't take chances. Let someone else die for his country. I have your return date marked on the calendar. Every day I cross off one more box.

Love, Mom.

That was my Mom at her best. I penned her a quick reply, emphasizing that I was in a safe place, no weapons, no VC for miles. I omitted the actions that got me here. The only good thing about serving in Vietnam was that we could send letters postage free. The PX was handy, so I dropped off the letters and bought a few items to bring back to my platoon.

There were women around, mostly US government employees, nurses and a collection of college age girls called the Donut Dollies. The government hired them as morale boosters. The proverbial girls next door. The average age of a grunt was nineteen, and most of them wanted more action than they could get at a government-run R&R resort. A lot went AWOL into Danang or hamlets strung out along the way whose sole purpose was to supply the horny Americans with prostitutes. I was horny but not that desperate. I stopped by a coffee shop staffed by a few Dollies, who treated me with respect. The sister I never had. No chemistry erupted. I expected none anyway.

After that I sat on the beach. The hot sand felt clean. Looked clean. Vietnamese workers policed it every morning as if it were an exotic resort instead of respite for war-weary men. Two more days of peace and then back to war. I was so inured to the routine of base camp and patrolling, that I was at a loss for what to do when not cleaning my weapon, keeping my feet from getting jungle rot and filling sandbags for defense. Reminders of the war came into view everywhere I looked. A line of slicks ferrying troops or supplies. A low-slung gray silhouette, destroyer perhaps, cruising a few miles out in the South China Sea.

"Hey, Marine!"

A girl's voice jolted me out of my trance.

I spun around, disbelieving, seeing a miracle called Lauren.

She'd traded the field cap for a beret and the fatigues for a sundress with black and white stripes intersecting in a series of Vs that flattered her curves. Not out of place anywhere else in the world. A trailing pack of servicemen jostled for position, taking pictures like paparazzi stalking a film star.

I ran to her and we embraced like old lovers. The GIs and Marines all booed but retreated quietly.

"I don't believe in coincidences." I said.

"It's not," she said as she sat down next to me, smoothing her dress over her knees. She kicked off her flip flops and gave me a long look. "Mr. McNamara may not have been so good at running the war, but he made a great system to track of all his chess pieces."

"I guess he figured that out at Ford."

"You like being a pawn in a war?"

"Lauren, we're all pawns. You and your boss. Different chessboard, same idea."

She kissed me on the cheek. "That's fair. Only we aren't flesh and blood targets."

"Over here you are. I figure your boss will want to get close to the action so he can send some titillating footage back home and impress the big boys at CBS, or wherever he's aiming."

"You've got that right. He's picked the operation and everything. I'll say one thing for the military, despite the hammering they get from the networks, they continue to give us everything we ask for. It's sad, in a way. We send negative reports, politicians get angry at the military, they turn around and have more correspondents reporting from more places. They don't seem to know the definition of insanity."

"Which is?"

"Doing the same thing, over and over, and expecting different results."

Exactly what Mel told me last year. "Heard it from a psychiatrist?"

"Therapist in New York. Anybody who's anybody is in therapy, you know."

"I didn't know."

"Kidding." She patted my cheek. "I stopped going. It wasn't helping."

"Helping what?"

"You name it. I thought I had everything wrong with me. Believed that the world was rigged to frustrate me, hamstring everything I did."

"Did anything help?"

"I stopped listening to people who wanted to give me a list of excuses for why I hadn't succeeded."

"So, everything is right with the world?" I said.

"You're giving me a hard time, but that's OK. I know you don't think so. You're not in this crazy war because your draft board told you too or because of something you read at school or because you wanted to conform. Your reasons are not easy to understand, but you made your choice and you're walking the walk."

We sat in the sand staring at the azure water. I couldn't figure out if our meeting again mattered as much to her as me. She did work with that sleazy reporter Taylor, after all. I didn't care. Nothing before or after counted. I could be dead next week. Or the bullet marked 'to whom it may concern' might strike her down.

"Let's stop analyzing and pretend we're two people who are interested in each other, and we've got this great beach to explore for the rest of the day. Whatever happens, happens," I said.

"Deal," she said, rising out of the sand like a sea goddess from the deep, lifting her skirt in the process and flashing me with the sight of a lifetime.

The beach at low tide extended seaward flat and shining. A few surfers caught the minor swell rolling in from the east. Flocks of terns and gulls patrolled the shallows, scooping up their breakfast from the bounty exposed by the outgoing tide. The war did seem a long way off. Our hands bumped, rebounded, and finally clasped with assurance. My sideways glance met hers full on and the question of "if" was answered. It became solely a matter of when and where.

"I'm staying in an old French colonial villa just outside of Danang," she said.

"I'm staying in some flophouse they call a barracks on the grounds here."

"They won't miss you for a few hours, and if they do, how can they punish you? Send you to Vietnam?"

"Hey, that's my line," I said, laughing.

She'd gotten a cab driver from the city to wait for her, exposing her sordid plan of entrapment, with which I fully agreed. I contributed some black-market dollars to the fare and off we went. I asked about security. She said the VC knew the place was used by journalists, so it was spared.

"Until after they've won the war and they decide they no longer need you. Especially if you start reporting about all the shit they've done to the civilian population."

"History is written by the winners," she said, not smiling.

"And we're on the wrong side of it. Or so my former roommate would have me believe," I said.

She let go of my hand, grasped my head with her hands and turned it to kiss me full on the lips for an eternity it seemed. "I'm sorry you lost the one you loved."

"She loved me back tenfold. I'll never see that kind of love again."

"You sure?"

Twenty minutes later we were in the villa, naked and on top of the bed. Overhead a fan spun its lazy course, circulating humid air laundered of the usual kerosene/shit smell. Today of all days, the foul land odor had lost its battle with the sea breeze. Not that it mattered. I was awash in the smell of Lauren's body wash, which had collected in all the places I needed to explore: behind her ears, under her chin, between her breasts, around her navel and further down than that, as she pushed my head and exploring tongue to caress her as fully as I wanted.

She breathed her appreciation in soft moans and then used to her hands to arouse me more fully than I thought possible, and I entered her. Time vanished from perspective as we coupled over and over. She climaxed first, I not long after, and then we lay in glorious afterglow on the sheets.

"You're a great lover," she said, offering me a cigarette.

"I didn't know you smoked," I said.

"I don't. I brought them for you. You can quit when you get home if that's what you decide to do. I'm not about changing people."

"Easier said than done, from what I hear."

"When is your DEROS?"

I told her.

"Then we can meet up somewhere, continue where we leave off today, and we can talk about the future."

"Waiting for the future to arrive, hoping we both survive."

"I'm sure you will, Pax. You have an air of invincibility about you."

I thought back to the ambush and how the lives of several men turned on it. I knew playing God invited consequences I couldn't imagine. Did I possess a predetermined destiny? What aftereffects awaited me, if any?

Lauren must have seen signs of my internal conflict, because she stroked my chest and said: "Something troubles you."

I used a tangential reply. "Do you think everything happens for a reason?"

"I'm not sure. Used to when I was little. After what I've seen in the war, I'm convinced, no. Not good reason anyway. But you were thinking about something else."

Maybe I should tell her the truth and see what happens? After today, chances of our meeting again ranged from slim to none. I had arrived at the point in a warrior's life when he accepts his fate. He cannot cheat death. He proceeds knowing he will die, but not taking counsel of it. Only in that way can he survive.

"Forget it. Don't mean nothing. Let's talk about New York. How about the Plaza Hotel?"

"You have expensive tastes, Pax."

I explained about Eve and me, and her face grew serious. "It would be your first time?"

I nodded. "How about for you?"

She laughed. "Oh my God. I never shacked up in any place as fancy as that. Brent tried to get me drunk in LA at the Beverly Hills hotel. I knew he wanted to fuck me, but I had zero interest. Then, or now."

"Even if he promises you a network job?" I teased.

"Especially not then, because he'd do me once but try to keep me around while he fucked every young pussy that walked by. That's how those guys operate."

I walked over to the window and stared out at Danang and the mountains to the west, where my fate might be decided in a few weeks. "Not a great career decision," I said.

"Turn around so I can look at your good side, honey. Not that your ass is bad, but oh my golly, what a view you give a girl."

I gave her what she wanted.

"As far as it not being a good career move, I can be the judge of that," she said. "Don't worry about me and Brent, or any other guy."

"What time is lunch around here?"

"The kitchen is always open for you," she said, rolling on her back.

Operation Lionheart

When I got back to An Hoa, a savage energy consumed the firebase. Slicks brought many new faces to join the battalion, adding five companies in strength. The arriving grunts milled around, experienced, but strangers.

Rumors circulated that MACV planned to send us on a big-time operation near the Laotian border. Spitting distance, in fact, which meant that if some of us happened to wind up on the wrong side of the border, it was 'Sorry about that' time.

"Operation Lionheart," I remarked casually to Lt Burke.

He got in my face right away. "Who the fuck told you that, Marine?"

I gave him a laundered version of the truth, not mentioning Lauren at all. She told me about it the last time we kissed before I caught the slick returning me to the war. It all came from Brent Taylor's big mouth. He'd been drinking with a major who knew a colonel who knew a general. So, word got out in the press that we were going to take it to the PAVN divisions known to be based over in Laos.

"And I'll have fucking TV cameras to worry about. I want best behavior when the cameras are around," said Burke.

Wow. He acted like I was a sergeant, not a lowly PFC. I had new respect for Burke. Maybe for myself. I knew exactly what I needed to do. Now the question was to put it into practice so we wouldn't get wiped out or get used for anti-war propaganda produced by Taylor. Lauren was sure to be out there. I hoped not right in the middle of the action.

We spent the next two days getting ready for the operation. A carbon copy of the last one, which hadn't satisfied the top brass. Not a big enough body count. Our platoon was the only one to make contact with the enemy. Either the NVA had evaded us or they were never there in the first place. They surely knew about it. By now they had to believe they lived in the heads of our generals. They would either pull back deeper into Laos or offer up some sacrificial troops to lure us into an ambush.

Col Schiffer, battalion commander, landed in his personal chopper to give us a pep talk. We knew his ass was on the line for not killing enough gooks. He made that crystal clear. Midway through his speech I whispered to Doc that I was ready to start a game in which I'd drink a shot of vodka every time an officer said the words "body count."

"You sure you don't mean take a drag of weed?"

My self-medicating had never been a secret.

"Why break my balls, Doc? I'm not the only one."

One thing I didn't mind hearing was that if we were chasing down some NVA and they happened to get across the Laotian border, we could continue to engage them until either they were all dead or we ran out of ammunition. I got the feeling that some of the brass wanted to take off the gloves and try to win the war. On the other hand, it wasn't D-Day in Normandy. If the NVA decided not to show up, the operation would be an expensive and muscle wearying hump for us, Journalists like Taylor would mock our efforts as a failure. If we happened to lose grunts to snipers or booby traps, more evidence of the futility of the conflict. If a company of NVA wiped out a platoon of Marines, fresh film of the dead being placed into body bags would be on national networks by the next day. And if we did, purely by accident, manage to engage, outmaneuver, outshoot, and destroy our adversaries, well, it was another rock being rolled up the mountain by Sisyphus. Surely it would roll down to the bottom in no time.

A day in August. Almost a year before, I had set foot on the Blaze College campus, a freshman. Circumstances beyond my control turned me into a professional killer. Whatever remained of the former Pax started an argument in my head.

You can't blame circumstances for choices that you made.

Andrew Barrett III chose to bomb a campus building.

He didn't force you to join the Marines. You weren't a flag-waver before despite your heritage.

I want justice for Eve.

Bear isn't waiting for you by the border. Just a bunch of scared teenagers bullied into volunteering to march south. Why didn't you kill the boy with the pith helmet?

Seemed like he needed a second chance. He wasn't with the main bunch. Maybe he didn't want to shoot any Americans.

Why did you keep his personal stuff?

I stopped the self-talk when my platoon and I climbed into the slick preparing to fly to the LZ. Only when we climbed out of the humid lower atmosphere and enjoyed temporary air conditioning a few thousand feet up did the question recur. True, I had stuffed the gook's wallet with photos into my rucksack. Later, out of sight of the rest of the platoon, I looked at them. One showed him standing with an older couple. Parents. Another, him with a cute girl smiling at the camera, holding hands, dressed in formal attire. Wedding? I didn't think a small country like North Vietnam went in for Senior proms. Several lines of text in Vietnamese provided one clue: a date. One dash three dash nineteen sixty-eight. First of March. If the picture taking happened for a wedding, he'd had a couple of months at best to enjoy married life before marching down the Ho Chi Minh trail.

I tucked the photo into my wallet and discarded his. I hoped the ARVN hadn't taken him. At the end of the war, he could go home to his bride. My gift to him. From now on, no more mercy.

The slick continued its journey. The beauty of the countryside no longer held any attraction. I saw only terrain good or bad for attacking or defending.

The battle plan called for Golf and Dog companies to land first, secure the LZ and move out toward where intelligence claimed we would find the enemy. Charlie company landed at a separate LZ to wait in reserve. That could be a good assignment, provided the gooks weren't nearby and waiting to spring an ambush. Rumors circulated that our colonel had asked for B-52 strikes in Laos behind the suspected enemy camps to drive them at us. Request denied.

The choppers banked without warning and the jungle came at us in a rush. Skirting the tree tops we hurtled forward. We were the third chopper to land. As far as I could tell there was no firing on the ground. Cold LZs were good to start, although sometimes it advertised a fruitless five-day hump. I jumped the six feet to the ground and stuck the landing for once, pushed ahead behind a couple of other platoon members through the elephant grass toward smoke marking the rally point.

The platoon hung on Lt Burke's words. He pointed on his map to our location and destination. Three klicks of humping, none of it on trails. We'd be lucky to finish before dark. We'd be the second platoon in line. No smoking or talking, tape down objects that could cause noise. Down deep we knew that made little difference. A western style force punching through jungle made plenty of noise. Our precautions might keep us from giving away our size, and that could encourage attack. That's what we came for. Not to avoid contact but to seek it and put fire on the enemy.

I wanted Bear on the march with the NVA, the People's Army. Love to catch him in the sights of my M-16 and shoot, not to kill but to maim. A nice sucking chest wound. He could lie on the fetid jungle floor and feel his lung fill with blood as every breath stayed trapped in his chest cavity and further compressed the good side. His breathing rate would increase to no avail. Unless something was done to stop the air entry, he'd die in minutes. Maybe I'd shoot off his balls while we waited. He wouldn't be needing them where he was headed. Then, when he was just about dead, but still able to feel pain, I'd take my kabar and cut off one of his ears as a souvenir. Put it in a shadow box with my medal. Lieutenant Burke had told me he put my name in for a Bronze Star. I didn't care for hardware. I wanted a flesh and blood trophy. A pirate's reward.

"Pax. Don't bunch up."

Philly spat his words in my ear after I'd collided with him from behind. I'd been daydreaming, not paying attention and missed his hand signal to halt.

"Sorry, Philly. What is it?"

"No idea, asshole. Can you see anything in this shit?"

We were under triple canopy, dark as twilight at high noon. Visual cues were few and misleading. Overhead the chatter of birds filtered down. Sweat trickled down my face, assaulting my eyes. I ignored it. At times like this I almost wished for contact. Anything to break tension. Of course, if the clatter of an AK did so, I'd be down in the dirt cursing my luck.

Whatever had halted the column remained a mystery. Philly got the signal to advance and grabbed my shirt. "Stay the fuck off my ass, FNG."

"I'm no FNG, cocksucker." I'd learned to dish it right back. He smiled and flipped me the bird before pushing on.

We broke for lunch after five hours of humping. The platoon set up a perimeter in a small clearing and we dove into our C rations with aggression, if not enthusiasm. Burke had been on his radio and word passed that a grunt in Dog company had stepped on a booby trap on the far side of the ridge we marched parallel to and would soon be medevacked. We heard the chopper coming in shortly after. Also heard the colonel's chopper circling higher up. He was stewing because nothing had happened. Burke couldn't bitch to us officially, but I could see he felt under pressure. As if he could do anything to start a fight.

Night came with no contact. We found a defensible area on a small hillock that didn't have a name or number and dug foxholes, set out Claymores and flares and got assigned guard duty. I was on tap for the 2 AM shift. Zero dark thirty. The best time to carry out a night attack. Philly was convinced we were being shadowed.

"You smell 'em?" he said.

"Not this time around. Your ass stinks so bad, I can't get a breath of clean air."

"Fuck you, I'm serious. The fishy smell mixed with smoke."

I sampled the air around us. I was only half kidding about Philly's body odor. I was used to it by now, but he stank more than most grunts. "I don't know Philly. Maybe mid-afternoon I caught a whiff of smoke that could've been from a cook fire. But not long enough to make a report."

"They are all around us."

"Good. That fucking colonel will be happy we have the chance to raise the body count." I patted my M-16 and fitted myself as best I could in the shallow foxhole I'd dug. Sleep didn't come easily, but in brief segments I relaxed and let the hum of insects lull me to semi-coma status.

The touch of a hand jerked me awake. Or was it the crackle of small arms fire? Somebody was getting thumped. I checked my watch. 1:30. That would be the right time. I couldn't see Philly in the pitch black, but I knew he had given the alert.

"A klick away, you think?" he said.

"If that. Could just be somebody got spooked. I don't hear any AK fire."

"Could have been a probe."

The gooks weren't afraid to send out teams of infiltrators and sappers, much like the Japs in World War II, according to the older non-coms I'd met. They might knife a sleeping grunt or frag him, then get away in the dark. We'd crossed a trail shortly before securing our bivouac area. The danger being easy access for the gooks, but the advantage of high ground negated that. Or so Burke argued. He'd sent an ambush team of one squad to welcome any nighttime visitors. We were scheduled to relieve them at 2.

"Let's go early," I said.

"Negative. They expect us at 2, we arrive at 2. Otherwise, they might light us up."

He was right. We waited, and at 2 Philly, Pearl, Cherry, Stretch, Grub, and I crept over to the ambush site and relieved the first team. Philly manned the M-60 with me as loader, aiming directly down the trail. We had some Claymore mines set about fifty meters from our position for Pearl and Cherry to blow when the first two gooks were ten meters past in order to catch the middle of the column. Then they were supposed to open up on anybody still standing. Stretch and Grub were in position to lob grenades in the same general area.

I estimated that a gook patrol sneaking down the trail would require about fifteen minutes of quiet walking to arrive at the ambush. It turned out to be closer to thirty. They were that good. I heard and saw nothing, but Pearl and Cherry sure did. I wasn't asleep but my attention had drifted to an unhealthy level when the concussion of the Claymores smacked me alert. Cries of pain emanated from the kill zone, competing with the steady bursts of M-16 fire put down at the head of the ambush.

Philly racked the M-60 and fired straight down the trail at knee height. The frags tossed by the other two ambushers punctuated the percussive symphony in doublets. I saw no return fire from the gooks, who would've been using green tracers to shoot back at us. After a couple of minutes, Philly stopped shooting and yelled "Cease fire."

A couple of bursts later, they did. And things stayed quiet the rest of the night. I was high on adrenaline and kept awake until the next watch came on at 4. By then, nothing for them to do but watch the trail. It was too risky to set out more Claymores in case some gooks had survived, but we had plenty of grenades and an M-79.

At first light Lieutenant Burke led us into the kill zone. And there was plenty of it to see. The Claymores had shredded, literally, three NVA who had been a few feet from the blast. The uniforms identified them, and little else remained that looked human. Behind them in the column lay two dead ones who carried satchel charges that hadn't gone off in all the shooting. The M-60 fire had smashed their knees first and then chopped up the torsos as they fell to earth. The last remaining member of the squad had crawled 25 yards back down the trail before bleeding out from a leg wound.

Lieutenant Burke radioed in the body count as we searched the dead for documents and souvenirs. I never saw any grunts mutilate corpses, but in this case, the Claymores had taken care of the mutilation. Grub and Tree each put things in their pockets they had no business keeping, but I wasn't going to say a word about it. The uniforms looked to be brand new, so maybe these were inexperienced troops. We could only hope.

"Looks like they sent their junior varsity squad on sapper patrol," said Philly.

"Fuck, it don't mean nothing," said Pearl. "That just makes the rest of them that much more pissed off."

As if to punctuate that observation, mortar shells started dropping in. The first few were well off the mark, giving us time to get into foxholes while Burke called it in. The bad news was that no artillery could return fire. The colonel was aloft in his chopper and although the likelihood of a round hitting him was small, no one would take that chance.

"Let's get the fuck out of here," said Philly.

Lt Burke wasn't afraid of taking suggestions, but this time he waved it off.

"They'll have spotters calling our positions back to the tubes, especially when they realize we aren't shooting back. I'd rather be under relative cover then exposed."

He did order us off the hilltop and we spread out next to a ledge that offered some defilade from the incoming rounds. After that, nothing landed more than fifty meters away. Then it stopped, just in time for an airstrike that probably cleared out some jungle and little else. Like a lot of output in this war, too little, too late.

We packed gear after some C-rations and humped toward the next big rally point, another 5 klicks distant. The jungle gave way to rice paddies and savannah-like fields of elephant grass. It made me miss the jungle, almost. Out here snipers could pick a target at leisure.

We linked up with the rest of G company. Burke and the other officers yelled at us not to bunch up. Two replacements stopped next to a five-foot-tall anthill for a smoke break. Two sounds broke the silence: a "thwap" as a bullet hit human flesh and the supersonic crack of its passage. The soldiers dropped like stringless puppets. I ran to them a few steps ahead of Doc Steinberg. The rest of the column had hit the dirt, which I should have done.

"Get your ass down," screamed Doc as he checked for signs of life.

"Dumbasses," he said with a sob. The fatal bullet hadn't been an ordinary one. It hit one grunt dead center in his back, left a large exit wound in front. Second grunt, same story, larger holes. Occasionally we'd capture a weapon with a more exotic pedigree than the generic AK-47. Russian or Chinese mostly. We used sniper teams too. Perhaps the sniper assumed the two grunts were officers. Or maybe he just wanted to see if he could kill two men with one bullet. Which he most certainly had done.

I lay on the ground, my face inches from one of the dead grunts. His vacant stare bothered me, even though I knew he couldn't see. I reached out to close the lids, heard the slap of another shot on target and Doc crumpled, a river of blood surging from the hole in his neck. Must've hit a major artery. He too, died silently except for a hideous gurgling sound in his chest for about fifteen seconds.

I lay still, too scared to move, praying the sniper would assume I was dead and not fire again. In the distance I heard the grunts who had seen the horror show open up with their M-16s on full auto in the general direction of the sniper. Somebody yelled at me to run, and so I did, at full sprint speed, until I dove behind another ant hill. One more round hit the hill as the sniper signed off with a flourish.

Capt West called in an airstrike and for a chopper to take away the dead. In a few minutes, an F-100 made a pass over the coordinates West had called in. The welcome orange and black fireball erupted. We cheered half-heartedly. Doc Steinberg and the grunts he went to help were still dead. The Medevac landed and we loaded it in silence. Nobody said: "It don't mean nothing."

Capt West called the colonel with an estimated body count of three from the airstrike. He didn't believe it any more than we grunts. Sounds of battle reached us from places we couldn't see. Occasionally another F-100 would streak overhead on a bombing run. It was midday and scorching hot. Our canteens were dry. Capt West ordered Lt Burke to investigate a possible bunker complex northwest of our position. Second platoon, about 500 meters distant, were taking sniper fire from the tree line. The colonel, two thousand feet above, wanted the bunkers taken. Our platoon, angry from our loss, wanted vengeance. Nobody griped about the assault.

I asked Burke, "Sir, who are we going to use as a corpsman?"

"Second platoon still has one, I hope."

We had taken Doc's medical knapsack from him and divided it up, just in case. I could put a pressure dressing on and syrettes of morphine were easy to use. I didn't want to have to stick myself, that was all.

The air grew smoky as we advanced. The buzz of overhead AK rounds became more frequent. No one reacted. Second platoon lay between us and the source. I spotted the antenna their radioman and passed the word for Stretch to call them. We got an "all clear" and walked up on their right flank. Ammo and water from our dead buddies went to those without. I slurped several gulps from a new canteen.

The objective was another half klick in front of us. West got on the radio again. Calling the Colonel, I figured. Just wanted to do it smart, not waste lives. We waited and took a smoke break.

"How you holding up?" said Philly.

"I'm so fucking mad that Doc got killed. Fucking new guys."

"They don't know shit. It's getting worse all the time."

We spent a quiet night, unmolested by harassing fire or sappers. A guy got bit by a snake, but it wasn't poisonous, so he got to stay. We needed every rifle in good hands. In the morning, the relaxation was palpable. Burke tried his best to motivate us. Yesterday our blood got up when Doc Steinberg died. I would have charged a company of gooks. Today I wanted out.

The two platoons managed to set off by about nine in the morning on a day that promised to be even more stinking hot than before. Water came in with the hot food, so I felt I wouldn't get dehydrated at least. Some of the grunts objected to carrying all the ammo that Burke had requested. He stood firm that they couldn't leave it around. The gooks had their share of captured M-16s. They'd love to send a special delivery bullet into one of us.

We hit the tree line in no time. Burke was off on the flank and the lieutenant from Second platoon told the point guy to start down a trail about fifty meters away. It looked well used. The kind that always meant trouble. I walked over and politely suggested we check with Burke and got a nasty glare in response.

"You can take the point," he said.

Fuck all this shit, I thought. I did what he ordered, hoping the gooks had split for Laos. The trail was a meter wide. A superhighway by our standards. The good part being that trip wires would be easier to see. The bad part was that a command mine could take out just as many of us. I started fantasizing about Lauren, angry that Taylor got to ride with her in the chopper.

I stood still at one point, staring at nothing. Philly walked up behind me and slapped the side of my helmet.

"Get back in the game, Pax, or you're dead."

That brought my focus back. I gave him a peace sign and scanned the jungle ahead. Saw nothing. Smelled nothing. Heard nothing except occasional chatter from the grunts behind me. They needed to shut up.

A flash in the distance halted me. I dropped to a knee and put up my hand. That got everybody's attention. I turned and signaled I was moving up; the others should wait. Then I proceeded. The wind was whipping fairly good aloft. Sounded like whispers. It could be. I had to pray if a sniper saw me, he'd put me down for good and not leave me lying wounded to scream for an hour before dying. I advanced fifty, then a hundred meters, then I saw the bunker.

Constructed of tree trunks and covered with moss and ferns, it was a product of skill and imagination. I could see it only from one spot on the trail. Before and beyond that single point, it was invisible. I stood frozen, watching for movement, letting the breeze push human scents in my direction, listening for anything indicating human presence. I didn't dare look at my watch for fear of creating motion. If I'd been seen, no one had acted. I counted to five hundred, slowly. Still nothing. I took a step, then two, then three. Other than a very residual odor of cooking fire, no human sign. Now I was near enough to see inside the bunker. Close enough to drop a frag in if I'd wanted to. I was this far, why not go all the way.

I raised my head over the parapet and scanned the interior. Not a soul. No weapons. No anything. Looked like the fulfillment of the prediction. A dry hole. I sauntered back to the rest of the column.

"Zilch," I told Burke. He got on the radio and talked to West. Ten minutes later Burke assembled the platoon. We did a more careful search, checking for booby traps as well as any items like maps to send back to Battalion HQ. Burke spoke on the radio to Schiffer. The buzz from the receiver suggested agitation. Burke looked aggrieved.

"Saddle up, boys," he said.

He put me on the flank, and I started circling back around our path to check for gook scouts on our trail. I slid into the jungle, moving in semi-circles to check for pursuit. My mind kept returning to thoughts of Lauren. This time I didn't have Philly to harass me. After an hour of no contact, I figured the gooks had indeed left the area. Time to report back.

I listened for the familiar noises of my platoon. Heard nothing.

I checked my compass and map. I had let a small ridge lead me away from the line of march. A dry creek bed lay in front of me. I could follow it and catch up. I drained my canteen and took a deep breath.

Holy shit.

The familiar odor of cooked rice and fish sent off mental alarms. The NVA. They might be fifty meters away. Maybe closer. I'd have to circle around the creek bed and bushwhack in the general direction of the platoon. Discovery meant death.

I checked my gear to insure silent movement. Left the canteen behind a tree. I couldn't wait longer. Then, twenty-five meters away, the rocky side of the creek stood up and began to move. A hundred or more gooks with leafy helmet camouflage advanced down the creek bed like a slow-motion silent movie. I prayed for them to make haste into Laos. I could've tossed a frag at them and killed a few before they greased me good. I followed, looking for a way around them. In ten minutes, they had dropped me.

That's when I got scared. Just before the shooting started.

Some firefights begin with a pick and a pop. Some are noisy but brief. This one sounded different from anything I had heard before. The roar of automatic weapons was continuous. As if an ammo truck had hit a mine and exploded all at once.

I moved hard left to skirt the area of maximum firing. I started to hear yelling and screaming in English. It didn't sound good. Out of nowhere, an RPG flashed from my right to a position ahead and to the left. I heard and saw the explosion. More screams. I got low to the ground, not wanting to surprise my guys and get shot accidently on purpose.

There they were. Or some of them. Three grunts hunkered down behind a log. I scurried over to join them, landed in a warm, red-purple mush that had exploded out of their bodies. Direct hit. I could only recognize one of them. Black Pearl. He looked at peace despite dying with such violence.

I closed his eyes. "Don't mean nothing," I said.

A sobbing sound caught my attention. I crawled towards it.

"Hey! It's Pax. Anybody. Make yourself known," I said.

"Stay the fuck down. They're up in the trees." It sounded like Grub. I caught a glimpse of the silhouette of a Marine helmet not far away. I crawled to him.

"Are you hit?" I said.

"Don't know. RPG hit near me. Killed Lieutenant Burke, maybe others."

He had shrapnel in his face but no other injuries. Burke blown away. I felt sick. "Tell me what happened."

Grub seemed to be in a trance. He stared dumbly, so I slapped him. Repeated my order. That helped. He started choking out words, then phrases until I got the story. They had been on the trail when the point ran into what they thought was a rearguard defense. Couple of gooks with AKs who ran away. The column picked up the pace and about five minutes later walked into a classic box type ambush. A heavy machine gun at a turn ahead and well concealed, probably dug into a spider hole, had opened up straight down the line of march. He found himself pinned down in a group with Burke and his RTO.

"How about the radio?" I said.

"Don't know. Don't care. Got to get the fuck out of here."

I slapped him again. "Listen to me, Grub. If you don't stop shitting your pants, the gooks are going to eat your liver for supper, and they won't waste a bullet on you first."

He nodded, whimpering. We crawled to where Pearl lay next to the unrecognizable Burke and his RTO. Anybody else hit had already crawled away. The PRC still worked. I got on the net and got somebody in Dog company, also under attack but holding on. I gave our approximate grid location.

I pulled Grub into a spider hole dug next to a pair of dead gooks and watched for targets. It didn't take long. An NVA officer came striding over to us, unaware we had replaced his men. His uniform looked out of the box new. A burst of fire from somewhere to his right sent him running for cover elsewhere.

We stayed put the rest of the day and night, fearful of death at the hands of one side or the other.

Frag

Charlie company found us the next day as they went about the task of recovering all our dead. Grub had grown quiet by then, immersed in a private hell inside his head. They led him away to a waiting chopper to be Medevacked somewhere.

The gooks were truly gone by now, the living and the dead. Our guys found a few bodies, lots of blood trails and some abandoned equipment and a couple of NVA who had gotten separated from the main force and missed the withdrawal. A couple of grunts were guarding them from survivors like me who might want to exact revenge.

It was easier for us to do a headcount of survivors and estimate our losses that way. Most of the wounded who couldn't walk out had been executed. It turned out to be an elaborate honey pot ambush. Every Marine element had been gulled into advancing past the dummy bunkers and HQ setup. Dog and Golf companies went into the fight with 246 Marines. I and 31 others were uninjured. Eighty-four were walking wounded. One hundred thirty were dead or missing. Aside from me and Grub, our platoon was wiped out.

I sat on my helmet, smoking, and watching the CH-46 choppers landing and then leaving with their grim cargo. Despite the heat, a chill washed over me. I was ready to quit. Nothing we tried worked. The grunts working the battle scene had counted exactly 25 NVA dead. By the time it got inflated up the chain of command, we'd be announcing that we'd killed 250.

I watched Colonel Schiffer's chopper settle. He wore a clean uniform and mirror sunglasses. I wanted to ask him if the mirror reflected the truth or what he wanted the truth to be. But I didn't. I needed to shut up and get back to An Hoa. I'd never wanted to get stoned more than now. Couldn't feel worse and if I got wasted by a mortar round or sniper bullet, I didn't care.

A second chopper landed with the Press. Lauren got out first, followed by the sound guy Kevin and last, Taylor. He made Lauren start filming right away. Walked over to Colonel Schiffer and tried an interview. I couldn't hear the words, but Schiffer's jaws were moving like a jack hammer and his face was red.

I walked over and Lauren stopped filming when she saw me. Literally dropped the camera in the red dust of that shitty LZ and ran over. We met and did our version of girl greets surviving Marine Hollywood-style. She jumped in my arms and wrapped her legs around my waist as I turned in circles. I couldn't speak, she had her tongue down my throat so fast.

"Oh babe, I thought you were dead," were her first words after the kiss.

"I thought I was, too."

"What happened?"

"Can't talk about it. Don't want to think about it."

"I know. So, don't. And I'll never ask. Promise."

Taylor came striding over, his face a sardonic mask. He'd picked up the camera and shoved it at her. "You've got work to do." Then, to me, "Happy to see you're in one piece, Private. Sorry for your loss."

He half-dragged her over to where the body bags were stacked. Great. Bad enough we'd been destroyed in a battle. Now we had to allow the Press to do its duty by rubbing the collective nose of America into the shit-sucking mess. Not good enough for me.

Taylor posed in front of the bags and started speaking. Lauren filmed him with her back to me, twenty-five yards away. Colonel Schiffer walked over to Taylor and an argument started. Lauren kept filming. I remember thinking, this is going to be one great shit show for television. He's going to get his moment on camera and get a promotion or new job while Schiffer will likely get kicked upstairs like Westmoreland for fucking up and lying about it.

From behind me came shouts and one shot. Someone yelled "Frag!"

I spun around to see one of the NVA prisoners had somehow got free, shot a Marine and was now running at Colonel Schiffer. Something in his hand caught my attention. A grenade. Not a shitty Chicom grenade that half the time wouldn't explode. This was an all-American M-26 fragmentation grenade that never failed.

Time slows down in disasters. I learned that in my near-fatal car crash and again seeing Eve die. Despite that I couldn't react with speed. Like in a dream where the big shore breaking wave catches up and upends me far from safety. The frag rotated lazily overhead as I made my best attempt to imitate Pirate shortstop Gene Alley reaching skyward to snag a line drive. I wasn't close. I spun left as I landed, violating the cardinal rule of avoiding shrapnel: get on the ground. I pushed off hard in Lauren's direction and saw her eyes wide with disbelief, just like anyone in a battle acts surprised when the line of tracers shifts in his direction, the mortar shell falls on a trajectory where he stands, the tank track rolls over a mine. It can't happen to me. Not now. Not here.

She wouldn't have been saved by the reflexes of a track star. We assumed later that the gook had intended to frag Colonel Schiffer, but his delivery was rushed. Lauren had turned to run when the grenade landed right at her feet. It made a crump to match the flash and she spun head over heels like a gymnast, arms loose as only a dead person's can be, and landed in a heap. Her camera landed a few feet farther away. I rushed to her side, hoping for something to quell my erupting rage but finding nothing. Blood welled out of shrapnel wounds. The blast spared her face, leaving her with a graceful but vacant smile below half lidded eyes. I held on as tight as an Alpinist holds onto a vertical rock wall. Then I saw him.

Taylor had picked up her camera and was filming us, muttering some stream of consciousness garbage in the direction of Kevin, who hadn't dropped his microphone in the chaos. I don't even recall what he said. It doesn't matter. Anything he could have said was inappropriate.

I set Lauren down and rushed Taylor like he was the quarterback on a bootleg, and I was a linebacker sent to drop and crunch him. Which I did with enthusiasm.

"You motherless fuck," I screamed as I headbutted him. His nose broke with a loud crack and sprayed blood over my face. I was just getting started. I smashed his cheeks with the heel of my right hand and delivered my elbow just above his upper lip, slicing it cleanly against his fractured teeth. Then I went for the kill. Both hands around his skinny neck, thumbs jammed into the angles where the combat instructor told us housed the carotid arteries. I shut off all blood flow to his brain. He went limp in ten seconds, but I knew I had to hold him for five minutes to complete the job.

A voice behind me called out a warning. "Stand down, Marine. Let go. Let go now."

But I wouldn't, not even after the first blow to my head, which stunned me and blew up a galaxy in front of me. The second whack worked. Blue billowing clouds that became black.

Second Opinion

The lights came on for me, and Taylor was gone. I was in a CH-46 chopper, cruising the treetops, flying out on Operation Lionheart. Another time translocation. My elation at getting a second chance diminished as words from the past surfaced to haunt me.

Stewart had been talking to me about the chance to alter history. "It's all very well to back up a day or a week and re-take an Astronomy exam since you know the questions in advance. Or to win a race you would probably have won in the first place. Do you know anything about chaos theory?"

Of course, I didn't, so Stewart gave me a micro-seminar. When he began adding equations, he lost me, but what I gathered from the early part was that in any complex physical system, if initial conditions aren't identical, the result can be wildly different. So, during one trip back in time I might encounter a person walking down the street. On the next trip, if I paused to look at some flowers in a yard, I might not see the person again, missing some important interaction that would have an impact on events later.

In other words, I might take part in the same operation, but because conditions were slightly different on the second trip, I could get hit by a bullet and die. I got scared. More so than I'd ever experienced in my short career as a grunt. Because now I had something to lose. I could try to warn Lauren about the grenade, but what if I didn't make it that far? Bugging out AWOL wasn't an option. I was better off with my squad around me, try to make the best of it. Warn Lieutenant Burke about the ambush. He could pass the word up the chain to Battalion HQ and maybe that insufferable moron Schiffer would change plans.

"I can't do that," said Burke.

"But sir, I have got a really bad feeling about what we're going to run across out there."

"Private, I have a really bad feeling every day I spend in this country. But we are Marines, and we obey our orders. No improvising unless extremely provoked."

I didn't care if he thought I had lost my mind. I had to fling something in front of him to make my argument believable.

"What if I predict something that happens exactly as I say it does?"

"You mean, who wins the World Series?"

"Something tomorrow. We'll be in the open. I can tell you who is going to get hit."

His eyes narrowed, creating little white lines in the laterite grime that coated his skin. "You'd better not be shitting me, Private. You're a college boy, not one of those rednecks from Alabama or a brother from the ghetto out to mess with Whitey."

"I'm not shitting you, sir." I wanted to add, you're my favorite turd.

"Tell me. Who's going to buy it?"

"There." I pointed at the nameless FNGs who were destined to drop from the same sniper round.

He shrugged. "So, they're new guys. High risk to get killed when we make contact. If we make contact."

"They will stop for a smoke while we're walking through an open field. Before the second one's cigarette is lit, boom. NVA sniper drops them from a quarter mile away."

Burke laughed. "You are one crazy fuck, Private. Trying for a Section Eight? You almost had me there." He slapped my shoulder and moved ahead. I didn't have the balls to tell him how he'd meet his end. The point of this was not to ever get ambushed in the first place. I walked over to the FNGs. I wanted to ease my conscience.

"Hey," I said. They stared with suspicion. They'd been outcasts up until now. I could hear them thinking, what is this motherfucker trying to pull?

"Smoke?" I offered both a Lucky.

They accepted and took deep drags.

"Just want you to know. No smoking when we're moving out on the operation. Right? Makes you a target."

They shared derisive smirks. "Go fuck yourself, lifer. Just because we're new doesn't give you the right to boss us around. We know what FNG means. Not funny."

I felt a little unhinged. I reached out, had my hand smacked away.

"Beat it. We'll hump it our way."

My conscience somewhat assuaged, I let them go. I had my own ass to think about. My ass and Doc's. I didn't want him to die attending to the two losers who ignored good situational awareness by bunching up, stopping, and smoking. At the same time, I didn't want the sniper picking me instead. My sense of timing was jumbled. In the wide-open area, there were a lot of ant hills like the one where the shooting happened the first time. I wanted to keep alert and at the same time, watch the FNGs. And Lieutenant Burke. He had to see the men go down together or he wouldn't buy in to me prediction. I noticed him off to my right. Not where he'd been before. So, he must have a fragmentary belief that I'd be right. Now I had to worry that he would be a target with his radioman. Nothing says shoot me first more than an officer and his PRC-carrying RTO.

There. They stopped. One fumbled in his webbing, pulled out a pack of smokes. I stifled the urge to yell at them. What would it accomplish? They needed to die. That was the paradox of combat. Officers understood. Or they rationalized sending men to certain death in order to save others. I was going to save Golf and Dog companies from annihilation, but those jokers had to die first.

They stood fifty yards from me, laughing, grab-assing like a couple of real rookies, which is what they were. I said a prayer for their souls.

Crack! The round buzzed overhead for the second time in my crazy universe. And for the second time the FNGs dropped. My gook sniper had been eating his green and yellow vegetables. I didn't know where Doc Steinberg was. Somebody bellowed for a corpsman. That hadn't been true the first time. I ran over anyway, taking the risk of getting shot. I dove headfirst up against the anthill and rolled around it to get defilade from where I thought I remembered the sniper waited.

A shower of red termite nest cascaded off my helmet from the second round. Close but safe. I wiggled around a bit more. Doc ran in a crouch toward.

"Get back. They're dead," I called out. Then I heard a moan. Fuck. Stewart's curse. Different results when initial conditions changed. At least one of the FNGs still lived.

Doc didn't hear me. Or ignored me. Anyway, he came sliding in next to me. "You do your job, Marine, let me do mine."

"I might have been wrong about that," I said. A third round smacked into one of the pair. Not the one who'd moaned. Doc and I pulled the survivor under cover. There were no more shots.

I could see Burke on the radio, probably calling for the airstrike. When that was completed, he joined us.

"What you got, Doc?" he said, looking squarely at me.

"One KIA for sure. Head shot. The other took it in the jaw, but he'll live. Brand new set of choppers courtesy of his rich Uncle."

"I called in a Medevac," said Burke. Be here in fifteen or so. You good?"

"Aye-aye, Lieutenant," said Doc.

Burke crooked his finger to beckon me away from the anthill. We got into some shade from a solitary tree, and he grabbed my shirt collar, put his face in front of mine. His breath smelled of stale C-rations, not enough water, and non-stop tension.

"OK, PFC Pax. Start explaining. How the fuck did you know those two yo-yos were gonna get shot?"

I was too tired and scared to make up a story. He'd know I was lying. But if I told the truth, he'd think I was nuts. I tried an indirect approach.

"OK, I'm going to say some things that will sound odd. No, they will sound fucking crazy. I'm sorry. I have to tell you."

"Spill it."

"Sometimes I travel backwards in time."

"Say what?"

"It's when I take a blow to the head. Get knocked out. But not always. I have a friend at home who understands. He might be able to explain it better than me."

"I have no doubt. Who is it, some loony 4-F?"

"He's a student. At college with me. Really bright guy."

"Kind of an Einstein?"

"You might say."

"Well, I'll be fucked."

Burke looked off to the west at the mountains. Seemed like a long time, but probably not. Finally, he turned back to me.

"There's something about this that makes me start to believe you. I don't want to. I'm a Christian. Or was, anyway, before I joined the Corps and learned how to kill. So superstitious crap doesn't hold any sway with me. Even the shit about miracles. Didn't really happen. They're stories made up to get people to calm down and join churches. The other day something real queer happened. The day you volunteered to take the point from Grub. He said to me later he dreamed he'd been on the point and got shot. Died. I figured he was starting to lose it. Been out here too long. Sooner or later we all go through it. Now, I wonder if maybe something did happen. Something I sure as fuck don't understand. If I'm wrong about this, we might be walking into the world's biggest clusterfuck. But I'm going with my gut. It says you're on the up and up. So tell me, PFC Paxton Knox, what should I do?"

I gulped. My chance lay before me. "Get out your maps and I'll draw it up for you."

After I finished, Burke spoke to the other platoons' leaders and then Captain West. Got him to adjust the plan. Cancelled the hot food delivery. I didn't want Lauren around to catch a to-whom-it-may-concern bullet. Burke pulled me aside and said: "Your fellow Marines are gonna be pissed about that."

"Part of the plan," I said. No budging on that point.

They didn't clear it with Colonel Schiffer. A spot of mutiny had soiled the integrity of the Corps. But as we were fond of saying, what could happen to them? They already were in Vietnam.

The next morning we swept wide around the phony bunkers,

sending only a couple of squads out to persuade any NVA scouts that we were taking the bait. The rest of us flanked the large group of NVA I'd seen in the stream bed. We stayed well back on account of the next part of the plan. Burke called in airstrikes. Lots of them. Starting at where I knew the real bunkers were, hoping to catch the gooks outside. Another wave of F-100s flew over the creek bed and soon it was practically flowing with napalm.

Dog company had gotten into position between the NVA and the border, so as we moved out and started mopping up the survivors of the airstrikes, the retreating NVA ran up against the anvil of angry Marine riflemen. They'd all lost friends in the weeks leading up to this. Nobody had to tell them what to do. It got described as a turkey shoot, but it seemed to us that real turkeys would've had better odds of survival.

We spent the day and night on the move, smashing all resistance. By sunrise, the next day an eerie quiet settled over the battlefield. The last broken NVA elements had fled in disarray over the border. The rules said we couldn't chase them, and in truth it might have been stupid to do so. They had fresh reserves there and we had no intelligence telling us where to look.

So, Captain West called a cease fire. We started tending our wounded, collecting our dead, destroying captured supplies and weapons. All told our side lost 3 KIA from a lucky mortar shot. The body count was a guess. A lot of bodies weren't intact or else had been deep fat fried by the napalm into a carbonized mass of protoplasm. Scores had died untouched in bunkers, asphyxiated when the napalm sucked all the oxygen from the air. Death on a scale we hadn't seen before. Total war was brutal. I didn't have to ask my Dad. He'd seen it. Vietnam wasn't different. If anything, the casualties were fewer. The scope of the conflict might have been a limited McNamara war. On this battlefield that wasn't true. We didn't fire a few shots and ask if the other fellows were ready to negotiate. We used all the force at our disposal to make sure of it.

I insulated my mind from the grotesque tableaux of total war by fantasizing about my plan to meet Lauren in Hawaii for my real R&R. She didn't know about it. I didn't think she'd be a tough sell. Burke interrupted my reverie.

"Snap to, Private. We're going back to the LZ and I'm going to have the pleasure of watching the air go out of Colonel Schiffer's sails when he meets the Napoleon who led the Marines on the biggest ass-kicking of the war."

"Excuse me, sir. I don't believe we ought to mention the, um, time travel aspect."

"Hell no. I'm crazy, but not stupid. I'll give credit where credit is due. You deserve a promotion. You pulled it off. You've been on the line for a while. Maybe move to G-2 and show those cocksuckers how real Intelligence works."

I didn't argue the point, even though I didn't think I wanted to serve in the rear. My mind wandered back to endless sex in a hammock with Lauren.

Burke was on and off his radio on the march to the LZ. We met another column from a different platoon escorting some prisoners. The Marines were giddy from the victory and this was good for the well-being of the gooks. The fact that we'd taken any prisoners at all was amazing. I recalled the wholescale murder of Marines I witnessed on my previous passage on the timeline. Information I would not be sharing with the guards.

We hit the LZ around noon. Colonel Schiffer's bird was on the ground and Burke wasted no time running me over there. I stood by in silence as Burke recounted an edited version of the truth.

"PFC Knox saved the day, sir. He had an idea the NVA might be setting an ambush, so he scouted their positions undetected, and we were able to call in air strikes that obliterated them. The kid showed more ability than most of our Recon teams."

Schiffer fixed his beady eyes on me.

"If he's that good, what's he doing in an infantry platoon? Why the hell didn't you anticipate an ambush? Damn lucky you caught the gooks asleep. Could've gone bad for you. Who the fuck authorized those airstrikes without me knowing about it?"

Burke had a bullshit story about the radio net going in and out of commission, forcing him to improvise. He added the magic words body count and suddenly Schiffer's attitude went about face.

"Well, turn in your PRC and get one that works. I'll sign the requisition. Can't have junior officers operating in the dark."

Burke's plan to get me re-assigned to the rear was going off the rails, which pleased me no end. I maintained my poker face, shook Schiffer's stiff hand when he offered it. I knew it was time to go.

"Permission to return to the platoon?" I asked Burke.

He nodded. He was having trouble hiding his disappointment. Instead of the imagined promotion to Captain, he'd probably get a shittier assignment than ever. Schiffer didn't like being upstaged.

I heard the whop-whop sound of incoming choppers and ducked involuntarily as they set down 50 meters away. I looked closely and watched the supposedly cancelled food drop get unloaded. My stomach twisted from anxiety, not hunger. Not supposed to happen. Lauren hopped out of the second chopper, camera in hand, followed by the sound guy and of course, Taylor.

I tried waving Lauren back to her chopper, which she didn't do, just waved back, with a smile on her face.

The next couple of seconds would replay endlessly for me in the coming months. An overwhelming wave of déjà vu swept over me. Despite things being different, they were the same. Dangerously so. The damn food delivery, the news crew. Worst was the small knot of careless Marines guarding the prisoners we'd passed earlier. Three of them squatting in a circle, hands bound. Except one gook's wrists were free, I realized, and I saw him look up at the nearest Marine, a pair of grenades clipped lazily to his belt.

My throat closed in fear. I yelled, but the racket produced by all the chopper traffic muffled it. I assumed, anyway. I knew no one heard me. I was caught in no man's land. Lauren and the Colonel were behind me, the gooks in front by not close enough to reach. I took my only avenue. I didn't invent the phrase. My JAG lawyer used it later in pre-trial.

I hoisted my M-16 and put a single shot into the gook, blowing his brains all over the startled Marines, who scattered like barnyard chickens. The other prisoners screamed and flopped around in the dirt, no doubt expecting a similar fate. I ran up to the dead man and kicked him hard. His empty palms faced the sky, his body crucified.

I turned; adrenaline charged. I wanted to scream out a cry of victory, and started to, abandoning the attempt as I face Lauren, who had impulsively followed me with her camera grinding away. She'd filmed the whole thing. American Marine runs amok, shoots unarmed North Vietnamese prisoner. Violation of the Geneva Convention and all canons of decent wartime behavior. The Marine with the loose frags had vanished into the crowd of tired warriors. Would he volunteer to identify himself and support my alibi?

It hardly mattered. Lauren tried to rush off and dispose of the tape, but Palmer had smelled Pulitzer, made sure it survived and shipped back to Saigon before he flew to New York to narrate and edit it. I learned later that the clip got almost as much air play as the one of General Loan shooting a Viet Cong prisoner during Tet. The My Lai massacre had happened, but its existence still a secret. Nothing sells the inhumanity of war better than showing it on the 6 o'clock news.

I surrendered peacefully to the MPs who arrived at An Hoa to arrest me. Lieutenant Burke had confined me to quarters, I'd turned in my weapons. I didn't know what to expect.

"Hell, Pax. There's nothing they can do. You shot a gook. He was going to frag an officer," said Burke.

"He was going to frag my girlfriend. If it had been just Schiffer, I'd have let him. I can't prove it. He didn't have a thing in his hands."

"Don't worry," said Burke.

The MPs took me to the brig in Danang. No big deal. The other prisoners were mainly enlisted men being held on drug charges, AWOL and so forth. Lots of them were black. They didn't have a problem with me or my crime. In fact, they congratulated me.

I wasn't reassured. The concept of a jury of one's peers doesn't exist in the military. Court martial is heard by a panel of officers, not twelve grunts from Camp Pendleton. After spending two days staring at the walls in Danang, I traveled under guard to Saigon. They put me in solitary somewhere inside the vastness of Tan Son Nhut airfield.

My first visitor was a genuine doctor, not a corpsman like Doc Steinberg. He asked a lot of pointed questions about my medical history. Questions that hadn't come up at the time I enlisted. Why was I taking anticonvulsants in college? I told him exactly what my neurologist told me.

"Spells. Possibly epilepsy."

"You have any spells in the Marines?"

"A few."

"Don't think that's going to save your ass, private. As of this moment people at home want to see you punished."

The next day the guards brought me several unmarked capsules that they watched me swallow. I knew from the side effects the doctor had ordered what I used to take.

My attorney, Major Crandall told me to cooperate. He had no good news.

The court martial was being moved stateside.

"You picked a great time to murder a prisoner," he said. "Your government, in its infinite wisdom, is doing its best to have you tried in the court of public opinion. They must figure it will take the spotlight off their lack of success in the war effort."

"That's not true. We're kicking the shit out of the NVA."

"All the American public remembers is Tet, and now they have seen an American Marine execute a prisoner of war. The war is over for the American public."

"It wasn't like I had any choice of times. He was going to frag my girlfriend."

"Is that still your story? Jesus H. Christ."

"What do you suggest?" I didn't mean to sound sarcastic. I wanted him to suggest a good alternative.

"Anything. Your weapon malfunctioned. You fucked up and put your finger on the trigger instead of the trigger guard."

"I'm a Marine rifleman. I don't make mistakes like that, sir."

"Excuse me for insulting you. What else do you have?"

"How about the truth?"

"With a capital T?"

"You decide." I took a deep breath and told him everything, starting back at the cross-country race when I ran into the tree. I didn't leave out any details.

Major Crandall listened impassively. He didn't take any notes. Just let me talk. When I finished, he pulled out a pack of Marlboros and offered me one. We sat there smoking in a windowless room that had no doubt held its share of liars, cheats, murderers, cowards, and thieves. Never had anyone made the case I was making.

He stubbed out his butt and put on his cover. Before he knocked on the door for the guard, he spoke.

"That's it. We're going for the insanity defense."

Will the Defendant Please

Over the course of the next year, media interest in the story increased. Anyone looking for proof that America deserved to lose the war needed only to point at me. It didn't matter if I managed to gain acquittal by reason of insanity. That made their case.

I knew none of this at the time, held in the brig at the Quantico Marine base only fifty miles from Blaze. I had no access to radio, television, or newspapers. I was permitted one hour of exercise in a small, fenced in area screened from the view of prying telephoto lenses. Because it was a military base, the networks couldn't overfly with a small plane or helicopter.

I had infrequent visitors. My parents could visit. My Dad didn't on account of the cancer advancing like a blitzkrieg. I couldn't attend the funeral after he died on New Year's Eve. My Mom spent most of her time crying. Smelling her favorite perfume gave me more relief than any words.

Lauren couldn't visit. She was a witness, though hardly a cooperative one. Through my attorney she wanted me to understand that she would do as little as possible to help the prosecution. I didn't want her going to jail for contempt. She had to testify. Conjugal visits were out of the question. We weren't married anyway. My mail was censored, blunting that avenue of affection. She said she'd wait.

"Does she know I could get the death penalty?" I asked my attorney.

"Not from me," he said.

Stewart got to visit once. I asked him how because I thought he would be on my witness list. He winced.

"Your lawyer said he didn't need me."

"But I say I need you. I can't explain time translocation without you."

"He wants you to explain it on your own. Better yet, don't explain it. Just say that it started happening to you and you don't understand it. That way you'll appear to be crazy. If I stand up and relate a lot of the theoretical astrophysics, it makes you and I conspirators. That will piss off the members of the court. You'll be standing in front of a firing squad in no time."

"You know about that, huh?"

"Could be hanging. I'm not sure. I did some research. Spies and collaborators in World War II were often shot, but not always."

"Guess it depends whether the local hardware store has enough quality rope."

My irreverence made him cry. He had such a tender heart. "I'm so sorry. I feel like this is my fault."

"It's not, Stewart. You were there to explain something that made me really feel crazy. I know I'm not. That means a lot."

"Well, the computer center is up and running again. I'm working on solving the problem of going forward in time. I think I may have an answer in six months."

"Don't bother. I'm taking those pills again."

"Why?"

"Not my idea. Every day two guards bring them, and they don't leave until I've swallowed them, and they check my mouth. My lawyer told me the prosecutor got my medical records."

"That means they believe you can time travel." I thought he

might explode with indignation.

"Maybe so. They aren't taking the chance I'm telling the truth. My lawyer is pleading me not guilty because of insanity. He said for the prosecutors to admit time travel exists would help my defense. Plus, I'd be able to escape."

It wasn't long after that the military psychiatrists started to examine me in earnest. I'd had a brief psychological assessment not long after I arrived back in the US. Designed to exclude crazies from enlisting. Nothing subtle. What happened next made that look like amateur hour. Interviews, intelligence tests, personality tests. A Polygraph. Lots of blood tests and X-rays. An EEG. One of the shrinks had the idea to fly me over to England where a medical engineer named Hounsfield had built a scanner that could take images of the brain. He was still testing the prototype, but I learned later, in 1971 it got used for the first time. But the court nixed the idea. Said it was too farfetched and likely would never be of practical use.

Mostly I sat alone in my cell. No TV, no movies. I had an hour in the exercise yard weather permitting. I did pushups, sit-ups, handstands, running in place. Weekly meetings with Major Crandall provided me with knowledge of world events.

On what turned out to be my final day at the Quantico brig he arrived with a new pair of guards. They waited in the hall while we talked.

"No baseball news," he said.

"I know. All-Star break."

"You might be interested to learn that American astronauts landed on the moon yesterday. Senator Edward Kennedy had more difficulty than they did just driving across a bridge in Massachusetts. He put his car in the water."

"Is he OK?" My parents believed the Kennedys were close

to saints.

"I guess so. He had a passenger, a secretary, who drowned."

"He needs to time travel."

Major Crandall ignored my sick humor. "Your trial begins next week. Camp Lejeune. Easier to keep reporters away."

I shrugged. My chances of acquittal looked about as good as the New York Mets winning the World Series that year. Brig food in Lejeune would taste as bad as Quantico's. I'd get to see, but not speak to, Lauren.

"If Lauren and I got married, wouldn't she be able to refuse to testify?"

"Doesn't work that way. Only for crimes that happen after marriage. Sometimes not even then. Good luck getting married in prison."

"You want me to pack?" I said.

Major Crandall just stared.

"I'm kidding," I said.

A helicopter flew us to Andrews Air Force base, where a waiting transport plane carried us to North Carolina. Major Crandall left me in the tender care of a new set of marine guards, even meaner looking than the ones in Quantico. I got a recruit-style haircut and a clean battle dress uniform to wear. I rated my cell one star higher on the quality scale than the one in Quantico. The blanket smelled fresh, not boot camp funky. The water lacked a metallic aftertaste and the faucet produced warm, not hot, water. A small, barred window high on the wall allowed morning sunlight to stream in for a few hours. My daily exercise expanded to include shooting baskets while the guards watched and smoked and said nothing.

On trial day they shackled me before walking me to a green station wagon. Interior smelled of sweat and stale tobacco. No door or window handles. Heavy gauge steel mesh guaranteed no attacks on the driver. The drive lasted five minutes and then the process reversed. Out of the car, across a well-manicured lawn bordered with flower beds and into a windowless building with pale green interior walls. The air conditioning felt great, a sign that officers used the place. I caught a glimpse of an empty courtroom before the guards put me in a small waiting room with two doors. The shackles came off and they sat me down on the only furniture, a high-backed chair on casters. Then they left, locking the door.

I sat still for a long time. During my time in jail I'd learned to accept long spells of inaction and solitude. My mind kept busy by replaying the good things I could recall from my former life: the routines of a loving family, an innocent youth, minor celebrity as an athlete, sex with Eve and later with Lauren. I'd given up hope of time travel helping me to escape. Part of me started to wonder if it was even real, not just a trick played by my brain. Major Crandall wanted to play that card. I saw no reason not to refuse.

My inner clock told me at least an hour had passed, strange even for the military. I heard no sounds except the hiss of the air-conditioning when it switched on. Shouldn't there be movement into the building? Where was Major Crandall?

On impulse I tested the doors. The entrance remained locked but the rear door opened soundlessly. I stood still, waiting for an ambush of guards. When nothing happened, I stepped across the threshold into a corridor I assumed communicated with other cells as well as the courtrooms. I tried every door in both directions and found them all locked. All except the one at the end of the hall under the red-illuminated exit sign, which warned of an alarm if opened.

What kind of sick game were they playing?

I pushed the bar and winced at the brightness that greeted me. The smell of magnolias and newly mowed grass delighted me. Birds twittered from the upper branches. In front of me: nothing. No platoons on the march. No deuce-and-a-half trucks. US and Marine Corps flags hanging limp on a flagpole. A hundred meters distant on the other side of the street was a chain link fence, at least ten feet high, with concertina wire fixed to the top. The door clicked shut behind me.

I turned and looked back, half expecting guards to rush me. What the hell was happening?

I got up the nerve and strolled to the fence, senses on maximum alert. Beyond the fence lay a blacktop road. I assumed it circled the perimeter of the camp. The sound of a vehicle broke the silence. A non-descript gray sedan approached from the right and rolled to a stop opposite me. US Government plates, tinted glass. I stayed frozen like a rabbit waiting to die under the wheels of a car. The driver's window rolled down. A man in a fedora stared at me.

"Get in," he said.

"You're joking. How do I get over the fence?"

"Take a closer look."

I did. Someone had with great skill cut out a section of fence large enough to admit a crawling person, then replaced the breach with a few strands of twine. I snapped them and crawled out. I picked up the loose piece of fence as if to replace it and conceal my escape.

"Don't bother. There's a crew coming to repair it," he said.

Not sure if I could trust him, I stood there.

The passenger door opened.

"Hello, Pax," said Lauren.

Underground Railroad

I fell into her arms and closed my eyes, certain that I was tripping out on something. She smelled like a field of lilacs. She started kissing me, washing my cheeks with her tears. "I missed you so much," she said.

The driver dropped the car in gear and accelerated. He made a hard right onto a gravel road. In a few seconds, the smell of red pine filled the interior, and sunlight flickered through the gaps between the trees.

"I missed you too. What just happened?"

The driver shot me a glance in the rearview mirror. Steely blue eyes and a sandy crew cut. He lit a cigarette from a lighter on the dash and passed it back to me. I took a drag.

"Who do I thank?" I said.

He had lit a smoke too and exhaled out his window. "Turns out you have a rich uncle."

He and Lauren burst out laughing.

"Uncle Sam," she said.

I tried to make sense of it. "You mean the uncle who put me on trial for war crimes? Plans to execute me?"

"Don't be dramatic. No American has been executed in the military for quite some time."

"Then a long vacation in a cool, damp cell."

He nodded. "Possible. But seeing as how I've got you in custody, that doesn't seem likely."

"On whose authority?" I said.

"If I told you, I'd have to kill you. So, I'll call it the Agency and leave it at that. The point is the US government has more to lose by allowing the trial to go forward than not. Something much bigger than your case is about to break. When it blows up, hardly anyone in America will support the war effort. All the same, the government wants to punish the hardcore anti-war people for their actions."

"Prosecute them for treason," I said.

"Easier said than done. Smart lawyers would work for free to defend them."

"And use the trials as a platform for spreading their message."

"Exactly right. In exchange for dropping charges against you, the government asks you to perform a valuable service."

"Like I was doing over in Vietnam?"

"Far more valuable. Less risky."

"I'm all ears. But tell me, not that I mind, but how does Lauren fit into this?"

I squeezed her hand.

"She's your accomplice. Your rescuer. How else could you bust out of jail?"

"Not very plausible." I gave her a long, searching stare. I wanted to believe in her. We had a brief but hot wartime relationship. I stood to end up in prison or dead or exiled.

"Why not?" she said.

"You're a news photographer. I'm a story."

"You're the guy who saved my life back in the Nam. Even if we never make it in the real world, I'll give you leave to cut me loose, no strings attached. I owe you that. If we stay together there's no story. I'll kill it."

I leaned forward and said to the driver, "What am I supposed to call you? I know it won't be your real name."

"I like birds. Make it Hawk."

"OK, Hawk. What's my end of the bargain? And why should I trust you, other than Lauren vouching for you?"

"We're going to take a break for refreshments in a little while. I'll explain then."

The car paused at a two laned paved road and turned right. Highway 24 read the first sign we passed. We headed north, parallel to the coast. Within a mile we crossed the city limits of Swansboro. Hawk parked in front of a café.

"Are you nuts? I'm an escaped prisoner. The cops here may be a bunch of Bubbas, but they are able to arrest people from time to time," I said.

"Relax, Pax. You haven't officially escaped yet." Hawk opened Lauren's door and I followed her onto the sidewalk.

"When will I?"

He glanced at his watch. "Around four. I'll have you in Rocky Mount by then, just in time to catch the Carolina Creeper."

"What?"

"Inside joke. It's the train called the Champion, run by the Seaboard Coast Line. There's an express and a local version that makes so many stops we call it the creeper. Got you Pullman car reservations to New York."

Hawk led the way inside the café, a steamy place with a counter and four booths on the street side. Awnings blocked the direct sun rays but allowed plenty of reflected light. He sat diagonally from me in the corner booth. When he took off his hat, his countenance took an even more fearsome appearance. A pale scar ran from the corner of his left ear to his jaw. When he talked, the facial muscle weakness testified to a vicious knife stroke.

The waitress arrived with a thermos full of coffee. The menu was brief and unpretentious. I ordered eggs, toast, and grits. First non-jail food in a while and I was ravenous.

"What's the plan?" I said.

"The guy that planted the bomb at your college. Your roommate."

"Ex-roommate."

Hawk shrugged. "He's still at large."

"Left the country."

"Probably. His comrades in the radical movement operate a people moving service for draft dodgers, bail jumpers, anybody in their circle who's wanted by the cops. He ever talk about it?"

"No. I had nothing to do with his business until he tricked me into moving the bomb from their factory to campus."

Hawk attempted to smile; the results hampered by nerve damage.

"Not the first or the last person they conned," he said.

"Eve was my first real love," I said, not looking at Lauren.

"Sorry for your loss," said Hawk. "Anyway, we think he used the service to get away. They called it the Underground Railroad."

"After the anti-slavery network before the Civil War."

"Shows they learned something in college," said Lauren.

"And you want me to get on board," I said.

Hawk smiled. "All we have is a New York phone number. By the time you arrive there tomorrow morning, your escape will be front page news. So, we hope the Underground Railroad people will take the bait before NYPD spots you. We can't share anything with them for obvious reasons."

"What if they won't go near me? I'm radioactive. They're trying to remain underground. They don't need more attention."

"That's where I come in, Pax," said Lauren.

I didn't get it. My facial expression must have said so. She continued.

"You're not my story, but you are a story. If you thought the press has it in for the US military, you wouldn't be totally wrong. I know a reporter who knows a reporter who sympathizes big time with the radicals. A week ago, I reached out to my colleague about the escape plan and your desire to use the Underground to get to Canada. She talked to her contact and word came back that they would love the propaganda impact of America's number one war criminal blowing the lid off the military."

Hawk chimed in: "Go along with them. Stay at their safe house. Meet as many of them as you can. Memorize names and faces. They're still beginners at spy craft. The Soviets would take you to several places, blindfolded, never talk to you except behind a screen. We think these radicals won't be quite that clever."

"Then you move in."

"Not until you are all the way at the end. We assume it's Canada or northern New England. Pretty porous border for them if they want to move you across. Lots of leftists live up in the woods in communes or on their own in secluded cabins. They'll have a way to sneak you over. Even then, there is likely a network of sympathizers in Canada. Don't stop until the train has shut down for good. Then call me and head for a US consulate.

Breakfast arrived. It was better than I'd dreamed. The cook had fried the eggs in bacon grease just to where the yolk had not quite solidified. It erupted with yellow lava and I greedily mopped it up with toast. The grits were ho-hum, nothing special, but a Southern staple. Eve used to fix them.

"I'm going along, right?" said Lauren.

"Absolutely," said Hawk. "I think the radicals will cream

their jeans—pardon my French—at the idea of having a media person there. They take perverse pleasure in taunting us. Feel free to promise them anything in terms of free and sympathetic publicity."

Lauren beamed. At last she'd be scooping her old boss. With the added benefit of staying with me. Hawk excused himself to make a call.

"Will this be hard for you?" asked Lauren.

How could it not be? The radicals had aided Bear and shared his values. Strangely, I'd stopped supporting the war now that I'd lived through it and seen how the average grunt or GI had come to be used as tools for promotion of officers. Whether the cause of stopping Communism in Vietnam was wise or foolish, I was looking out for my brothers in arms. If the war couldn't, or wouldn't, be won, it was time to come home. I knew I could look at Bear or anybody on his team in the eye and make that claim.

"You have a personal score to settle with Bear. You can't let that upset the larger plan," said Hawk.

"I will make them believe me. They'll accept that I'd kill for their cause. They will stop looking for reasons to suspect me. When they time comes, you and your team take them down for good."

Hawk drove to Rocky Mount, where we stayed out of sight until the train arrived at eight. He gave us tickets to a sleeping car berth and a thousand dollars in cash. In the trunk of his car was a backpack for me with a small quantity of clothes, toothbrush, wallet with a fake ID card, cigarettes, lighter, playing cards and a highway map of the Eastern US. He made me memorize two phone numbers: the Underground Railway's and his.

"Safe to assume you'll be searched one way or another," he said.

The low moan of the approaching train horn signaled departure time. Only a few passengers stood waiting on the platform. No police. Nobody who looked official.

Hawk said as he shook our hands, "All I can promise is that there will be no New York police on the platform in New York when you arrive. Other than that, you'll need to keep your wits about you. Don't try to be heroes. Collect information. Travel to the end of the line."

"When it's over, what then?" I said.

"Try to cut you a deal with the government. They want someone to answer for the war crime charges. Like I said, soon enough they'll have that."

I started to protest, and he waved me off.

"It's a bad deal for you. I get it. Here's the problem. There are people in the government who believe what you said about time travel. They think it can be used as a weapon."

"You don't think it happened?"

"Don't ask, and I won't lie to you. All I'm saying is that you're looking at twenty years in the brig versus a new life as a government guinea pig. Two choices, neither very appealing."

He didn't stay to wave goodbye. Lauren and I boarded, and the Pullman car porter showed us to our compartment. By day, a comfortable pair of seats. By night, a fold down sleeping berth that was a snug fit for two. I gave the porter a generous tip and said we were tired, wanted the bed made up soon. We ate in the dining car. I finally sated my ravenous taste buds with the Salisbury steak and mashed potatoes. Compared to C rations and jail food, I might as well be eating at Windsor Castle with the royal family.

The porter prepared our sleeping compartment. I pulled the shades and we stripped, too full of desire to bother with foreplay.

Lauren saw my readiness and rode me with aggression. Climax came in under a minute. As we snuggled spoon-like in the bunk, I whispered, "I'm not done with you."

"I hope not, Marine. Treat me as rough as you want. Use me like a toy."

"For real?"

"Totally."

We spent the rest of the night carrying out her wishes. By dawn I was sleeping next to her, sated for the time being. The porter's call arrived way too early. I could have used another 24 hours in a sex coma.

"Duty calls," said Lauren.

She gave me a final glance at her breasts before slipping on the harness of a bra. "It's not Danang."

"I don't want those Movement guys making a play for you anyway."

"Aren't they all supposed to be liberated and respectful of women?"

"The ones I saw at college were as randy as any Marine," I said.

"Should be an interesting generation to watch," she said with a laugh.

We spilled into the terminal and quickly mixed with hundreds of other passengers. I doubt any police in the area would have been able to spot us, given our ages and non-descript clothing. True, my hair was still short but contemporary standards, but plenty of soldiers and Marines traveled by rail and I didn't stand out from the crowd.

I found a phone booth and shut the door. Put in my dime and dialed. The line purred a few times, then someone picked up.

"Hello?" Female voice. Neutral tone.

Now came the hard part. Hawk didn't know if I had to use a password or another recognition signal to initiate the process. It could end right here and now if I raised suspicion.

My cover story was as near to the truth as I could make it.

"Hello. I'm in trouble and I need help. I heard this was a place I could call."

A long pause. "What kind of trouble?"

"I'm a US Marine and I'm AWOL. I don't want to go back to the war." Better to be open-ended, not real specific.

Another pause. I heard a voice in the background. Two people discussing me. Better than a total hang-up.

A second person came on the line. Male. New York accent.

"We aren't a law office. Maybe you should try Legal Aid."

He'd said "we." First clue that this was a group. I needed to push a little.

"Maybe you don't understand. I've had legal help. It's gone farther than that."

"OK, then. What are you saying?"

Starting to take the bait. I let out some line.

"You read the papers? Watch TV?"

"Yeah."

"What's a big story today? I'll give you a hint. Camp Lejeune."

Longer silence except for a rustling noise. Newspaper?

"OK. Got it. How did you get this number?"

Another critical point. I had a plausible answer.

"Got it from another Marine in the brig. He was going to go to Canada before he got drafted, decided not to, ended up in Nam and then fragged an officer. He's looking at life."

I thought the fragging reference would be catnip for an anti-military radical. I was right.

"That was righteous, brother. He didn't get out with you?"

"No. I had outside help. Girlfriend. She's with me. We need to get out of the country."

Another pause. Longest yet.

"Can you call back in an hour?"

I didn't have a choice. "Sure."

The line went dead.

Lauren and I used the time to take the subway north to 59th street and Lexington. She'd spent time in New York, knew her way around. I'd told her my plan and she was agreeable. We walked west until 59th changed to Central Park South. It was only a jump away now. The Plaza Hotel. Should have spent New Year's 1968 there with Eve. Gone to Rockefeller Center to skate. Joined the celebration in Times Square when the ball dropped at midnight. It had been bitterly cold that day. Wouldn't have mattered with Eve at my side. Now it didn't matter as much. Lauren more than filled the void, but there was always going to be the late-night dream, rousing me from sleep, feeling and hearing the blast that took her away. Watching her vanish in a fireball. That vision trumped the memories of the horrors I witnessed in Vietnam.

We took a room for a night, not knowing if we'd stay there. Made love right away with the windows open and the traffic noise muting our passionate cries. Afterwards we looked down at the green expanse of Central Park, promised each other we'd take a ride in one of the horse-drawn carriages that night if our destiny hadn't drawn us further along its path.

Time for the call. One ring and then a pickup.

"Hello?" Same voice.

"Yes. Call me Pax."

"Call me Che." The thought crossed my mind it might be

Bear. Just his style.

"Is there space on the Underground Railroad?"

"Yes, if you look right to us."

"Where? When?"

"Where are you?"

I didn't want to say the Plaza. Didn't fit the image.

"Near Central Park."

Che didn't say anything for a few seconds.

"I'll meet you under the arch in Washington Square Park. Know where that is?"

I didn't think I was supposed to know.

"No, but I can find it. Marines are good at directions."

"Fair enough. One hour." The phone clicked.

We discussed strategy. We had to leave the Plaza. Che would either want us to stay in his safe house or with a comrade. Now I was starting to talk like them.

We headed for the subway. Took it south to the 8th Street Station and walked a few blocks to the Memorial Arch, in the heart of NYU, surrounded by a colorful mélange of hippies, artists, street musicians and regular students. Not at all like the scene at Blaze.

We slowly circled the Arch and then sat on the edge of a fountain. Lauren found a bag of popcorn abandoned by a tourist and tossed the kernels to the pigeons. We had half an hour to kill. I watched people. I didn't know what to look for. He could be any one of them.

Lauren tossed the last handful of popcorn to the birds and dropped the bag in a trash can. I stood to stretch. The nearest street performer launched into his interpretation of the Dylan song. *Masters of War*. I wasn't a fan and considered moving farther away. I took Lauren's hand and looked for another place to sit.

A couple emerged from the onlookers and came right at us. A man with dark hair, shorter than average, a moustache and beard, tortoise shell glasses, wearing a scruffy sport coat above faded jeans. An assistant professor or grad student, perhaps. The girl with him had a pageboy style haircut, unlike 99 percent of the coeds, and wire rimmed glasses that failed to hide dark circles under her eyes. They walked side by side without ever touching. Not even the brush of a hand. Nor did they make eye contact with me. At the last moment they passed by on either side of us and vanished behind the arch.

"What do you think?" said Lauren.

"Recon mission, I'm certain."

"Should you have said anything?"

A fair question. "Don't know. Have to wait for them to make the first move."

At the one-hour mark we walked over to the arch and stood underneath it. No point in being subtle. It was now or never. I was nervous for the first time in months. In combat I learned how to detach. That was my defense. I'm not going to get killed today because of reasons X, Y, or Z. Didn't matter that it was bullshit. I knew it but believed it anyway. Then I could let my brain focus on the more important stuff. What I needed to do in order to survive. Guys that focused on anything out of their own control were more likely to be unprepared. And they died for it.

"Knox?" I turned around before answering. Playing it cool. Sport coat guy and his page were back.

"Right. I go by Pax. This is Lauren, my girlfriend."

The woman sniffed.

Lauren said, "I'm a girl, and his friend."

"I'm Ted. This is Diana," said sport coat guy.

"Where's Che?" I said.

"He couldn't come. He's traveling today."

"We need to go. This place is crawling with FBI and their spies," said Diana.

They walked us out the north end of the park. It crossed my mind that Hawk, or somebody like him, might be tailing us. Diana kept looking all around, including behind. The Cold War spy game continued with an hour-long subway ride that took us back through Grand Central, the Shuttle to Times Square, then south again on the Blue Line to Washington Square. All to throw off pursuers, I supposed. Ted and Diana stayed mum except to point out what direction to walk. Our destination was within Greenwich Village. Turned out to be on 11th Street.

Ted led us to a townhouse in the middle of the block. The building looked old but had been kept up over the years. A three-story walkup, brick, that matched perfectly with the neighboring structures. I could smell the aroma of freshly baked bread after we climbed the front stairs and walked down a hall to the back. A large, sunlit kitchen greeted us. A rear window offered a view of a back courtyard, little else.

Diana greeted the woman who had just taken the bread out to cool with a tight hug. Then she poured herself a cup of tea and sat at a massive oak table.

"I'm Cathlyn," said the woman. She gave Lauren a hug and offered me a handshake.

"Where's Terry?" said Ted.

"Out at a steering committee meeting. He should be back soon," said Cathlyn. She looked at Lauren. "The bread is too warm to eat, but can I offer you some tea?"

Lauren accepted, I demurred.

Cathlyn could have passed as Diana's sister: same light

brown hair, cut short, lacking the eyeglasses. She sat next to Diana while Ted remained on his feet, pacing the floor.

"I read about you," he said staring at me. "And I don't like a lot of what I saw."

I didn't reply. I wasn't on trial. I had the sense he wanted to get me talking so if I was working for the government, I'd make a mistake and contradict myself. I wondered what he'd do then. He wasn't a big guy. He hadn't spent the last several months of his life learning how to kill and then following through with the training. If it came to a fight, I'd win.

"You weren't drafted. You volunteered. You went into combat and you killed liberation fighters as well as civilians. Then you fucked up more than your masters could allow by killing an unarmed prisoner in front of a news camera."

At that point, my throat tightened. I wondered if he knew Lauren had taped it. I forced myself not to look in her direction. Nothing to give her up. I relaxed when he continued down a different path.

"You defended yourself with the absurd excuse that you had traveled back in time, knew that the liberation fighter was going to throw a hand grenade, so you shot him in self-defense, sort of."

My inner Marine was having trouble restraining itself. The guy I shot was not a "liberation" fighter. He was a soldier of North Vietnam who had invaded the South through Laos. He wanted to kill me as much as I wanted to kill him. He would have succeeded in killing Lauren on the second go round had I not intervened. I wasn't sorry.

"What have you got to say for yourself?"

I was raised in a household with two diametrically opposed philosophies. My Dad believed in not starting fights, but never losing them either. My Mom counseled turning the other cheek, agreeing to the other guy's arguments in order to defuse the situation. I chose her path, much as my Dad would've protested.

"You're right. I'm sorry for what I did. I came from a military family. There was an explosion at my college. I harbored angry thoughts at the activists who set it off. I realize now they didn't intend harm. But at the time, I was vengeful and didn't think about the consequences of my actions. I thought I could defeat the activists' cause by going to Vietnam and fighting against liberation."

Ted beamed. I imagined never in his wildest dreams had he imagined he'd be able to verbally confront one of his enemies and get him to admit his guilt. In another place, another century, he would have had me taken outside to be shot.

"What do you see yourself doing if we give you the chance to escape to freedom?"

Making sure assholes like you go to prison, I thought. But I said: "Working tirelessly for worldwide revolution. Telling the truth about the murdering imperialists running the American empire and oppressing the Vietnamese people."

Ted walked over and hugged me. I swear there were tears in his eyes. He smelled like stale tobacco and bad BO. In other words, like a grunt in Nam, only without an excuse like humping in the boonies for a week.

He started up again. "Tell me, Pax, did you learn much about explosives in the Marine Corps?"

I knew where he was going but I couldn't walk back what I'd just said about working for revolution.

"Yeah, something. I mean, the engineers did most of the demolition work: blowing up bunkers, ammo, rice, and stuff. But we grunts got into the act from time to time when we didn't have any engineers with us."

"You, personally learned how?"

This was excruciating. "Yeah, I did."

He pulled me out of the chair. He looked more animated than when I'd made my phony confession.

"Follow me."

We walked down the hall and descended to the basement. He led me to windowless room. It looked like a storage closet: boxes piled up, some furniture, an old refrigerator with the door removed. The lighting was bad. I couldn't see much until Ted aimed a flashlight across the room.

Tools lay scattered over a long work bench. Lengths of lead pipe a foot tall stood like Atlas rockets on launch pads. A shoebox held coils of wire, black tape, and dry cell 1.5-volt batteries like we'd use for science experiments in 5th grade. Only this wasn't any science experiment. A larger box on the floor contained the real prize: fifty or more orange-colored cylinders I recognized as industrial grade dynamite. Not the cool C4 that we used in Vietnam, but not lacking in power.

I gave him one of those looks that say, "I know what I'm seeing, but I don't believe it."

He grinned like a middle schooler who'd spray painted a swear word on a wall.

"What do you think?" he said.

"I think that you are more than likely going to blow yourself up with this shit."

"So, help me out. You wanted vengeance. But first you picked the wrong target. Now you can correct your error and strike a blow for the oppressed."

Always with the recycled commie rhetoric.

"Sure, I can give you some technical assistance. When do you want to have the fireworks display?"

He grinned "There's a dance at a USO in Fort Dix. Soon. Like to give them a taste of their own medicine."

He pulled a box out from under the bench and opened it. Inside was an assortment of hardware: screws, nails, nuts, and bolts.

"Just like the bomblets they drop on Vietnamese peasants."

I whistled. This guy was playing for keeps. A few sticks of dynamite packed with those items inside a lead pipe would kill dozens of people within 50 meters of the blast. If he got lucky, over a hundred. Nobody in the room would escape unhurt.

We got to work. Laid out the dynamite, blasting caps, wires, wire caps, pipe and shrapnel, batteries, and alarm clocks. Fit everything inside two pipes and screwed them shut with threaded caps. I drilled holes through the lead for the wires and taped the batteries securely. He just had to connect the wires and start the clock to give himself enough time to plant them and bug out.

"Hook up the wires before you leave home. Red to red, black to black. You don't want to be in a hurry or having bad lighting when you make the connection. Otherwise it goes off in your face. Got it?"

"Got it, comrade."

We walked back upstairs. At the top, he gave me a bear hug and said, "I'm sorry I didn't trust you. Now I know victory will be hours."

He'd watched too many corny Hollywood productions. I decided to try for a little intelligence.

"Who's this Che guy I was talking to?"

"Nobody." He winked. "Just the brains of the cell."

"You suppose I can meet him before the—um—railway takes us away to safety?"

Ted chuckled and slapped me on the back.

"Hell, he's going to be driving you there."

El Che Llega

Lauren and I slept on a comfortable bed on the upper floor of the townhouse. Turned out that Cathlyn's father owned it. He was wealthy and spent most of his time in Europe with his wife. Rich people tend to keep up their homes. This house was no exception. Not a hippie flophouse. No cockroaches, rats, moldy ceiling tiles. The hot water supply seemed endless. Towels and sheets, immaculate. I wanted to ask if this kind of opulence would disappear after the revolution.

We closed the door and screwed like bunnies. Hard to tell if we'd have this kind of privacy for a while.

"Do you care if people hear us? See us?" said Lauren.

"Not a bit. I love you and want the world to know it."

"If only we were back at the Plaza, you could screw me right next to the window."

"Lauren, you are hornier than any Marine I ever met."

"I know. I got propositioned all the time."

My heart fluttered at that, hoping she hadn't succumbed in a moment of lust mixed with alcohol.

"Didn't go for it. Not until I saw you."

"What was the appeal?"

She dug her fingers into my ribs until I squealed.

"Handsome. Obviously intelligent. And you hadn't lost that look of humanity, despite where you were, what you'd seen."

I had to add a phrase. "And what I'd done. Don't forget that."

She kissed me long and slow. Took a breath and continued.

"You had to make choices nobody should ever have to make. At the end of your life, you can be proud of yourself."

With that and her kisses in my ear, I slept.

The household awoke early. Ted knocked on the door at six.

"Sorry. The train will leave soon. Thought you'd like to eat first," he said.

The members of the Collective packed the kitchen. That was what they called the group. Terry and Kathy were the two we hadn't met. They remained quiet as we tried to fill up on a mixture of oats, honey, ground nuts and yogurt. A stark contrast to the southern fried eggs and grits the previous day. No coffee, just tea. Kathy explained that coffee represented imperialism in South America. No coffee drinking tolerated.

"I'm not asking for a destination, just a time estimate. Will this be a long day?" I asked.

"That's up to Che. He's driving you. He might be making more stops, picking up other riders, other material," said Ted.

I wondered if the material was for more bombs. Couldn't afford to ask. I changed the subject, sort of.

"Cool. When is the package we made up going to be delivered?"

The instant look of fire from Diana spoke volumes. Ted stared at his cereal and mumbled, "Can't really say. It's a decision for the Collective."

I pushed. "I thought there was some military dance at Fort Dix. There must be a band hired to play, tickets to sell."

Ted ducked his head further and replied. "Yeah, that's in a couple of days. But the question is: will the event be symbolic or definitive?"

"Inside or outside the dance, you mean?" I said.

Diana put a finger over her lips. "I don't think it's a matter for non-cadres to discuss."

"Christ, Diana. He helped me make the bomb. His fingers are all over this. Don't you think he has a right to know what's going to happen?" said Ted.

She answered in deliberate, icy tones. "All of us will vote on where it gets placed. Demonstration versus annihilation. Once we cross that line, there's no going back."

I looked at each of them in turn. Trying to read intent from their faces. Ted and Diana were known quantities and cancelled each other. Cathlyn had pressed me hard on my motivation. Somehow, she didn't strike me as a pacifist. Her parents tacitly supported the use of their house. That spoke of militancy. Terry served on a steering committee. A leader. Blood had been spilled on the Blaze campus. They surely knew that. Momentum rolled in favor of more action. Like the Vietnam in microcosm. Once the decision was made by the White House and Pentagon to commit ground troops, the die was cast. Thousands of lives were decided in counsels far from the scene of the action.

I figured Kathy for Cathlyn's foil, but the vote would still be three to two at worst. They would put the bomb inside the dance hall. I doubted I'd have the chance to get to a phone and warn Hawk. I had to focus on my mission. Sweep up the rest of the network. Put them on trial for the world to see their true colors.

I grabbed Lauren's hand under the table and squeezed. She smiled and returned the gesture.

"It's time for you to go," said Diana.

"Che on his way?" I said.

She nodded.

Five minutes later we stood on the curb, just the two of us.

"We could leave now. Call Hawk. Or not," I said.

"Then what? Miss the chance to find out what happened to

Bear? Arrest the network? Make one of them roll over on his comrades?"

I had those thoughts too. And an even bigger one.

What if Bear was Che?

The Wages of Sin

The Resistance ran on time. At least the New York branch. Diana had assured us she'd call our ride and we'd be picked up in ten minutes. I saw something moving behind a curtain in the townhouse, figured they'd watch us, just in case. Another reason not to try to call Hawk.

A blue VW van chugged down 11th Street and flashed its lights. The signal. We hoisted our packs and waited. It ground to a halt and the passenger side door opened. A woman with long brown hair got out, smiled, and opened the rear door.

"Get in," she said.

I went first. If I saw Bear, I planned to put him a chokehold while Lauren ran to call. There was a small grocery store on the corner with a phone booth in front. The presence of the woman wasn't foreseen, but unless she had a weapon, nothing was going to stop me.

I had my own plan. I jerked open the driver's door.

"Got you, Che," I said, reaching for his throat.

But not Bear. A studious looking fellow with wire rims and a mop of curly brown hair. He laughed in a nervous way. Put up his hands in mock surrender.

"His plans changed. I'm Bill. That's Bernadine. Just us two. You know Che? He's a righteous one."

"Yeah, kind of. Through college. I'm Pax. This is Lauren. Thanks for taking the trouble," I said. My heart still hammered from my readiness to fight. I felt out of breath and dizzy.

"No trouble, brother. You OK?" He put a hand on my shoulder.

"Yeah. Well, no. This whole thing is stressful on us. Just want it to be over."

He laughed. "Out of one war and into another. Don't worry. You're on the right side of history now."

I'd heard that phrase before. Saul Stone. History was a polygon, I'd decided, not a two-dimensional sheet. The winning team got to write its version.

Bill drove us out of the winding streets of Greenwich Village to FDR Drive, took that north along the East River. He gave us a touristy monologue when I said it was my first time to New York. The UN building. The Queensboro bridge. Gracie Mansion, home of New York's Mayor.

I pressed him a little for details of the Underground Railroad, but he coyly deflected my questions.

"You don't want to know too much. I don't want to tell you too much. You might get caught. Cops put pressure on you. You talk. We get caught too. This revolution business has risks."

"Fair enough," I said.

By now we had left New York and Bill drove us through Connecticut to Interstate 91, where he turned north. We'd left urban America behind. Green rolling hills appeared in northern Massachusetts and when we crossed into Vermont the land in all directions was primitive and verdant.

"Hungry," said Bill. Not a question. He pulled off and followed a two-lane highway into a small town, past a river with an old mill and a touristy spot calling itself the World's Largest Basket Store.

"I have friends here. They'll take you the rest of the way," he said.

We turned off onto a series of well-maintained gravel roads that climbed gradually to the west. If there were street signs, I saw hardly any. I hoped Lauren was taking mental notes. This could be tough for the FBI to locate, which I supposed was the whole point.

Finally, we pulled into a winding single lane that narrowed into a driveway. It ended in front of a collection of outbuildings. All carried the stamp of Yankee craftsmanship: white paint, generously applied over clapboard siding, green shingles that matched the background of birch, maple, and pine. A house with similar trim stood in a clearing beyond, a thin curl of smoke rising from a chimney built of granite set in gray mortar. We got out and set down our packs while Bill walked up to the house. I half expected Robert Frost to walk out and greet us.

Instead, a couple dressed in utilitarian khaki met Bill halfway down a gravel path. They embraced like old friends. They walked nearer and I saw they were in fact elderly but moved with a vigor usually denied those past the gift of youth.

"Scott and Helen, meet Pax and Lauren," said Bill.

I felt bad they might get arrested for helping us. "It's like turning my grandparents over to the police," I whispered in Lauren's ear.

"Forget who they remind you of based on appearance. It's about actions. They make choices, they take the consequences," said Lauren.

"True," I said, rationalizing in my mind I might not remember accurate directions. I thought about phoning them a warning but saw no wires leading to the house. Back to the land, indeed.

We entered the house and passed through a large living area with four walls of bookshelves. Shakespeare, Dostoyevsky,

Twain, Melville, Milton, Marx, Adam Smith, Kant were a few of the names that sprang out.

Scott and Helen turned out to be strict vegetarians and expected the same of their company. Lunch was a vegetable-based gruel that owed its sparse flavor to pungent herbs and spices. I looked in vain for droplets of fat that might sustain me. Scott appeared to weigh about 120 pounds on a five-ten frame. Helen the same. They ate as much as the NVA and VC cadres I'd been chasing around I Corps in South Vietnam. Those guys were tough though. Nothing like deprivation to make for an aggressive state of being.

After eating, Bill and Bernadine left for parts unknown. I tried fishing for a hint about their destination and got nowhere. Nor were they much help directing us to the next leg of the trip. Just an assurance that Scott would send me off in the morning. The price for lodging turned out to be a shift of gardening. Scott and Helen didn't believe in artificial fertilizer or pesticides, so we plucked beetles from squash, cucumbers and tomatoes and hoed in a foul-smelling slop that Scott had obtained from a nearby farmer. That pretty much took care of the rest of the day. The positive effect was that we were all too tired to argue, though I was damned if I'd ever go to work in a socialist collective.

That evening we sat around eating homemade ice cream flavored with maple syrup Scott and Helen made from maple trees on their property. Their farm covered several hundred acres, and they turned a small profit on the proceeds. Although Scott couldn't make himself use the word profit. He called it a surplus.

They retired at nine. There was a comfortable bed in a guest room that doubled as an office. I started snooping around, hoping to find a scrap of paper with an address I could turn over to Hawk. That came easily out of the waste basket on an envelope with an invoice they'd paid. I also found a statement from the First Bank and Trust of Boston informing Scott that his trust account had earned a solid 8 percent interest in the quarter ending June 30. The principal amount stunned me. I showed it to Lauren.

"How the hell did they get that kind of money? Not from raising zucchini and selling half gallons of maple syrup to tourists," she said.

We snooped some more, eventually jimmying open a file cabinet and locating documents identifying Scott as the beneficiary of a paternal inheritance of a million dollars. Perhaps the guilt of receiving the largesse had turned him into a flaming radical, much like Bear. Maybe he really believed people could live off the land in a subsistence economy. If so, he was a raging hypocrite.

Next morning, we ate a farewell breakfast. Helen made fabulous pancakes that I drowned in maple syrup. Scott was cordial. Reasonable, even.

"Sometimes I act my age. I forget that young people must make their own mistakes. I made plenty in my time. It's hard to admit being wrong about so much. The ideas were right. The execution was messy. A lot of people died because of those mistakes," he said.

"It's still happening. I've made my own. Others do. The biggest danger is being so assured that one has figured everything out," I said.

"If you ever come this way again, stop by," he said.

I knew I wouldn't, but I lied and promised I would.

Scott and Helen didn't own a car, so Lauren and I walked a couple of miles to state highway 30 and hitchhiked into Manchester. Scott gave us written instructions including a phone number, which turned out to belong to a guy named George, a

Harvard dropout who drove a truck and spent his free time trying to organize other drivers. His problem was that they mainly belonged to the Teamsters Union and believed in the teachings of Jimmy Hoffa, not Karl Marx.

George had a fresh black eye from his latest attempt to organize and educate the workers. They hadn't been in the mood to listen to his message, but we were a captive audience.

"The answer lies in applying the doctrine of who does what to whom. The working class is who and the capitalists are whom. They get squashed. It's as simple as that."

He was hauling a load of picnic tables made in Cuba. Trees felled on land confiscated from American companies in the revolution were loaded onto ships flying the Liberian flag, which sailed to Mexico. The lumber was milled there at facilities owned by an anonymous Portuguese millionaire and then trucked to an assembly plant in New Jersey, where it was fabricated into the tables.

"That's quite a trek," I said.

"Everything was handled by union workers."

"How well are the tables selling?" I said.

George shrugged. "Last trip they were running out of room in the warehouse."

"It's summertime. Maybe it will pick up."

"Doesn't really matter."

"Doesn't matter?"

"Absolutely not. Eventually, there will be buyers."

Someone needed to educate George about economics.

"My Dad works for US Steel in Pittsburgh," I said.

"That's great. I hope he's a union member."

"I don't think he has much choice in that. My point is that times aren't all that great for the steel companies. Steel made in other countries is priced under his product, so the company ends up with steel it can't sell, meaning it must cut prices, so profits are less. The competition can produce steel for less because its government subsidizes production. American steel companies then lay off workers because less steel gets sold."

George wasn't fazed.

"Our government should buy steel to raise the price."

"Buy with what?"

"Money."

"Money from where?"

"Raise taxes on the rich."

"The rich are making less money because industries are going out of business. So, tax revenue goes down."

"The government can print more money, distribute it to its people, everybody wins," said George.

We went on and on for a long time like that.

"I can agree to disagree," I said.

"You're just wrong," said George. "Dissent is tolerable for only so long."

He drove us to Montpelier, a beautiful small capital city with a gold domed State House flanked by a pair of ancient cannons. The warehouse lay a few blocks distant on the banks of a river. Lauren and I helped George unload the truck. Inside the warehouse dozens of unsold tables stood stacked to the rafters. Many had defects in workmanship, splinters on the seats, and nails protruding recklessly upward.

George argued with the manager when he learned no more orders were being accepted.

"You can't do that. Workers down the line need to get paid."

The manager said: "We aren't selling any picnic tables. Customers are angry because they are shitty. They return them, asking for their money back. We haven't been able to pay ourselves in the last two weeks. We're behind on rent."

"Don't pay rent. You're being exploited," said George.

"We're getting kicked out."

"Resist."

"How?"

George climbed into his truck. "I never liked him anyway. He doesn't employ any black people."

I thought for a moment. "Just how many black people live in Vermont, anyway?" I asked.

"That's irrelevant," he said. He said nothing else on the ride to Burlington. He dropped us off in front of the bus depot.

"Be out front at eleven tonight," he said.

"Good luck with your organizing," I said.

We went inside, found a payphone and I called Hawk, who wasn't there. I talked with an assistant. The conversation was one-sided. I gave names, addresses, and the route we'd taken.

"We're waiting for a pick-up in Burlington. We're not far from Canada. My guess is the border crossing takes place over the water."

Lake Champlain lay a few blocks away. It seemed the obvious route.

"What time are you going?"

"Pickup at eleven."

"OK, keep to the plan. Cross the border, then contact us again. We have some contacts within the RCMP that can meet you afterwards."

"One more thing," I said. I told him about the Greenwich Village townhouse and the bomb. I got no sense of urgency in reply.

"Think the FBI or ATF should check it out," I said.

"I'll pass it along to Hawk."

"God damn government bureaucracy," I said after hanging up.

Lauren gave me a searching look.

"Maybe you should think about staying there."

"In Canada?"

"Sure. I know people in Montreal. You could go underground. Wait out the war."

"I don't want to live in Canada. I'm sure it's a lovely place. Not my home. I'll take my chances. I trust Hawk to do the right thing."

We found a café and ate. Strolled over to the lakeshore and gazed at Lake Champlain holding hands until dark and lights on the New York side twinkled randomly. I enjoyed playing the part of a young couple on a romantic getaway. Someday we'd do it for real.

"Promise?" said Lauren.

"Promise," I said kissing her.

Back at the depot a TV with a bad vertical hold blared from a perch above the ticket counter. I ignored it until Lauren poked my ribs with her elbow.

"Look," she said.

On screen a reporter stood in front of a barrier of sawhorses draped in yellow tape. Clouds of smoke roiled from a building behind them. Firemen shouted orders and pulled hoses closer to the conflagration. At least three massive streams of water arced into the disaster. It looked like a scene from Dante's Inferno. And it looked familiar.

"That's the townhouse on 11th Street," said Lauren.

The reporter shouted into his mike. He described a massive explosion without warning in the quiet Greenwich Village neighborhood. No one had reported the smell of natural gas. The utility company was in the process of shutting off the supply.

People milled around. Most stared silently, a few seemed to be crying. I didn't recognize anyone.

"What was in the basement?" said Lauren.

I kept staring at the screen, waiting for Ted or Diana to walk away from the wreckage. I didn't want to believe what I was seeing.

"A bomb factory."

"You helped him, didn't you?"

"Up to a point."

"What point?"

"When it came time to attach the wires from the battery to the detonator."

"Then what?"

"They were going to put it in a dance hall. There was shrapnel packed into the pipe. He had it all set aside. Would have killed or maimed everybody in the room. Maybe a hundred. Maybe more."

I stared at Lauren.

"I reversed the wires. Told him to arm it before he left. It was going to be soon if they voted to do it. Mass casualties. I couldn't let it happen. I thought about Eve. I thought about the Vietnamese I killed in the war. My brother Marines coming home in body bags. I thought about calling Hawk then, but they were watching us too close. Somebody died. Ted, for sure, maybe others. I don't know. I don't know if there will be enough left to tell."

"How do you feel?"

"I'm not sure."

"Avenged?"

"No. Bear is still out there. He needs to answer for Eve."

Lauren held me for a long couple of minutes.

"I'm so sorry," she said.

Charon's Ferry

Our cross-border boat left after midnight, skippered by a young, bearded guy dressed in black coveralls and a watch cap. He wouldn't say his name. I memorized the registration number of his boat to give to Hawk. I'd call the boat a modified fishing dingy. The cabin was closed, giving us relief from the cool night air. I nicknamed the skipper Charon, after the mythical Greek ferryman who took the souls of the dead across to Hades. It seemed appropriate.

Charon smoked a joint as he stood at the helm. If he wasn't worried, neither was I. The overhead sky was brilliantly lit with stars. I used my incomplete knowledge of astronomy to try to impress Lauren.

"There's Polaris, the North Star. See how we're headed right at it? If Charon needed navigational help, that would be what he'd use," I said.

"The lake runs north and south. How difficult can it be?"

Turned out to be a little tricky as we crossed the boundary. Despite there not being a ton of security guarding it, Charon took no chances, turning off his lights and creeping along the shoreline. I would've thought a straight shot down the middle would be less likely to attract attention, but it wasn't my call.

We made it safely across the border and continued north. There were a few boats out and Charon gave them wide berth. Dawn light brightened the Eastern sky as we sailed the final few miles. I knew I was tired, but the adrenaline of the adventure keep sleep at bay. I didn't know what awaited us. The end? Or a beginning?

A small motorboat puttered out from shore to meet us. Charon gave the pilot a friendly wave and announced unnecessarily that our ride with him was over. No celebration. Take your crap and get off my boat.

Motorboat guy proved more talkative and friendly.

"I'm Gary. Been here five years. Either of you from Boston?"

"No. Pittsburgh for me."

"New York," said Lauren.

"Doesn't matter. Always looking for someone from Beantown. You hungry?"

"Starving. And sleep-deprived," I said.

"Got solutions for both problems."

He tied up the boat at a small dock at the base of a path that led up the bank to a parking lot. His was the only vehicle there. A French Deux Chevaux. Two horses. Gary's voice swelled with pride. It was air-cooled like a VW, with the same noisy rattle. He wouldn't buy an American car again. Driving into Montreal over the St. Lawrence River he pointed out the modern concrete highrise apartment complex called Habitat, constructed for the Expo 67 World's Fair.

We bypassed downtown and ended up near the campus of McGill University. Good. Among students. We'd fit in. As soon as we got caught up with sleep and got fed, it was time to call Hawk and get brought in. I thought about telling Gary we'd find our own lodging. I had lots of cash, after all. But I didn't want to act suspicious. He parked the car and led us up a few flights of stairs in an older looking apartment building.

Inside we found ourselves in a warren of activism. It was the

Collective, Canadian version. Posters themed with revolutionary slogans covered so much of the walls the wallpaper was obscured. A table in the kitchen was laden with food. Bread, cheese, and fruit. Not knowing when or where I'd eat again, I gorged until I thought I'd burst.

A serious-looking young man with a wisp of beard interviewed us. Like most of the others he wore jeans and a blue work shirt. His face carried the pallor seen only in prisoners or agoraphobics. As I repeated my carefully rehearsed story, he wrote it down in a loose leafed binder.

"What happens now?" I said.

"The committee will meet tomorrow to decide."

A thin girl with stringy red hair a bad case of acne led us to a small room with a single bed and unwashed sheets. A European youth hostel would have seemed luxurious in comparison. Too tired to complain, we fell asleep in each other's arms.

I jerked awake later. I had no idea of the time. Heard no noises, darkness ruled. Zero dark thirty again.

"What's the matter, baby?" said Lauren.

I shivered and pulled the blanket under my chin.

"I was dreaming, but it seemed so real."

"About what?"

"Promise you won't call me crazy."

She gave me a knowing smile. "About us having sex?"

"I wish. But no. In fact, I'm quite sure I wasn't dreaming at all."

She stared at me like she thought I was crazy but she couldn't bring herself to say the words. "Go on. What happened?"

"I time traveled. A bunch of times and all over the place. First, I was in high school, taking a social studies test. Pretty boring. I had to answer a question about the bill of rights in the

Constitution. True or false: The Second Amendment protects freedom of speech. Out of the corner of my eye I could see Tim O'Gara trying to crib answers off me."

"Did that really happen?"

"Sure. He sat to my right. He was always trying to cheat."

"Why do you think it was time traveling and not just a vivid dream?"

I opened my mouth and pointed to a place I didn't need to see to appreciate. The bloody gap left behind when Tim knocked out one of my teeth. He ambushed me after class for turning him in.

"I never minded him cheating before, but for some reason it bothered me that time. He caught me alone in the hall and hit me with his lunch bucket. It stunned me but didn't knock me out. I went into the bathroom to wash off the blood and started feeling dizzy. I opened the door to the toilet stall in case I needed to throw up and found myself walking through it into a strange house. I knew I'd never seen it before, but it seemed familiar, like I belonged there. There were pictures on the wall. Pictures of Eve and me. I wore a tux and she wore white. It was our wedding."

Lauren didn't speak at first. Taking it all in, I supposed. No way could she believe it unless I showed her the proof. Which I had in my pocket. I took out the photo, unfolded it, and gave it to her.

"Wow," she said at last in an emotion-laden voice.

"It seemed like a dream until I woke up next to you again. My sore mouth was a tip off and I could feel the picture in my pocket. I wish I could ask Stewart about this, but that's impossible."

"I want to know one thing," said Lauren.

"Go ahead."

"Did you make a conscious choice to come back here? To this time?"

I was asking myself the same question.

"The room had two doors. Behind the one facing me I could hear conversations. Laughter. Like a party was going on. Next to it was a mirror. A full length one. I caught a glimpse of what I looked like. It wasn't me. I mean, it was, but it wasn't. Older, gray hair, wrinkles. I'd guess maybe sixty or so. I could walk through the door and resume whatever life was going on, skip the forty years leading up to that moment. It seemed unfair, for one thing. Cheated out of the prime years of life. I turned around and walked to the other door, into a murky darkness blacker than a moonless, foggy night. Woke up here."

We spent the rest of the night clinging to each other. Too scared to sleep, too tired to leave. Lauren stroked my hair and gave me tiny kisses. I had hoped a rescue attempt would come in the night. That Hawk's team had followed us and were waiting to spring the trap. Early morning sunshine reflected off clouds high above our window. Perhaps the Canadians did things differently. I tried to reject the alternative, that the US government just wanted me gone.

"Let's go," I said.

We tiptoed past sleeping revolutionaries who didn't post guards and raided the kitchen. I took hunks of bread and a couple of bananas. We had plenty of cash, but no place to spend it creatively. We attracted no attention. I wanted to find a pay phone and call Hawk. It was time to drop the curtain on the operation.

We walked the streets until the city started waking up. I got a pocketful of change at a grocery store and called from a booth outside.

The phone rang twice, and a voice unlike Hawk's southern

twang answered. Nor was it his assistant.

"Where's Hawk?" I said.

"No one here by that name."

"Whose phone is this?"

"You tell me. You dialed it."

"Hawk has blue eyes. Light crew cut hair. A scar on the left side of his face."

A long pause. "That would be Major Diamond. He doesn't work here anymore."

"How can I reach him? It's important. National security issue."

There was no way I could avoid giving up my identity. The man listened with few interruptions as I blurted out the story.

"Can you help us?" I said.

"Where are you, exactly?"

I gave him the street address.

"Don't leave there. Don't talk to anyone. You understand?"

"Sure." Seemed simple enough. The store had a small deli. I wanted a drink to wash down the bread. The shop owner was French speaking, but not a problem for international traveler Lauren. She ordered a couple of cokes for us and we waited.

It didn't take long. In ten minutes, five uniformed cops entered the store, invited us at gunpoint to surrender. They forced us to the floor, searched and cuffed us. In the street an unmarked van waited. They put us face down on the floor and the van drove away. Lauren tried French on them, got no response except "Shut up."

They put hoods over our heads and the van lurched off. It made a series of turns before the engine noise increased to a level that convinced me we were on an expressway ramp.

"Where are we going?" I yelled.

"Shut up." Punctuated by a kick to my ribs.

The van continued at high speed. Half an hour, at least. It slowed and turned right, rolling us like loose cargo, then braked hard. The sound of jet turbines drowned out everything. The pungent aroma of kerosene assaulted my nose. We weren't just at an airport. We were on the field next to the beasts.

"We'll be OK," I said to Lauren.

I got another kick in the ribs.

The doors creaked open and a pair of men lifted me out. I couldn't tell if another team picked up Lauren. The noise of the engines didn't allow it. The men slung me onto what I sensed was a conveyor belt moving Into an airplane. I reached the top where another team picked me up and dropped me into a seat. A belt snapped closed and tightened across my lap

A voice from behind me: "Got it ready?"

"Affirmative."

"Then shoot."

I prepared for my messy execution, thinking, this better not hurt. But instead of a gunshot, a needle pierced the crease of my elbow. The pain radiated to my fingers. Whatever drug he gave, it worked fast. In seconds I felt my tongue getting thick and the darkness under the hood became absolute and infinite.

Part 3: Curtain

Velvet Prison

A silky hood covered my head. Consciousness had returned, bringing with it a dull, drugged sensation. I took stock of the situation. Aware that I sat strapped into an airplane seat, free only to breathe and wiggle fingers and toes. I smelled a human presence in the seat next to me. Tobacco and inexpensive cologne failing to mask nervous sweat. I tried to speak but couldn't because of the tape across my mouth. I had to stifle a visceral panic at being so close to asphyxia. It wouldn't take much. The South Vietnamese soldiers used to torture VC prisoners that way. Some said ours did as well. Highly effective, often fatal.

The plane descended steeply. Civilian planes didn't dive that way. The bump of landing gear and the roar of thrust reversers followed soon after. My guards unstrapped me as we taxied, handcuffed me, and hustled me down a ramp as soon as the engines stopped. A hundred steps from there they put me in an open-topped vehicle and removed the hood.

The outside light nearly blinded me, not before I confirmed that the plane was military, probably C-130 Hercules, a capacity for a hundred troops with their kit. Not the case today. I glanced at my seatmates, who stared straight ahead, outwardly oblivious to me. Their hard, lean look bespoke abilities to take me down without a sweat. They reminded me of the Special Ops recon Marines I'd seen occasionally. Men who leaped off slicks across the border in Laos to carry out sabotage, prisoner snatches, and intelligence gathering. Resistance was futile, and their attitude confirmed it.

No one minded my checking the surroundings. Distant mountains shimmered through waves of hot air baking off a desert landscape. Overhead the sky was a deep blue without even a wisp of clouds. California or Nevada.

The vehicle lurched forward and in the near distance a remote-controlled gate slid open at the touch of a button. We accelerated down a two-lane asphalt road across a pancake-flat wasteland unchanged in centuries. The breeze of passage did little to cool me. The road curved right and a boundary fence came into view. Twelve feet tall with rolls of concertina wire on top. It wouldn't keep out a squad of VC sappers but out here, miles from anything, secure enough. And perhaps the fence was designed to keep people in, not out.

We stayed within 100 meters of the fence until a group of three buildings emerged from the shimmering air above the pavement. All built of concrete without identifying marks. No windows except by the front entry. We stopped in front of the tallest of the three. I guessed eight stories, but without windows to count, who knew?

"End of the line," announced the driver.

The guards hustled me to the entry, a dark tinted double door that opened as we approached. A blast of air conditioning hit me with a welcoming smack. Ahead was a curved reception desk manned by two more generic guards. They didn't salute and they didn't speak. They wore gray coveralls without rank stripes, nothing to suggest a particular service branch. One of the two took me by the arm and pulled me through another automatic door into a hallway of pale green linoleum, matching pale green paint covering the concrete block walls. Overhead, white acoustic tile dulled the sound of his clicking boot heels. I was still wearing my government issue sneakers acquired in the Camp Lejeune brig. Soundless.

The destination lay down another corridor to the right and up six floors on an elevator. I was right about the height. The top floor was eight.

"In you go," said the guard, unlocking a door and pushing me through. He took off the cuffs and left. The Spartan décor included a bunk, metal commode and sink. I turned on the faucet and drank greedily despite the briny aftertaste. Reminded me of Quantico.

I looked around the rest of the cell. No windows, but a second door at right angles to the entry. Connecting cells? Weird. The ceiling was perhaps ten feet and adorned with two fluorescent fixtures with a dark bubble in between that I assumed was a camera. I thought about flipping the bird to whoever was watching, but merely waved.

The camera was equipped with audio. A voice blared loud enough to startle me.

"PFC Knox, stand at attention."

This seemed like a James Bond spy novel. The secrecy laughable if it weren't my life on the line. I'd rather fight some angry GIs in a bar than deal with cloak and dagger crap.

I stared at the camera.

"I'd like some answers," I said.

"You'll get them when we're ready."

"When does my trial start? Where's my lawyer? Where's Lauren?"

No answer. Only the hum of fluorescent lights.

Then, the second door opened with a click and soft whirr from inside the wall. I walked with caution to the threshold and peered into the other side. No guards. Only a short hallway that led to an unlocked door. Behind it a room decorated in government issue style. I had sat in dozens like it. Bland linoleum floor, battleship gray walls, rows of folding metal chairs arranged with precision that faced a lectern.

A woman stood on a riser behind it. The height disparity made me feel powerless, no doubt the intent. She wore a short white starched lab coat over a gray skirt. She had refined features but lacked makeup except a blush of lipstick that gave contrast to an otherwise pallid face. Her expression remained neutral, betraying a hint of haughtiness, like a royal meeting a commoner. Which was how she beckoned me: a come-here wave of her palm.

I walked to the base of the lectern, stood at ease like I'd learned in Basic training.

"I'm Dr. Marks. Ellen Marks," she said.

"What is this place?"

"A research facility. U.S. government. We study paranormal phenomena."

"I'm a phenomenon?"

"You prefer being a war criminal on trial for murder?" A smile briefly flickered on her face. Then the clinical mask returned.

"I'm neither. Where's Lauren? Where's Hawk? That SOB double-crossed us."

Dr. Marks shook her head. "Your girlfriend is safe and unharmed. No longer in custody, assuming she agrees to cooperate."

"How? Like I'm 'cooperating'?"

"You're still in custody. In her case, all she has to do is sign a stringent non-disclosure agreement."

"Then she's free to go?"

"As long as she doesn't try to find you, or hire someone to find you, or divulge anything she's seen in the last few days."

I felt light-headed with relief. Someone else could write the story and Lauren could live her life.

"Can I sit down? Get something to eat? The water was great but I'm starving."

She stepped off the riser and put a hand on my shoulder.

"Of course. How thoughtless of me. Come this way."

She led me to a cafeteria. Long tables with attached benches, a window for food service and one for tray disposal. Standard institutional layout, able to serve a hundred or more. Now it stood empty, but the smell of cooking grease hung in the air. In the kitchen she opened an industrial sized stainless-steel refrigerator. I helped myself to a carton of milk, a banana, and some crackers, then slid onto a bench across from Dr Marks.

"Better than C-rations or the slop in the brig," I said between mouthfuls.

"You aren't here for your health, but you deserve decent food."

"What *am* I here for? What's paranormal research?"

She was more than willing to tell me.

"This facility opened in the early fifties. At the time, interest in UFOs, little green men, or what have you, was high. Not in the scientific community. They knew better. A few maverick congressmen and Senators attached an amendment to a defense appropriation bill that built the facility and staffed it. They believed it only a matter of time before an alien from outer space would fall into our hands. The creature could be studied here, out of the prying sight of the press."

"What happened?"

"Naturally, no aliens ever appeared. But as you know from

your brief military career, once a government program starts, stopping it becomes a challenge."

"Like the war."

"Exactly. Eventually the mission broadened to include the study of mental telepathy, telekinesis, and time travel. The kind of things illusionists carry out in night clubs all the time. People want to believe that is possible."

"Do you?"

"No. At least not in the way popular fiction presents it. I'm a scientist. I have degrees in medicine and psychiatry from a major university. I was an associate professor on a tenure track. I had a big office, all the graduate assistants I needed, and government grant money flowed my way like the Amazon River. My research interests revolved around the study of psychotropic drugs like LSD, psilocybin, and MDA. I believed they had a future place in psychotherapy. I had many volunteers from the undergraduate ranks. Screening them for disqualifying conditions became a job for my assistants. Word got around to the students that the protocol drugs produced powerful effects they considered desirable. Eventually the wrong subjects gained admission and a scandal upended the program. A girl became psychotic and killed herself along with four others. She was the daughter of a university Regent. I was convicted of manslaughter and faced a long prison sentence. Or I could work here."

"Kind of the arrangement you're offering me."

"Face the facts, Pax. May I call you that?"

"It's my name. No more PFC Knox."

"That's how the world looks at you. Symbol of the imperialist United States. A man who killed an unarmed prisoner in cold blood."

"You talk like my ex-roommate and the people I met in New

York."

"The ones you blew up?"

I feigned disinterest but inside I boiled. What other surprises awaited me? I performed wet work for the government and my actions gave them leverage to keep me in servitude.

"Uncle Sam turned me into a killer. I learned too late that he expected me not to exercise my own judgement."

"I'm only repeating the conventional wisdom. I don't judge you. But most people do. They'd like for you to go away and not remind them about what really goes on in wars."

"Be like my Dad. Stoic, tormented by his memories. I wish I could time travel back to 1941 before he enlisted and tell him what really happens in wars, even the good ones."

"Be honest, Pax. That isn't what you want. You'd stick out like a sore thumb if that were even possible to carry out."

"Tell me what I want." I imagined she'd read my service record and my interviews with Major Crandall. I had not concealed anything."

"You think that's what a psychiatrist does?"

"I have no idea. Help nervous people. Lock up the real nut jobs. Listen to bored rich movie stars complain about how screwed up their lives are. Help queers go straight."

She laughed. A girlish giggle that evolved into a convulsion of mirth until I thought she might tear up her insides. Tears ran in twin streams down her face for a minute until she regained control and returned to her therapist's demeanor.

"I'm sorry Pax. I had no right to set you up like that and laugh at you."

"Forget it."

"I want to help you get your old life back."

"For real?"

"Yes. If you really can travel in time, it has unspeakable implications."

That sounded dangerous.

"Meaning what?"

She raised her gaze upwards, like a priest searching the heavens for a divine signal. Then she looked me square in the eyes.

"I feel like I imagine Einstein and Fermi and Heisenberg and the other physicists felt when they realized they were just steps away from being able to split the atom and unleash an incredible source of energy. The world will never be the same afterwards."

"You don't think I'm nuts."

She shook her head.

"The government does. That's why they sent you here. I get to evaluate a half dozen kooks a month who think they have magic powers. You're an embarrassment to the politicians who are trying to wage a war without winning it. Fortunately for you, an even bigger embarrassment awaits the military. Journalists have learned of a worse incident than yours and the attempt to cover it up. In the end, they'll release you after I certify that you aren't a security risk or a danger to yourself and others."

"What's next?"

"I'm going to repeat a lot of the tests you took before. I don't trust anyone but myself to perform or interpret them. Then I'm going to use chemical and physical means to push your brain into a place where you can slip across the boundary. This time in a direction that I can control. It won't be random like before."

"My friend Stewart thinks that's not possible. I'm a freak of nature."

She smiled the way a mother smiles at her child when he speaks nonsense.

"I read his interviews with Major Crandall. And I talked to him once on the phone. Stewart is a very smart young man, but confirmation bias undercuts his ability to put his ideas in practice. He takes pre-conceived ideas and picks out facts to justify them. A common pitfall in science. He's not the first or the last."

For all his genius, Stewart seemed a little flaky.

"I know he'd be all over the idea of UFOs," I said.

"He wrote a letter to this program about it. In 1959. Very precocious lad."

"He could help in many ways, I'm sure."

The look on her face told me she disagreed. I persisted.

"We were roommates before Eve died. If I'm going to be your guinea pig, couldn't he be here to give me some company?"

She didn't have to grant my request. But she needed a cooperative subject.

"I'll think about it," she said.

Testing started right away. Vials of blood, cup of urine, EKG, EEG, x-rays of my entire body. The techs kept me busy until late in the evening. Dr. Marks was long gone before my escort—guard, really—took me back to different quarters from the one where the day started. It was locked, to be sure, but more like a dorm room with Spartan but fresh furnishings. I had a desk with a small bookshelf inhabited by a collection of paperbacks, mainly detective potboilers written by guys like Chandler, Spillane, and Erle Stanley Gardner. A dresser in one corner contained a supply of khaki coveralls, briefs, and socks. Best of all: a private lavatory out of sight of the omnipresent ceiling camera. I was starving but tired as well. Sleep won out.

All the Time in the World

The techs at the facility were Dr Marks's workhorses. They operated with military grade precision, from the team that brought me from the transport to the ones who cooked the food. All wore the same uniform, had recruit-style buzz haircuts, and were non-communicative unless absolutely necessary.

The next day a tech brought me to the cafeteria and waited while I gorged myself on eggs, sausage, and pancakes made by a bored-looking tech who would have looked at home in any of the mess halls I'd frequented in the Marines. The staff had already eaten and left. I counted fifty trays piled in the dishwashing window.

The escort tech ignored my questions. How did he get his job? Volunteer or draftee? What was his duty schedule? Where was the nearest town? They smiled and said nothing.

Then it was back into test mode. Intelligence tests, personality tests, the relevance of which I doubted, but it wasn't my play to direct. Dr. Marks remained out of sight and sound. She let her underlings proctor my efforts.

I ate lunch, heavy on the grease, and waited for the next phase. It didn't take long.

A pair of techs escorted me into a cavernous white room. Two stories tall at least. In the center stood a cylinder perhaps six feet in diameter and ten feet long, like a rocket laid on its side. Dozens of cables emerged from its equator and snaked to an oversized junction box at the rear of the chamber. The cylinder was open at its front, revealing a sheeted mattress on drawer slides fixed to a pedestal in the center of the cylinder. Engineered like the hideous morgue cabinets I'd seen holding my friends' remains. A hinged hatch could be swung over the opening to close it. Next to that stood a console with multiple TV screens and a keyboard.

Dr. Marks walked into view from behind the cylinder, holding a clipboard and talking to an assistant, who also wore a white lab coat. She didn't look in my direction.

"Dr. Marks," I said.

She looked up and snapped, "What?"

"What's the plan?"

She waved to the techs. "Put him on the gurney."

I shrugged them away and climbed on without help, feet first.

"What's going to happen?" I said.

The techs tightened leather straps across my chest and legs, immobilizing me. They rolled an IV stand next to me and washed my arm with antiseptic. An assortment of large IV catheters waited on a tray next to rolls of tape.

I distracted my mind with a visual inventory of the interior. To my right blinked a panel of lights, each one centered above a switch or a dial, each marked with scientific jargon on embossed plastic tape. The techs placed a modified football helmet complete with a chip strap on my head. I caught a glimpse of its interior: wiry plastic stalks, like inverted mushrooms, had replaced the conventional padding. It fit snugly but not uncomfortably. They fastened a single cable to the crown. Visions of convicts strapped to the electric chair with a primitive version of the helmet flashed through my mind.

Dr. Marks walked to my side as one of the techs started an

IV. She had a faint smile.

"I'm sorry I'm so pre-occupied. This," she waved her hand at the enclosure, "is the culmination of many hours' work and millions of dollars. It's the culmination of my career if it works; a catastrophe if it doesn't."

That wasn't reassuring. I was the guy with the power cable next to his brain.

"What's about to happen?"

"Calibration. The helmet is an EEG transceiver. Put it on and it works like all the individual electrodes in a diagnostic EEG. The computer in the shell gets inputs from your brain and constructs a signal algorithm of voltages that will send you back or forward in time."

"Will it hurt?"

"No. You may experience some mild seizure activity."

My heartbeat jumped to its maximum.

"What the fuck?"

"No worries. You'll get a mild sedative through the IV before we start.

Out of the corner of my eye I watched the tech drawing up an injection. Milky fluid, like cream.

"I guess the straps are to keep me from flying off the tablet when you throw the switch. Are you going to yell, 'It's alive'?"

Her puzzled look told me she didn't get the joke.

"From the movie Frankenstein. I'm kidding, Doc," I said.

"Any more questions?" she said.

"A million. You're in a hurry. Let's do this and I'll ask you later."

"Just relax and count backwards from ten," said the tech.

He slipped the needle into the IV and gave me the full syringe.

I got to seven and the rush hit. Heroin had started making the rounds in Nam during my time, but I never indulged. Users described rapid onset of euphoria within a couple of seconds of an injection. I know I received a painkiller injection with my appendectomy, but it didn't compare with this.

I tried to speak, found my tongue too dry and spastic to produce more than mumbles.

"He's under," said the tech.

"Initiate sequence," said Dr. Marks.

The cylinder vibrated. I felt my muscles twitch in response. The familiar blue shimmering began. Sounds became crisp, more distinct as my vision faded.

"Reciprocal voltage detected."

"Increase the gain."

"Stay at a hundred millivolts?"

"For thirty seconds, then increase by ten every minute."

"Receiving output."

"Is the computer recording?"

"Affirmative."

"Keep the frequency under a hundred."

"The phase appears harmonic."

"Good. Standby to induce first order jump."

"On your command."

"Go."

The lights went out for an instant, then re-started as if a circuit breaker tripped and re-set the circuit. My vision came back, and a pressure wave punished my ears, like a near miss of an RPG. I found myself sitting in the cafeteria, a sandwich and bowl of soup in front of me. No cylinder, no techs, no Dr Marks. The cook stood behind the serving area, his back to me. A clock on the wall read 22:16. Military time for 10:16 PM. I had never been there at that time. The cook turned around and showed no surprise.

"How is it?" he said.

I had no idea. The bite mark in the sandwich told me I'd eaten something.

"Fine," I said.

"Heard they really worked you over today. Bet you're starving."

Before I could answer, the blue fog rolled back in. My surroundings vanished and I felt as if I were floating on a raft. Rain started falling. Lightning flashes triggered stroboscopic glimpses of my surroundings. Four walls and a roof, rows of double bunks, skin-headed boys standing at attention until the scene dissolved into a steamy cauldron that smelled of equal parts shit and dust. Something hit me from behind. I turned at the instant I realized I wasn't sitting but standing and walking.

"Knox get your sorry ass moving before the column drops us. You're a lousy excuse of a marine, even for a fucking new guy."

Sergeant Sender shoved me again with the stock of his M-16. The rain intensified.

I stumbled forward, unable to reply and knowing that to do so amounted to back talk. Not appreciated by platoon sergeants.

"Sorry, Sarge," I managed to croak.

It hit me. First week in Nam. First patrol. First day of a five-day hump that saw no enemy contact until day four. For that I felt relieved. Then scared. My own time drifts had been minutes to a few hours. I'd just gone from September of 1969 to June of 1968. Dr. Marks had built a true time machine. Could she send me anywhere and return me?

In a few more steps I received my answer. My stomach flip-flopped like I was riding a slick diving hard and to the right, levelled off and let down softly. My vision cleared as a warm breeze brushed my face while I stood staring at the chalky lines of a cinder track. On either side of me fidgeting boys in shorts and singlets. I glanced down, saw a similar outfit plus brand new track spikes, a birthday gift from my parents.

"Runners to your marks." On our right, the starter raised his gun.

Junior Olympics, twelve-year-old finals, 1962. A race I lost in a heartbreak finish. My fists closed with tension. *Not this time.*

"Set."

The crack sent the group of fifteen hurtling down the track, jostling for position. My archrival, Steven Hurley, took the lead in the first hundred yards. I moved wide to avoid tripping, saw him extend his advantage by the end of the first lap. By then I ran in a group of four, eight seconds back. The timer called out splits as we passed. Steven hit a minute ten seconds and looked not to be straining. I had never run faster than five minutes for the mile. Still, my breaths fueled a rhythm I knew I could maintain.

The next half mile served to winnow out my trailing group. I held second alone at the bell in three minutes forty seconds. Steven still led by ten yards. At this point, the first go around, I had faltered, started to sprint early, and overtook Steven at the final turn before my legs tied in knots, leaving me a disappointing fourth as he took the tape in four forty-eight. This time I focused on staying the course.

He will come back.

Back he came, allowing me to pull even on the final straightaway. I sensed him dig deep for a final charge. I answered before he began with a monstrous surge of my own. One step, two steps, three steps in front. The heat of a blast furnace seared my lungs without slowing me. The stretched tape beckoned and wrapped itself around my waist as I won.

Four-forty-six. A final lap in sixty-six, one second slower than my best quarter ever. I jogged up and down the track, fearful of fainting. Shook Steven's hand. His face betrayed the horror of losing to a runner he had dominated.

I waved to my parents in the grandstand. They jumped up and down in a manic joy. My triumph lasted one more second before the shimmering dissolved the scene, hauling me back into a blue soundless hurricane that buffeted me and in another second pinned me down. The fog began to lift, a light probed my eyes, then moved away, revealing the anxious face of Dr. Marks.

The Chronokine

"How long was I gone?" I said.

"Half an hour. I won't say any more. You are supposed to answer my questions."

"What happened?"

"Pax, you're the subject of the study. I'm running things. Debriefing begins now."

A tech rolled a movie camera on a tripod into the cylinder and after turning on some lights, started it. Dr Marks was the director, I the subject.

"I don't want you leaving things out. Tell me where you were, what you saw, what you did."

My brain overflowed with questions, but I knew better than to resist. I recounted every moment of the experience. Dr. Marks hung on every word, her eyes scanning my face like an anxious lover seeking affirmation. She didn't interrupt the narrative, holding her questions until I ended the story.

She consulted her clipboard and looked at a screen embedded into the interior of the cylinder. Using a keyboard, she adjusted the position of a horizontal line bent into a pair of sine waves. She moved a small blinking arrow by turning a dial until it rested on the midpoint of each wave form and pushed a single key each time.

"When did you say the track meet occurred?" she said.

"April 28, 1962. I'll never forget it. Especially after I won the race this time."

She pressed her index finger into my chin.

"During these excursions you need to resist the temptation to change events."

"I thought that would be the whole point. Why not change things for the better?"

She shook her head. "It's not for you to decide, Pax. I know you did it on your own before. I can't allow you to continue. I'm mapping your timeline, past and future. I don't want you to change the past. I'll do my best not to send you into a situation where the temptation will strike you. However, if you hope to be freed from here, you will carry out orders. You might think you have been discharged from the Marines, but in fact you weren't. I insist on full obedience if you are participating in the experiment. When did the incident in Vietnam happen?"

"The dates are vague. I had been there a few days. Call it the middle of May. Best I can do."

Her frown telegraphed her displeasure as she made additional adjustments to the control panel. I had no chance except to lie there passively and await my release. What seemed at first to be an exciting scientific experiment had turned into another hurry up and wait government exercise. She expected me to be compliant and participate without wavering in whatever task she created.

"Can you at least give me a rundown on how this time machine works? Stewart had a bunch of ideas. But he isn't here to explain them to me," I said.

"OK, I'll try to keep this simple. It's got a more elegant name than 'time machine.' I call it the Chronokine. Chrono, from the Greek word for time; and kine from the word kinesis, meaning movement."

"You are a natural Chronokine. Your brain cells

communicate using electrical signals. Billions of them firing at high rates. It produces a frequency unique to you. Think of it like a fingerprint. The energy travels outside of your brain just like light and radio waves. Your friend Stewart might have told you there are many parallel universes that are physically superimposed on each other but distinct as far as their inhabitants."

"Something like that. I'm fuzzy on the details. He wrote an equation that I didn't understand."

"What I'm trying to do is tune the Chronokine to your frequency and add just enough energy to deploy your consciousness to a different timeline."

"What good is that? I'm the same guy when I return."

"But you aren't. Your actions change the receiving timeline and that effects the transmitting timeline. You proved that yourself by intervening in tragedies. You gave life to dead people. That result pleases you but there are couple of reasons why I can't use this power merely to reverse individual misfortune. Developing a more complete understanding of the forces holding the universe together. Your friend Stewart would appreciate that."

"The other?"

"The US government believes the ability to place a man from the present into the past could alter the present in positive ways."

"How?"

"Anticipate natural and man-made disasters that will occur in the future."

"Like what? Another Presidential assassination?"

"Possibly. Or stave off a world-wide pandemic infection."

I didn't care to hear more. It sounded so clean and even idealistic. What could possibly go wrong? I knew very well from my time in the Nam, plenty. Murphy's Law always prevailed. And Murphy was an optimist.

Dr. Marks ignored me the next two weeks. When I asked about her, I got blank looks. The facility felt less of a prison because my freedom of movement improved. If for no other reason, location in the middle of a desert precluded escape. An unlocked door meant I could pass through. I explored as much as I could. The basement level held the Chronokine as well as laboratories and communication centers. The living quarters for the employees including Dr Marks occupied another entire floor off limits to me. Places I could go were the cafeteria, a library, a gym with a swimming pool, weight room and if I wanted, a running trail inside the perimeter fence. They let me smoke outdoors, despite Dr. Marks' specific disapproval.

"I starting smoking in the Marines when my life expectancy dropped to six months. If you let me go back, I promise I'll quit."

Her exasperation reminded me of my mother. They didn't share many other traits. She turned on her heels and returned to the facility. I dropped my Lucky Strike in the sand and crushed the butt. Noticed something I'd missed seeing before. Or maybe it hadn't been there.

A butt from a filtered cigarette. I picked it up to examine. In tiny blue letters just short of the filter: Marlboro.

A few days later I went to the library but found it locked.

I rattled the door handle, which attracted the attention of whoever was watching me on closed circuit TV. In no time, a tech approached, a surly one named Chad. We had one thing we agreed on: mutual dislike.

"What's the problem Chad? Do I have an overdue book?"

He didn't laugh. "Off limits. Head back to your room."

He gave no other information. I had no choice to comply. He

locked me in for a couple of hours, then released me in two hours.

"Stay in your room every day from two to four," he said.

"Says who?"

"Dr. Marks."

Dr. Marks wouldn't see me. Jack, another more approachable tech, said she was on a trip to Washington. Doing what, he couldn't or wouldn't say. Every day I went to the library at two until Chad or Jack appeared to lock me up. I was determined to get some answers. A plan occurred to me. The closed-circuit TV system had to have coverage gaps. The techs waited for me to go to the library before intercepting me. One day, they didn't arrive. I'd found the blind spot.

I sidestepped toward the library, back tight to the wall.

Waited.

Still, no response from the techs.

I knocked on the door. Not to request entry, but to communicate. My advanced infantry training included Morse code in case communication in the field had to performed without speech. Most Marines did poorly, but the PRC operators could handle it, so I paid attention.

A long shot that whoever was in the library could understand, much less care.

Hello my name is pax who are you I tapped.

I heard footsteps. My heartbeat was louder.

The person sent back Morse.

Chuck here are you in the experiment

Yes I can travel through time

He kept me waiting. Finally.

I knew I wasn't the first

As badly as I wanted to keep tapping, I knew I risked discovery. I sent my final transmission.

They don't want us to talk tomorrow I will slip letter under the door same time you as well

Roger that

I retreated along the wall and headed for me room via the gymnasium. I ran into Jack along the way. His face betrayed him before he said a word.

"Where have you been? Chad swears he's going to cuff you up in your room."

"Having a snack in the kitchen."

"Didn't see you on the monitor."

"Well, look."

I produced a banana I had collected at breakfast but didn't eat.

He didn't seem convinced but there was no way he could contradict me. The kitchen staff never hung around between mealtimes. They had their own quarters, their own diversions from the boredom of their jobs.

The next day I followed the same routine to deliver my message and didn't wait around to get caught after Chuck slid his under the door. This time I evaded the techs and got back to my room.

Hello Pax. Dr Marks recruited me from a VA hospital in Colorado. I had a seizure disorder the doctors couldn't fix. She brought me here and ran tests. Then she put me in the machine and sent me back in time. Crazy. Just for half an hour. I served in the Marines from 1921 to 1953. When I told her that I had been an embassy guard in London in 1923 she about went crazy with happiness. Told me I could literally save the world. She didn't say how. Do you know? Let's keep writing every day. I'm going out of my mind with boredom. Chuck Cutter USMC.

Dr. Marks returned the next day. Chad collected me after

lunch and brought me to her office. Four coffee cups stood like sentries on her desktop. Puffy eyes lent further evidence to over work and lack of sleep. A stack of computer printouts leaned dangerously to one side, threatening to collapse.

She waved me in but then ignored me as she studied a notebook for a few minutes.

Finally she spoke. "I need you back in the Chronokine."

"An order or a request?"

"Order, obviously. But you need to be an active performer. Otherwise the entire program may fail."

"More important than what I've been doing?"

"Critical to the success of the Chronokine."

"Does it have anything to do with Chuck Cutter?"

Her face blanched.

"What do you know about him?"

"I know you plan on time travelling him, that's all. He said he was a Marine guard in London in the 1920s and that you got very excited about that. What are you planning to do?"

"Make the world a safer place," she said, handing me a picture.

A multi-storied building filled the frame. I didn't know much about architecture, just enough to recognize it as European.

"What is it?" I said.

"The Grosvenor Gardens house in London."

"That's where I'm going?"

She showed me a map. A section of London, cut out from a larger document. A circle drawn in red ink made it into a bullseye.

"I want you to memorize the map in case you need to walk the final segment. When you arrive, you need to measure precisely how far you are from this building."

"Reason?"

"Not for you to know."

"Give me a small hint. It might help me if I'm off the mark."

"You're going to a different year and location. Precision counts. If the Chronokine fails to deliver you where we aim it, it makes a difference. Consider it a calibration tool."

"London, obviously. When?"

"A few days from now."

That made no sense.

"Don't give me more top brass bullshit. I had all I could stomach in the Marines."

I could see her wavering. Wanting to show how smart she was compared to her overlords in the government. After all, she had escaped a long prison term in exchange for her service.

"Chuck is old. Time travel is risky for him. I can only afford to send him out once. I need the Chronokine calibrated to an exact time and place for him to carry out his assignment."

"Which is?"

"It's classified. I've already told you more than you need to know."

"Send me in his place."

"Wouldn't work. You wouldn't fit in."

"Tell me then. I go ahead in time and return. You get the information you need for Chuck's mission. What happens next? I get to leave? Or perform more experimental work for your project?"

She lowered her eyes. I had the answer.

"We'll make history. Everyone in the project. Especially you. It's your talent I'm utilizing."

"Send me back in time. I want to save Eve from the bombing."

"I can't do that. That might affect the timeline in unexpected ways."

"Which is what you're doing, Doctor."

"I told you already. It's going to make the world a safer place. I can't allow pining for your lost love jeopardize that."

I launched myself at her, got her around the throat for a second or two before I heard a shout from behind and fists began to pummel me. I whirled around to face Chad and clocked him a good one in the face. Before I could put him away an intense pain straightened me up and dropped me. I wasn't knocked out but for a few seconds found myself paralyzed, long enough for Jack to slip handcuffs on my wrists and put his knee in the small of my back.

"Sorry Pax," he said.

"What the fuck just happened?"

"Cattle prod, sort of. Been modified for human use."

I could breathe again and my limbs weren't tingling. Dr. Marks left the room while Jack and the recovering Chad frog marched me back to my cell and locked me in. After a while, Dr Marks talked over the intercom.

"You're still going in the Chronkine to London. I don't recommend that you talk to anyone except to get the date and time. You'll just get locked up if you start raving about time travel. To be safe, I'm going to push the date ahead by a few years. It won't make any difference for the calibration. The main point is to send and return you. Don't lie about the day and year. That could kill Chuck. If you had an illusions about your services no longer being required. Forget them. There are plenty more things we can accomplish with this technology. You're going to die in this prison, but in the end you'll be famous."

London Bridge has Fallen Down

The Chronokine no longer scared me. I suppressed my fear, just as I had in combat. I told Jack to hold off on the medication. He started an IV anyway.

"Dr. Marks wants you docile. Don't need to get an electric shock just before your time jump," he said.

The drugs turned me into a peaceful hippie, more stoned than I ever felt on weed. I giggled and smiled as the helmet went on and Dr. Marks began adjusting the Chronokine's controls. I willed myself to watch and if possible, memorize what she did. The display was not complicated: two dials moved a blinking cursor over a grid composed of x and y coordinates. Location and time. I didn't know the units, but that didn't seem critical. She consulted a notepad for the task and tucked it into a slot under the controls.

I lay flat and listened to her count down the time, an unintentional mimic of a space shot. The following sequence of mechanical hammering from the Chronokine's innards, muscle twitching, and visual shimmering took place as before. The last thing I saw before blueness took over was her face, a portrait of anxious energy.

The fog became literal atmospheric fog, moist and white. As I got my bearings, people moved past and around me on a street corner. A large man nearly collided with me and looked at me with contempt, as if I were some kind of defective. He said something I couldn't understand and moved on. I had a moment of panic, thinking I'd materialized wearing no clothes, but I had the same gray jumpsuit issued when I'd arrived at the research center. I should have felt anonymous, but I couldn't shake a feeling of dread.

In front of me stood the Grosvenor Gardens building, no longer black and white as in the photo. Whatever its purpose in Chuck's time, it now looked unused. Plywood sheets covered the windows and a large chain held a barred gate closed in front of the front door. I had arrived at the right place. Now I needed to learn where I was on the timeline.

I followed the crowds, trying to blend in. Cars and buses filled the streets. I searched in vain for a glimpse of a Bobby, famous street cops of London, but to my disappointment saw none. There were a number of men in pairs carrying weapons. People gave them a wide berth, as if close contact might cause injury.

I stopped in a large square, amazed at the sight before me. A large screen, as big as any in a movie theater, towered fifty feet above the street. Color images of two people seated behind a desk alternated between filmed clips of what looked like a soccer match. I looked around for the projector that could produce such a clear image in the light of day. I saw nothing of the kind. A television? The screen was absolutely flat without a hint of the immense vacuum tube that would have been necessary in my time.

In my time.

Of course. I'd landed far into the future. Dr. Marks' warning hardly seemed necessary. I increased my pace lest the return trip began before I'd accomplished my simple mission. The TV screen provided the answer. Along the bottom, a moving strip of characters spelled out what I needed and more. The information consisted mainly of sports scores, but ever thirty seconds a time and date inscription appeared.

13:13 1 April 1999.

April Fool's Day, indeed. Footsteps in unison broke the spell. As loud as on any parade ground in the USMC. Ranks of soldiers streamed past, coming off a bridge in the distance. The soldiers didn't merely march in close order. They goose-stepped. No mistaking the gait for anything else. High stepping and with a quick tempo. Singing as well, but I couldn't make out the lyrics. After they passed, a hefty crowd of civilians followed. Curious, I joined them. Nobody spoke. I searched the faces in the crowd for someone who looked friendly, who might share a word with a stranger. No one like that existed.

We stopped in view of, but a long way from, a castle.

"What's that?" I asked the man next to me.

He stared at me, bug-eyed, and said, "Buckingham Palace," before he vanished in the crowd. A mixture of terror and disbelief.

I moved through the crowd, which yielded easily, each person shying away from contact. Ahead, spotlights illuminated a large fountain in a plaza. The soldiers had settled behind a fenced off area that I assumed held VIPs. The citizenry remained well behind it, but I squirmed forward until I reached a vantage point just below the balcony. I assumed the Queen or a major leader like the Prime Minister would appear. Did England still have a monarchy in 1999?

My attention drifted to the palace walls framing the balcony. Two large portraits flanked it, easily seen in the spotlights. They were of the same person. I didn't recognize the face. Why should I have? Not my country, after all. A middle-aged man dressed in a military tunic, with intense eyes beneath a unibrow of black hair. Some general, I supposed. Freshman year I took European history. Big help.

The band paused and the doors above me opened. A man walked forward to a podium, mounted it, and gazed over the vast crowd. The next thing he did stunned me to my core.

He raised his right arm, extended it up and forward away from his chest. I didn't need to look behind me because the sound made by several thousand arms imitating his movement was enough. Flags rolled beneath the portraits dropped open and I felt weak enough to faint, were I not suspended without support already.

"Sieg Heil! Sieg Heil! Sieg Heil!" the crowd chanted.

The flags ruffled in a slight breeze. Taunting me. Swastikas. The emblem of the long ago defeated Third Reich. What madness had overtaken the world?

The speaker started his address, in German, and I retreated through the rapt mass of people. They appeared transformed, robotic, somehow just not human. I needed to get away quickly, before something happened to prevent my return to the Chronokine. I despised the project, but I needed it more than ever. As I feared, a disturbance broke out at the rear of the throng. A man stood in the fountain, waving a British Union Jack.

"Fuck the Nazis! Fuck New Britain! Join the Resistance."

A second man joined him, waving a pistol, and echoing his outcries. A smattering of approval arose, then was drowned out. Opposing factions formed and collided with a keening frenzy. A skirmisher reached the flag waver and tried to tear loose the flag. Two quick shots put him face down in the water. The mob surged at the men. A final shot ricocheted harmlessly off the fountain and the pair vanished beneath the scrum.

Club-wielding bobbies beat a path through the mayhem and

emerged with the pair. Four bobbies lifted the first over their shoulders and walked forward. The man's arms and legs flopped in the familiar dance of the dead I'd seen so often in the Nam. Two more bobbies marched the second protester, still alive, to a black van that screeched away, siren moaning, after the they loaded the corpse aboard.

The mob took out its aggression on the flag, now laid out in the street. Flames licked away after they soaked it with gas.

"Sieg Heil! Sieg Heil! Sieg Heil!" they raged. I couldn't erase the image of what I'd just witnessed. I didn't need details of the calamity unleashed by Dr. Marks' intervention. The end result spelled the end of civilization. I took shelter in a park until the blue haze enveloped me, signaling my return to the as yet unsullied present of 1969.

The Plan

Jack wheeled me into Dr. Marks' office. I felt drained of strength and my mind recoiled from the enormity of what I'd witnessed.

She looked concerned. A sign of humanity long overdue. She dismissed Jack and checked my blood pressure and pulse.

"Seems OK now. The techs said you were incoherent and raving about something when you returned to the Chronokine. What happened?"

"I was in London. The year was 1999. April 1st at one-thirteen in the afternoon. I materialized at Grosvenor Square, just as you said I would."

"I know where you went. What happened? Did you interact with anyone?"

"No. I walked around in a crowd. I asked a man about a castle and he said it was Buckingham Palace."

"Exactly right. You were less than a mile away. Thirteen hundred meters, in fact. We calculated date and place of arrival well within the margin of error. I'm pleased."

"Now you will send Chuck off on his mission. To London."

"Didn't take much for you to figure that out."

"What if?" I stumbled over my words.

"What?"

"If something goes wrong."

"Such as?"

"He can't do whatever it is you're sending him to do. Make the world a better place."

"Nonsense. He's reasonably healthy for his age. He'll have instructions. He's a United States Marine. Like you. He'll carry out his mission to the letter."

"Wait here," he said.

"What if initial conditions aren't the same?" I told her what Stewart had told me about changing events in the past. It might not be as simple as one might like.

A smirk wrinkled her face and she laughed. "Your friend Stewart. The boy-genius who went through shock therapy. He's what we call a savant. One talent that makes him seem superhuman, where in fact he's quite ordinary in most respects. And deficient in others. I told you I'd had contact with him. He's a flake, as your generation would say."

Unexpected tears burst from my eyes and I slammed my hand on her desk.

"You don't understand. I saw Nazis in London. Germany must have won the war. They were goose-stepping, shouting 'Sieg Heil' and they murdered a couple of protestors."

"I suppose Hitler himself stood there and made a speech?"

"No. Some other guy. His face was on a poster. I didn't recognize him."

Dr. Marks pushed a button on her desk. I knew what was coming. I tried a final time.

"Why don't you delay Chuck's mission. Give it more thought. If you really want to get rid of Hitler, you want things to go perfectly."

"The Chronokine project has been on the drawing board for quite some time. We use a scientific approach at work. No guessing involved. We've created models that quite accurately predict what will happen. There will be other missions to alter the arc of history. This is the first."

Jack and Chad came in. I got out of the wheelchair and went with them.

"Give him a mild sedative," said Dr. Marks. "He's still quite stressed after his experience."

When we were down the hall far enough to be out of earshot, I tugged Jack's sleeve.

"I need a smoke in the worst way," I said.

He shook his head and grinned.

"Dr. Marks hates that you do that."

"There's nothing to do here. I'll quit someday. Just not right now, right here. She's right. I'm super stressed and I need a smoke to calm down. I'll take the sedative too."

Chad scoffed and let go of my arm. "He's all yours to coddle. I'm going to watch some TV."

Jack got my cigarettes from my room and let me out into the exercise yard. Except for a small spotlight, darkness ruled. Overhead the stars had emerged. To the east a full moon had started to traverse the heavens. It produced ghostly illumination of a distant mountain range, the only interruption of the sandy plain populated by cacti and sagebrush.

"I promise I won't try to escape," I said.

He laughed at my usual joke.

"Knock when you're ready. I can't stand the smell," he said.

I lit a Lucky and took a deep drag. If Chuck's smoking habits mirrored mine, he'd come out here in the morning before breakfast. The pattern of his extinguished Marlboros told me he stood next to the fence, due east. I think he liked sunrises. I usually stayed by the door because morning air in the desert bothered me with its chill. I couldn't recall ever finding one of his butts anywhere except by the fence. I hoped he'd remain a creature of habit. I had two Luckies left in the pack. I put them in my pocket and tore open the pack. With the pen I'd swiped when I banged on Dr Marks' desk, I scrawled a message while I stood under the spotlight, my back toward the walls. I buried the pack with the red Lucky logo facing up, covered all but the circle with sand. No way he could miss seeing it. But would he pick it up? Turn it over? I hadn't prayed since a nasty mortar attack in Danang right after I arrived in the Nam. Tonight, I prayed again.

I also hid the sedative pill I'd pretended to swallow and the paper clip off Dr. Marks' desk.

In the morning I asked to see Dr. Marks. Request denied.

"Why?"

"She's in Washington."

"When will she be back?"

"Two days."

They let me out in the yard at 10 for my morning smoke. I lit up and casually strolled toward the fence, not wanted to appear anxious. High on the wall two windows in the techs' quarters could provide a vantage point for somebody wanting to spy on me. Tinted windows, making it impossible to see in.

I walked a crooked fifty feet getting to the spot. My heart stopped. The pack was gone. In its place a Marlboro box. I squatted and leaned against the fence, legs splayed, and I slid to the ground, box trapped under my legs. In a minute I stood again and transferred it to my hip pocket.

Back in my room I read Chuck's reply.

I'm supposed to go AWOL from London in 1923. Travel to Bavaria and shoot Hitler when he tries to overthrow the govt. Suicide mission but I don't care. You say it backfires and Dr. Marks won't believe you. Tell me your plan and I'll work with you.

With Dr. Marks gone to Washington we had time. Chuck and

I used the cigarette pack post office twice more to set up our plans. All I needed to know was which tech would be watching the closed-circuit TV screen on the night we planned to move. That turned out to be easy. Jack told me when I told him I was through smoking.

"That's great. We should celebrate tonight. I'll bring a bottle of Scotch to your room and we can drink a toast to your improved health."

Evidently Dr. Marks hadn't told Jack I'd be in prison for life.

Jack showed up at around ten with the Scotch and two glasses with ice. I made a big show about being the bartender. He never saw the powdery fragments of my pill fall into his drink. The Marines I'd met in advanced infantry training had told me about making Mickey Finns to get a girl so drunk she'd pass out and they'd have their way with her. Disgusting, to be sure. I had other plans for Jack. Just a good night's sleep, followed by a court martial for falling asleep on watch.

At midnight I made my move. The paper clip lock pick was another trick from advanced infantry. I'd had two days to get competent, so I had the door open in no time and the same for Chuck's.

He looked like a Chuck. Over six feet, blue icy eyes, crewcut white hair, perpetual smile, bone crushing handshake.

"Welcome aboard, Sergeant Major," I said in a whisper.

"How'd you know my grade?"

"Good guess. You served long enough."

"OK, enough chit chat. Let's get this party started," he said.

First stop: the laboratory. Between us we held enough practical knowledge to build an improvised explosive with the materials at hand. Acetone, hydrogen peroxide, and hydrochloric acid combined to form a nasty, unstable explosive called acetone peroxide. Careful handling would allow us to place it inside the Chronokine. I'd light a fuse before departing and blast it to hell.

I wrote a note to Dr. Marks explaining the unintended consequences of her historical meddling and promising to make sure she'd never get the project started in the first place. I slid it under her office door as we made our way to the Chronokine.

By 4:00 AM we had things ready to go. I put the helmet on Chuck and started the Chronokine. I didn't know how much warm up to give electronics, so I waited five minutes.

"Pax, you'd better get busy. I have a nervous feeling about this," said Chuck.

"Everything will be fine," I said, but I had the same kind of butterflies.

One last adjustment of the instrument panel, double check the display for distance and time direction, and I flipped the switch.

A blue glowed enveloped him and his legs twitched a little. I didn't know what to expect. For the second time in as many days, I prayed.

The blue intensified to white, nearly blinding me, and then he vanished, leaving the helmet spinning randomly on the platform.

"Goodbye, Chuck," I said out loud.

"What the hell is going on? What do you mean by that?" said Dr. Marks.

She emerged from shadows, flanked by Chad. He held a .45 caliber Colt model 1911. Standard military issue. Its muzzle ready to pour fire into me. Five minutes had turned out to be too long after all.

Dr. Marks held up the note I'd left.

"Are you out of your mind?" she said.

"Are you out of yours?" I replied, trying to keep the edge out of my voice.

"You just ruined an effort to prevent the most catastrophic event in human history," she said, shaking the paper like she intended to kill it.

"I was there. Killing Hitler does nothing to stop the war. In many ways the outcome is worse. I only saw the tip of the iceberg. I'm sure the full picture is worse."

"My simulation shows otherwise," she said.

"Simulation?"

"I have access to the most powerful computers in the world. I ran multiple models of the likely effects of removing early Hitler in his career. 99.9 percent probability of success."

"Dr Marks, I can't argue math or statistics with you. I know what I saw. I also know what happened in Vietnam when my commanders listened too much to intelligence experts who claimed to be able to predict the positions of the enemy. Lots of dead Marines."

"Chad, put him in cuffs and lock him away. I'll decide what to do later," she said.

Chad might have a military background, but not one like mine. One look at him told me he'd never killed a man. That didn't make me proud, but it made me prepared. He advanced taking cautious steps. He kept the .45 extended, finger on the slide as trained. I closed in until I knew a left arm reach could grab the barrel, then I raised my right arm. His gaze flickered toward the feint and I grabbed the barrel with my left hand, twisting it backwards until the joint pain released his hold. I hammered him across the face with the handle and he fell backwards. The sound of his skull impacting the floor told me he was out for the count.

I leveled the .45 at Dr. Marks, who dropped to her knees, palms held meekly skyward. I didn't want to waste words or time. For all I knew more techs were on the way. I cuffed her behind her back and shoved her to the floor, then went to work. I laid the explosive to the rear of the Chronokine, thinking the blast wouldn't gravely injure Chad. I pulled him and Dr. Marks over by the elevator.

"Don't move," I said.

I dropped the magazine from the .45, noted Chad hadn't even chambered a round, put the mag in my pocket and put on the helmet. The fuse I'd rigged had an estimated thirty second delay. I lit it and worked fast at replacing the settings to pitch me back in time to September 1969, then lay flat, waiting for the shimmering.

"God damn you!"

Dr. Marks leaped over me and reached for the controls. The bitch had slipped her cuffed wrists under her feet and now could use her hands. I grabbed her right hand and pulled with all my strength. No effect on her. She resisted with a strength fueled by extreme stress. I smelled the fuse burning, out of sight but not mind.

A soft popping sound from the back of the Chronokine warned that the bomb had reached the edge of detonation. I pulled as hard as I could, hitting the "GO" button just before the hand of an invisible giant knocked Dr. Marks backwards. Blue starbursts blinded me, and the world went dark.

Re-entry

I saw only blurs but heard without trouble.

"He's coming around," said a female voice.

"I'm surprised," said another.

"Pulse ox is 94 on two liters."

"I'm not dead," I said. I tried to sit but couldn't.

Laughter. "No, Mr. Knox, you aren't."

"I need to pee," I said.

"No, that's the catheter in your bladder."

My focus sharpened by degrees. Two shadows became two people. They wore white. One blonde, one dark-haired. The blonde moved to the side. The dark-haired one spoke.

"Mandy, you can finish your charting. I'll talk to him."

Features appeared. Smooth skin, brown, almond shaped eyes, narrow mouth, petite chin, black hair pulled back. Not Dr. Marks, but female in a white coat with a stethoscope draped over her shoulders.

"Where am I?" I said. My dry tongue stumbled over the phrase.

She offered me a cup with a straw. I drank half of it, grateful for the care.

"Same place you've been the past few days."

I looked around. Walls covered with neutral wallpaper featuring abstract grass tufts. A window beyond my feet featured a view of just blue, cloudless sky broken only by the contrail of a distant jet. A television braced to the wall played silently. Two figures on the screen spoke to each other as a ribbon of text played across the bottom. The words meant nothing. Cool air bled into my nose from a plastic tube encircling my neck. Fabric restraints held me down. An IV line ran from my left wrist to a plastic bag suspended by a hook. A metronomic beep in the background was, I realized, synchronized to my heartbeat.

"Hospital. Tell me its name. Tell me your name," I said.

"Walter Reed National Military Medical Center. I'm Doctor Nguyen. Amy Nguyen."

I again tried to sit, but a sharp pain in my side stopped me.

"Sorry. Your chest tube will limit movements until we pull it out."

Chest tube. Grunts with collapsed lungs got those if they made it as far as the evac hospital.

"What? I got shot?"

She smiled and shook her head.

"You're on strong painkillers. I think it's messing with your memory. Don't worry, everything is fine."

If I was on painkillers, they weren't helping much.

"Bad news?" I said.

"I'm afraid so. A lifetime of smoking has consequences."

"Lifetime?" I got a bad feeling.

"We removed your right lower lobe. Took out the entire cancer. No sign of spread, thank God."

"Yeah. Thank God."

She checked the chest tube drainage and made stabbing and swirling movements on a plastic tablet. She turned it far enough sideways to reveal a miniature TV screen covered with printing, like a newspaper.

"We can pull the tube out today. It's been clamped for a day and there is no sign of air leaking back in. That will make you happy. You can start getting up and going to therapy."

"I have a question. Doctor…....?"

"Nguyen."

"When did you get here from Vietnam?"

"1975."

"With your family?"

"Me, two brothers and my mother."

"What happened to your father?"

"He remained behind. We never heard from him again."

"I know this sounds dumb or crazy. My memory is for shit, pardon my language. The war ended in 1975?"

"Yes. The Americans left in 1973 except for a small number of advisers. The final days were chaos. Helicopters flying from the American embassy to carriers in the South China Sea. North Vietnamese tanks driving up to the Presidential Palace. I didn't witness it. Saw it in newsreels."

My throat got very dry again.

"What year is it now?"

She smiled like she was used to stupid questions.

"Twenty-seventeen."

"I have another question."

"Go for it."

"Is there a mirror in here?"

She wheeled a bedside tray over my lap and flipped the tray up to reveal a small mirror inside the compartment.

I did my best to prepare for the shock awaiting me.

My hair had gone full gray. Creases ran across my face like mini-fault lines. Several days' worth of gray stubble completed the picture of an aged vagabond. The realization continued to impact me. Dr. Marks' final struggle had succeeded in altering the direction of time travel but not the displacement. Although I hadn't been anywhere on earth in the last forty-nine years, I'd aged and developed lung cancer as if I'd smoked the entire time.

After a few more days, the hospital discharged me to an extended care facility. I realized that I was withdrawing from nicotine. Really wanted to smoke in the worst way. The doctor ordered a patch that diffused nicotine through my skin and the cravings diminished. A fancy new kind of aspirin controlled my pain. I waited for a government agent to arrest me, but nothing happened. Another veteran told me about the pardon given to draft dodgers and deserters. I realized that nobody would come looking for me. Freedom belonged to me, paid for with anonymity.

A social worker talked to me about placement. Nothing on my record indicated a home address, which puzzled her. My parents long dead. It was as though I had dropped out of the sky into the hospital. I didn't let on that was exactly what happened.

"Can you locate a man named Stewart Lone? Friend from college. I know he went to Cal Tech, worked as an academic in astrophysics."

The social worker returned the next day.

"I found your friend. He said he's glad you're doing better. He wants to talk to you. He doesn't work at Cal Tech anymore."

"MIT, I suppose?"

"Not exactly."

She handed me a piece of paper.

Stewart Lone
Hanover Middle School
Falls Church, Virginia
703-248-5660

I called and felt a wave of relief hearing his voice.

"You work at a middle school?"

"I had a psychotic breakdown a long time ago. In my fifties. Maybe it was the pressure of my research. Or something else. Not sure. Ended up in a psychiatric hospital. All kinds of treatment. Drugs. Electroshock. I got help and crawled back into reality. Found out I loved teaching, especially young people. Got this job and it's great. I don't have to retire."

His voice cracked. I waited for him to compose himself.

"I'm sorry I never tried to contact you, Pax. The system swallowed you up. My own troubles consumed me."

"It's OK, Stewart. I mean it. Guess what?"

"What?"

"I time traveled to get here."

He fell silent. I guess the shock of it all left him speechless. His voice returned in a whisper.

"Oh my God. Say it's not so."

"You won't believe how crazy."

"Speaking of crazy. Before I really flipped out, I had a lot of dreams about you. Seemed so real. I began having delusions. That was the breaking point."

I didn't want to unload the entire story right then. I had plans.

"Stewart, it's almost summer. I'm guessing you get vacation."

"Sure, I do."

"I've had some health problems, but I'm getting better for the time being. I need help, I need to get a place to live, and I want to travel a little."

"Tell me where you are, and I'll come get you."

Reunions

Getting settled didn't require a big effort. Stewart owned a four-bedroom house he admitted was a mistake.

"I thought I might get married and need the space. Relationships are hard. I'm a solitary animal."

He had thrown his excess energy into creating a beautiful piece of property, inside and out. The yard was immaculate. Bermuda turf grass groomed to golf course standards, framed with century old bricks laid in a sawtooth pattern. A mature magnolia shaded the front walk, azaleas and day lilies competed in beds to be the Best in Show. The rear yard featured a screened gazebo overlooking a Koi pond with the corners anchored by a pair of flowering crabs. A nursery groomed by professionals wouldn't look as good. My room faced the back yard. Every morning sunrise woke. I started walking for exercise, even tried jogging. Checkups at the VA didn't find any residual cancer, but I anticipated eventual trouble. I wouldn't sit around waiting for it to happen.

Stewart helped with the nuts and bolts of integrating me into a world I found stranger than fiction. I needed a passport. I needed a social security card. Turned out the military bureaucracy had pigeon-holed my status, never formally discharged me. I guessed that making me invisible kept the Chronokine project under the radar as well. A search online for Dr. Marks turned up little useful information. That eased my mind about my past returning to spike my plans.

"What plans?" said Stewart.

"I'll tell you after you drive me to the airport."

Not being able to walk to an arrival gate bugged me, but I knew the reason. I managed to keep my emotions in check until I spotted the redhead walking off the bottom of the escalator. Tears erupted as we flew into each other's arms and kissed.

"I love you, Lauren. Will you marry me?"

"Wow, you sure don't waste time, Marine. Can I have a drink first?" she said.

We drove to a quiet bar near Stewart's and we sipped beers as she brought Stewart up to speed.

"I ended up back in journalism. Got married, had a couple of kids, got divorced, traveled around on my divorce settlement. Tried looking for you, got nowhere. Drank myself into oblivion. Got sober, wrote a couple of books, and one day Stewart sent me an email. Here I am."

We made love in my bedroom.

We lay in the afterglow, holding hands.

"I know you're on borrowed time," she said.

"The doctor said she got all the cancer out, but I'm not buying that, In the event I don't make it, you get my meager estate and some memories different than the way it turned out before."

I had a plan.

My passport took a while to acquire because of my odd status. I claimed amnesia from war injuries, which satisfied the government. Gave us time to plan an actual wedding. Right in Stewart's garden, him as my best man, Lauren's daughters as co-maids-of honor.

The honeymoon choice raised eyebrows.

"Vietnam? You can't be serious," said Stewart.

"It's where we met, after all. I hear it's as beautiful as ever, and as long as one doesn't step on an old land mine, safe."

I admit, the flight into Hanoi raised goosebumps.

"For them, it's been over forty years. For me, almost last week."

Stepping out of the plane relieved my anxiety. The odor of jet fuel, but none of the Danang shit burner stench. No one looked twice at me. More than a few Vietnam vets landed with us. They wore baseball hats with unit identification badges. Their nervous chatter quieted when they set foot on the tarmac. Warriors returning to make their own peace with the past.

The government mandated professional guides and interpreters. After all, democracy had never sprouted from the revolution. Not-too-subtle propaganda paraded before us as we toured museums and memorials. I mentally closed off my eyes upon seeing displays featuring the twisted wreckage of American jets. The victors get to write the history, I reminded myself. The people made up for the official coolness. They greeted us like long lost family, which we were in a twisted, paradoxical sense.

The city retained much of the architecture and Old-World atmosphere created by the French colonialists. Autos continued to be far outnumbered by bicycles and motor scooters. The crush of people never ended. Evidence of growing Western influence showed up in billboards advertising familiar consumer products: images of sneakers, jeans, beverages, and the like assaulted the eye. Air pollution from thousands of coal-fired stoves added to the burden on my respiratory tract. I wondered if the authors of the conflict would be able to recognize what their sacrifices had wrought?

I showed the guide the address I wanted to visit, along with a bribe to loosen him. He smiled, took the cash, and hailed a taxi.

I rolled down the window so I could savor the olfactory crush produced by humidity, cooking oil, frying fish and rice. This time I wasn't hunkered down in a foxhole praying a low flighted round wouldn't take off my head.

Our destination lay just outside city limits. Despite the passage of time, obvious bomb craters dotted the countryside. Farmers and their families shared the duty of maintaining the rice paddies that occupied the rest of the land. A sight that hadn't changed much in hundreds of years. I looked at Lauren and shrugged.

"Humanity is nothing if not resilient," she said.

The driver stopped in front of a high-rise apartment complex and pointed to one of the buildings. We got out with the interpreter, who led the way. The building had all the earmarks of a public project: low maintenance hedges served as boundaries for narrow sidewalks leading to each entrance. Some units had window air conditioning; others left windows wide open. A parking lot held only a dozen or so cars, a couple hundred bicycles and mopeds.

We entered building number six and slid into an elevator with an elderly couple carrying grocery bags filled with fresh produce. The interpreter said a few words and the couple smiled, bowed to us and got off at the third floor.

We stopped on seven and at unit 7333 the interpreter knocked on the door. In a minute, the door opened, and we entered a hallway covered with well-trodden carpet over hardwood. The reason for the trip stood squarely in front of me. A slim, slightly stooped man with thick but fully white hair. He bowed and said a few words.

"His name is Phan An. He is pleased to again meet the brave American soldier who spared his life," said the interpreter.

We sat in his kitchen and drank tea Phan had just brewed. It was sweet but with a hint of boldness. Phan apologized for the state of his home, which to me looked immaculate. His wife had died six months ago and keeping up the place taxed his energy.

"I am happy to see you after all this time and to meet as friends, not enemies," I said.

Phan related that after his capture he underwent interrogation by Americans, which he felt certain saved his life. Then he lived in a POW camp near Danang until the NVA invaded in 1975. Life there was difficult, but not nearly as much as life as a soldier fighting the Americans.

"You had powerful weapons that we feared. We could only prevail by choosing the time and place to fight. I felt no hatred for you or your comrades. We were soldiers obeying orders. The war ended, I came home and tried to make a life for myself. My wife gave me four sons and I am proud of them all."

He looked all around the room for a few seconds before speaking through the interpreter again. The interpreter cocked his head to the side and asked Tran a question for passing along his statement.

"Phan wonders if you ever dream about the afternoon you captured him."

"Yes, often in fact."

A look of relief crossed his face.

"Then he hopes what he has to say has meaning for you. He has two distinct dreams. In the first, he is passing through the forest and senses your presence but can't locate you. You fire your weapon, and the burst takes him down. Before he dies, he looks up to heaven and he sees you suspended in the air above him. You look sad and distressed. He wants to speak and reassure you that you merely did your duty as he tried to do his.

"In the second dream, he again passes through the forest but this time you capture him, take his pack and rifle and return with him to your unit. He wants to know: which version do you believe actually happened?"

I don't hesitate. "Phan knows they both are true. Fortune smiled on us both at the second encounter. I came to Vietnam an angry young man. I return older and at peace."

Day of Reckoning

When we returned home, a surprise waited.

Stewart handed me a phone number. "This guy called you. He claims to be an old friend. Knew you in the Marines."

"He give a name?"

"Hawk."

Lauren and I exchanged astounded looks. A man I wanted to thank before I throttled him into unconsciousness. The embodiment of ambivalence. I couldn't forget the betrayal in Montreal but I could forgive it.

I called the number, a local area code. Figured he'd be a retired colonel or general by this time. Maybe an adviser to one or the other political party, an expert on cable news shows.

He picked up right away.

"Hello, Hawk. Or is it Diamond? Or do you have another real name?"

"Diamond. How was your trip to Vietnam?"

"Still have sources in intelligence?"

"That part never retires. I'm not active, but I know people."

"You'll forgive me for not thanking you about our reception in Montreal. Or didn't you hear about it?" I said.

"I heard. I'm sorry. Sorrier than you'll ever know. If it had been up to me, your freedom would've begun that day. I got overruled and by the time I got into a position to do anything, they'd taken you to the research facility. The My Lai shit hit the fan, and nobody wanted you on the street."

"You say you know people. Did they tell you what happened to Dr. Marks?"

"She's alive. Never did any more work on the Chronokine project. The explosion blinded her, left her brain scrambled from the concussion. The government got spooked, shut the place down and used it for tank target practice."

"I'm not sorry," I said.

"No reason to be. Didn't learn what she intended to do with you."

I decided to keep the secret for leverage if I ever needed it.

"Can you help me locate another participant? He's older than I and maybe passed away."

"Name?"

"Chuck Cutter. USMC."

"Hang on a second." I supposed Diamond could access a database from his smart phone.

A minute later he came back. "Got a pen and paper?"

"Fire away."

"Section 2, grave 994, Arlington National Cemetery."

My eyes misted up.

"When?"

"February 20, 1945. At Iwo Jima. Posthumously awarded a Medal of Honor."

He wanted his life over. I wondered what he tried to change. If his soul rested in peace.

"He was a good man. I'll tell you more if I get the chance."

"You will if you agree to see me. There's more but I can't tell you over the phone."

"You'll have to kill me."

"Exactly."

Diamond arrived in half an hour. He had aged less than

anyone I knew so far. Same crew cut, grayer, same steely blue eyes. Walked with the look of coiled tension. He didn't waste any time, pulled out a packet of photos and tossed them on the table.

"Andrew Barrett III. I believe you're acquainted with him."

"Indeed."

The photos all showed Bear at various ages since I'd known him. Most were fuzzy and poorly focused, probably shot with a long lens. The newer ones were in color.

"How did you get these?" I said.

"I know people, as I told you. Barrett fled to Cuba after he bombed the building at Blaze. In those days, a lot of radicals took the trip. One by one they seemed to tire of the socialist paradise and left. Some went to other Soviet bloc nations, some returned to face the music at home or try to live under assumed names. Barrett stayed. He found employment with the highest levels of the government as a specialist in what we call wet work."

"He killed people for the regime."

"You're being blunt, but correct. He's semi-retired now. Runs a charter fishing boat in the Bay of Pigs. Little tourist town called Playa Larga. Fidel had a place not far away. Rumor has it when one of the inner circles ran afoul of the boss, Barrett took the guy on a fishing trip from which he never returned. Counterrevolutionaries have short shelf lives in Cuba, even after all these years."

"Why didn't your agency take him out?"

Diamond shrugged. "Not for lack of interest. American foreign policy doesn't condone assassinating US citizens without compelling reasons."

"Blowing up a college building doesn't qualify?"

"In the words of someone you'd recognize but I won't identify, that's yesterday's news. You'd be surprised how many sixties radicals ended up in the State Department."

"Shit. Hell." My inner Marine thought of lots of other words to use but didn't.

Diamond rubbed my shoulder. "I'm sorry for your loss. Can I tell you how you can do something about it?"

"Let's have a drink," I said.

Playa Larga

It's a beautiful day to die.

A blue canopy stretches to the horizons. The sea surface shimmers without concealing coral sand, broken only by dark masses of coral teeming with an aquatic community. My boat rides on the interface, rocking in a slow swell.

Later today, rising air masses will roil the atmosphere, sending cumulonimbus clouds into the troposphere. Rain showers and squalls will menace fishermen. Tourists back in Playa Larga will seek cover in their hotels or walk over to any of a dozen bars happy to serve them cheap local beer. The rain will keep the jungle green and cool the air. Same as it has for hundreds of years.

I won't be joining them. It's my last day on earth. But first, I need to kill a man.

Getting to Cuba, and specifically to the Bay of Pigs, took effort. Being seventy explains it in part. Last year I lost part of my right lung to cancer. A pink crescent scar shows where. Great White shark bite, I joke. The polite ones look away.

The truth is, not a Great White but 365,000 little whites, did the damage. Cigarettes, I mean. A pack a day for 50 years. Fifty years in which I took no active part but my body absorbed the damage of a bad habit. The death certificate won't blame cancer. I refuse to give the illness that satisfaction. Do I regret it? Sure, I do. But I chose it and I'm not going to pitch a fit about how unfair life is. Not like a lot of my brothers-in-arms, although I understand their point of view. The country they fought so hard to protect has turned into a mass of tribal misfits looking for excuses as to why their lives turned out so poorly. If you aren't a victim, just wait a minute and you can become one.

My condition requires that I travel everywhere with an oxygen cylinder. It's green to distinguish it from other compressed gases. A plastic tube runs from the regulator into a set of prongs that fits in my nose. I can carry a small tank in a backpack. It's good for a couple of hours before it runs out of gas, just my Pittsburgh Pirates last season. When I need an all-day supply, I use a larger bottle, which I pull on a mini-hand truck.

The agency that booked my trip happily certified my medical need for oxygen. Major Diamond saw to that. Despite special attention given to tourists in Cuban medical clinics, rationing reduces the supply of drugs and treatments. Looks like the Cuban medical system still has wrinkles. I signed a waiver. Couldn't get a tourist visa otherwise. Truth is, I can get by without it, but I enjoy skipping long lines whenever and wherever I can.

I travel unaccompanied. Lauren agreed to let me go alone. Hard not to. Our reunion, no matter how sweet, must end in sadness. We fly to Miami, rent a convertible, and drive to Key West. Neither of us has been there. She patiently explains over drinks on Duvall Street the meaning of a bucket list. Later we make love for the last time, lacking some of youth's vigor but none of the passion. I can still make her happier than a cat in a yarn shop. The next morning, we return to Miami and say goodbye at the airport, then I ride an electric cart to the American Airlines gates. I find a large crowd of American tourists. The fascination of visiting a previously forbidden land has stirred romantic notions in my fellow baby boomers. For some of them revolution is a drug. Others are checking it off their own bucket lists. My seat assignment puts me next to a friendly and talkative married couple.

The plane reaches cruising altitude in no time at all before the slow descent to Havana. A wall of tropical turbulence shocks the passengers from complacence to panic. The plane drops a thousand feet in a few seconds. I flash back to the Nam, recalling chopper flights taking fire and diving to the deck to evade the stream of AA fire. The memory fades but the dive continues. Passengers scream for their lives.

We level out; flight attendants scurry to comfort the afflicted. My seatmates hug each other and order drinks. I pass on the offer for free booze. Through breaks in the clouds the island appears. Verdant and lush, like Vietnam without groundfire. The runway looms below, and the flight ends on a good note.

I deplane in the middle of the pack. The mix of jet fuel and tropical humidity greets me like an old friend. Charcoal cook stoves in villages next to the airport add a smoky fragrance to the mix.

My seatmates ask about friends or a guide meeting me.

"Neither," I say.

"We're staying at the Hotel de Sevilla, if you get lonely."

"Thanks."

Before we separate at Customs, we exchange handshakes. In my college days we could have been friends. We had much in common then. Nothing anymore.

After I clear Customs, I find my way to a transit station and board a bus bound for the town of Playa Larga on the Bay of Pigs. The current generation of Americans knows little or nothing about what happened there, but Cubans will never forget. It's like asking a Bostonian why Massachusetts celebrates Patriots Day. In 1961, the US CIA sponsored an invasion of Cuban exiles that attempted to depose Fidel Castro, whose band of guerillas had toppled the Batista government. Soon after the Soviet bloc adopted him. This didn't sit well with Red-hating Americans, considering that Cuba was a short 90 miles away. The invasion was easily defeated and the propaganda value of humiliating the imperialist Yankees was exploited. I always wondered if JFK's decision to proceed aggressively in Vietnam was not in some way influenced by the disaster. When in a hole, the best move is to stop digging, of course. Hindsight is always 20:20.

Playa Larga itself played little role in the battle. Most of the fighting took place at Playa Giron, located at the mouth of the bay. Both locations have museums according to my guidebook. The easing of international tension brings more Europeans and Americans to Playa Larga for the warmth, azure water, fishing, scuba, and snorkeling. The bus ride is about 150 kilometers and not stressful. Fully air-conditioned for valued tourists like me. I have a pocketful of US dollars to guarantee all the help I need.

The bus stops in front of a squat cement block square building adorned with a small sign: Deposito. A short line of passengers bound for Playa Giron mills about. According to the guidebook my hotel stands 500 meters away. Half a klick. I could walk but I need to recon the address Major Diamond provided, so I hail a taxi.

When I show the driver the address, he shakes his head. I anticipated that. I flash a hundred-dollar bill and he reconsiders. "I'm an old friend," I say, hoping to reassure him.

"He expects you?"

I consider my choice of replies. I prefer being as honest as possible. Lying takes too much energy. "He has for a long time, but my arrival will surprise him, I hope."

He nods without smiling and we depart. It's not far, he says.

I give him another hundred to take care of my luggage.

"Keep it in your trunk. Come back in half an hour, *por favor*."

"He is probably out on his boat, Senor."

"I can leave a note."

The cab disappears in a cloud of blue exhaust. The 1960s era Ford needs new rings. I walk in the shade, avoiding puddles from the most recent rain. I don't want to leave footprints. The first obstacle is a six-foot-high brick wall around the property. I feel reasonably fit for a 70-year-old with lung cancer. The thought of confronting Bear provides all the motivation I need.

Using some fortunate toeholds between the bricks I clamber over the wall with a modicum of exertion. The builder didn't put broken glass on top or install razor wire. Any thief foolish enough to burgle this residence would pay mightily for his boldness. I dust off my shirt and visually check for security cameras. Not seeing any reassures me to a point. Major Diamond told me cameras ranged in size from cigar box to martini olive. A miniature lens with a live feed to the local cop shop could bring trouble fast.

The house features a Mediterranean-style villa look rather than a colonial hacienda. A torrent of Bougainvillea exploding up the walls and around the balconies. A crushed coral central walkway bisects a Bermuda grass lawn. A serpentine driveway swings past the entry before circling to the rear.

Seeing no further benefit in stealth, I walk to the door and ring the bell. Inside the house, chimes echo and fade. I wait thirty seconds and repeat. Still nothing. No scurry of steps. No voices. Go time. My bent paper clip method lets me enter in thirty seconds.

I close the door and listen for an alarm, but silence reigns.

So much the better. Always the careful guest, I remove my shoes.

The entry hall ends at a locked door, which I ignore for the moment. On either side of the hall are open entryways to living and dining areas. They hold no interest for me after I make a quick inspection. Wealthy patron artwork covers neutral-colored walls. A glass coffee table holds architecture magazines and a copy of the notorious Madonna book "Sex." Curious, I open it and find a personal inscription from the author.

A helical staircase spirals skyward from the living room and I follow it to the upper floor. Three bedrooms, three baths, and a large office/study. That's what I came for. Diamond shared a grainy photo grabbed by a miniature camera. A floor to ceiling window showcases the Bay of Pigs and the distant Caribbean.

Dead center of the rear wall sits a built-in bookcase divided into thirds.

In center hangs a 16x20 black and white photo of Bear. Recent because his naturally black hair has gone all white. Ditto the full beard, a mature version of the one he sported as a young radical.

Surrounding Bear are 5x7 pics of the company he keeps. Posing with Fidel and Raul Castro, naturally, and some lesser lights in uniforms I don't recognize. A cavalcade of celebrities smug with the swagger of the enlightened, showing off their connection to a romantic revolutionary. Ted and Jane, Angela, Huey, DeNiro, DiCaprio, Oprah, to name the ones I recognize.

The right-hand section features photos of Bear with a dozen or so nubile beauties wearing the briefest of bathing suits. I wonder what happened to Allison. The left-hand section contains behind glass an armory any collector would envy. A Who's Who? of international firearms. AK-47, AR-15, Browning Automatic Rifle, Colt 1911 .45 handgun, Thompson submachine gun,

Glock-17, Barrett M82A1, FN FAL 7.62, Heckler & Koch P2000 9mm and MP5 submachine gun, M1 Garand .30 caliber rifle, Nambu 7mm pistol, Luger p08 9mm. Perched above them all, hard to ID for sure but I have an opinion: a 6.5 mm Carcano 91/38. The rifle used to assassinate JFK. A replica, to be sure. Had to be a lot of them floating around in the early 60s. Next to it I find what I came for: the chrome-plated Colt Cobra he had at Blaze. I take it out and spin the cylinder. Empty. I change that status with six Federal .357 Magnum 125 grain cartridges from a filing cabinet and one more small modification. It fits nicely in my waistband, covered by my tropical shirt.

Would he miss the revolver? No idea, but doubtful, unless I leave obvious signs of entry or if the cabbie talks. In that case, nothing can save me. I plan to book an early morning fishing charter because he has similar plans at 8 AM. Before I leave, I stop for a look at the master bedroom. Befitting a man of importance, it boasts a king bed, walk-in closet, flat screen TV of 60 inches or more and a view of the water. I stand on the balcony, imagine him there every morning, master of his fate. His home for the last 40 plus years. Behind the scenes muscle for Castro. Now, with travel restrictions eased, a little more vulnerable.

I leave through the front gate. The cab idles there as promised, and we drive back to the hotel. I slip the driver another hundred. For his discrecion.

"In the morning. 6 AM, I need to charter a fishing boat." I say, and he nods.

"Si, Senor."

"I am going to challenge *Oso Negro* to a fishing contest."

His eyes bug out. He must be asking himself how crazy is this Gringo? But he doesn't turn down the cash.

"Si, Senor." He leaves in a blue haze.

Check-in follows. I hand over my passport for inspection and sign the register.

Even this end of the earth village hotel has a bellman. He hauls my suitcase, and two oxygen bottles up the stairs because the elevator is *descompuesto*. I tip him twenty and let him leave before I flop on the bed. It's five in the afternoon and the heat of the day wouldn't quit. I nap for twenty minutes until activity on the waterfront gets me up. Boats returning. I can look out the window and probably catch a glimpse of Bear.

I stare at the docks. Binoculars would help, but I don't have any. A robin egg blue boat has just tied up. That's the right color. The stern swings around to face me and I can make out the boat's name: *Che*. Of course, it couldn't be anything else. Then, he appears. Taller than the average American. Here in malnourished Cuba, a giant. Yes, the hair is white but full. Hemingway beard too. No stoop in his gait. Carries a couple of bait buckets to the gunwale and leaps to the dock with ease. For a moment I envy his health.

Andrew Barrett III. Bear. In Cuba, *Oso Negro*. Black Bear. *Oso Blanco* now. My body aged fifty years in the two I've lived since Eve's murder. I don't mind a suicide mission. I have tracked him here to even a score. Life for life. Then I can die. Will die, of necessity. Escape not an option.

A couple of middle-aged Americans follow him. He calls to the dock crew and they take a swordfish and a couple of mahi mahi from a cooler. Someone will have a good meal. They give Bear plenty of attention. More so than a typical guide could expect. He tips the crew from a money clip and walks to a nearby Vespa. He kick-starts it and spin-slides out of the parking lot.

Darkness falls like a curtain here but the streets stay quiet. No night life to speak of. Playa Larga is not Cancun. A few locals laugh and call out to friends. In the distance, roosters engage in a nocturnal crowing contest. On a weeknight, expect nothing out of the ordinary. I drift off to sleep and battle the usual dreams from the past. Some, I now believe, are portals through time. If one led me back to December 1967, I'd leap through in a heartbeat. No such luck tonight. I wake to pee at 3 AM, tell myself I should be assaulting Bear's house right now. Zero dark thirty again. Waiting is pointless and stupid. He could be on his way over now. Take one of his weapons and go all OK Corral here in downtown. He wouldn't ask the police to do it. For a guy who never served in the military, he's showed the right instincts before. Nothing will change that. I'll be careful when I walk out the front door.

At dawn, the roosters won't shut up. The sulfurous stink of exposed mudflats and dead fish herald low tide. I find a café and force myself to eat huevos rancheros on top of a pain pill. Do I want a Mimosa? Si Senor. The fresh orange juice tastes zingy from the snap of sparkling wine. I get a nice buzz that mingles with the opiate.

A nervous looking Cuban sits in one of the moored boats. I want him on edge. More likely to comply. I wave him over and introduce myself. He has more than a passing resemblance to my cab driver. They are cousins. Family ties are good for business, even if it's the Gringo who visited *Oso Negro*. We agree on a price. I don't haggle because, well, what's the point?

He starts the twin engines. They rumbled as he makes a few trips to the dock to transfer gear and bait.

"What's been biting lately?" I say.

"We catch mahi mahi, some red snapper, maybe swordfish."

"Tarpon?"

"Not where we go, Senor, unless you want to go up the

river."

I shake my head. Bear will be in the Bay later, and our business can't wait. I need only a hat, sunglasses, and the spare O2 tank. Some lucky villagers can have my luggage. I'm ready to go.

The fisherman's name is Eduardo. Born in 1962 in Santa Clara. I compliment him on his boat. Only ten years old. Twin hull, powerful diesels inboard. Faster than the *Che*, he replied when I ask. I casually ask more questions about Bear. Eduardo shrugs. Yes, he knows him, a little. He brings in clients from Havana that are connected. Strange that they don't want to ride in a nicer boat like his, but he's not going to make issue. Plenty of business for everyone these days. He asks if I ever met President Obama.

"Great man," he says.

"I'm not political," I say.

Eduardo takes me out to where he was killing it yesterday. Naturally, we don't get a strike in the first hour. Story of my life fishing. He offers me a cigar and I accept. I don't inhale. No need with a Cuban Parejo. I haven't smoked since before surgery. The nicotine rush makes me shake like a leaf. Cross Cuban cigars off my bucket list.

Second hour we catch four small fish that Eduardo tosses back in. He promises *mucho grande* fish. I give him a thumbs up and pull a beer from the cooler. It goes down smoothly. Feels like 90 degrees on the water. My senses need reorganization after the cigar assault. I scan the Bay with Eduardo's binoculars. In ten minutes I get a surge of emotion when I spot the blue dot that has to be Che. I tap Eduardo on the shoulder and point.

He gives me a WTF look. A rising panic replaces his earlier casual demeanor. Nobody in his right mind messes with Oso

Negro. I pull a hundred out and tuck it into his pocket. I point again. "Change course for that boat. *Mi amigo*," I say.

Eduardo shakes his head. "Is big shot. No friend of you."

I pull out the Cobra and point it at Eduardo. I want to see a look of terror in his face to signal compliance. To him, the muzzle must look like a 16-inch cannon on the USS Wisconsin.

I let the Cobra drift away from Eduardo. "That man is a friend. From way back. In America. I need to talk to him out here. Doesn't involve you. Once I get with him, you take his client back to Playa Larga."

I give him a few more direct instructions in case Bear decides to run or do anything other than allow me to board. Even if he tries, his piece of crap boat can't outrun this thing. I did my homework.

Eduardo agrees not to disobey or pull any funny stuff. I suspect he'll take the money and hide. Let his taxi driver cousin take over the charter boat business for a spell. We take a heading that looks good to intercept Che in about fifteen minutes. I check my O2 tank one final time. Connections tight. Just need to twist the red knob and flip two toggle switches.

Eduardo slows the boat as we pull within a hundred meters. Bear does the same, no doubt wondering what our intentions were. An emergency? Uncertainty becomes my ally. I pick up a grappling hook, taking care to coil the line properly.

"Let me talk," I say to Eduardo. I don't know enough Spanish to apologize. He nods, face now ashen. We pull parallel to Che and both skippers put their engines in neutral. I swing the grappling hook overhead and cast it across the gap. It lands dead center of the cabin and with a few hand-over-hand moves, I pull us gunwale to gunwale. After securing the line I toss the O2 tank over and follow.

I aim the Cobra at Bear. Cock it for dramatic effect. His expression runs the gamut from curiosity through surprise to fear. I brace against a chair in case he guns the engine. I motion with the Cobra for the passenger to jump into Eduardo's boat. He understands and leaps across. I toss the grappling hook overboard and the boats drift apart.

Eduardo gives the engines full throttle and roars toward Playa Larga. Bear kills his engine, and the soft lap-lap sound of the waves provides background.

He says something in Spanish.

"English, please," I say.

"Who are you? I saw you on my security video."

"Look closely."

He does. Still, no recognition.

"Do you know who I am?" he says.

I could just proceed. It shouldn't matter. Except that it does to me. I need his acknowledgement. Too late for apologies or mercies. Last chance.

"I can run fast. No bear has ever caught me."

A long pause. His mouth opens, jaw slack.

"Pax?"

"That's right."

Bear slumps in his Captain's chair, hands in his lap. I don't want to give him time to think, to plan, so I talk fast.

"Nice place you've got," I say.

"Glad you liked it. Gun theft is against the law."

"That's how you got it."

"You're thinking it's poetic justice to shoot me with my own gun?"

"Justice, yes. Let's leave the poetry out of it. Your hero, Che, was something of a poet, yes?"

"He didn't write poetry. His poetry was in the revolution."

"An unfinished life."

I know he wants to stall. Something in me wants to give him a last shred of hope before kicking it away. His gaze flits about, past me and at the shore. Perhaps a patrol boat has responded to the mayday call I expected Eduardo to make. I don't care. Nothing can spare Bear.

"I read about you, Pax. Not a very heroic life. War criminal and all."

"I got pardoned. You didn't. Why don't you come back to America and stand trial? I'm sure after all these years we could find an unbiased jury."

"I'd be crazy to think the warmongers who have taken over would allow that to happen."

Bear raises his gaze higher. I hear the low drone of engines in the distance. The rescue party. I'd let them get a little closer. I point the Cobra at Bear.

"Want to choose how you die? Two taps to the head?"

"Go fuck yourself." Bold talk from a dead man.

"I know what you're thinking. You removed all the firing pins from the weapons. Crazy not to. Invitation to murder you. You forgot I know as much about guns as you."

He leans forward. He needs to rush me. Grab my wrist before I shoot. I know how sick I look. I can't win a hand-to-hand fight. I don't need to. The oxygen bottle has a valve held closed by a cotter pin, like on a grenade. I need to pull it and twist the valve. Solid state circuits and a two kilograms of military grade C-4 will do the rest. Diamond gave me the option of a time delay. Plant it on his boat. I declined. I want no chance of a slip up. The enemy gets a vote.

The patrol boats arrive. Two of them. Military police in

abundance, all armed with AKs. Bear smiles. He shouts a command in Spanish.

"Kidnapping is against the law in Cuba. I told them not to shoot you," he said.

"You want to do it."

He gives a little shrug. "Perhaps. But we have due process. Trial first."

I toss the Cobra overboard. "Don't need it anyway."

I grasp the valve and pull out the cotter pin.

Bear stands up. No escape. Panic crosses his face. The patrol boats are doomed. No witnesses. Diamond will find out anyway.

"This is for Eve," I say.

I turn the valve and flip the switches. The world explodes into a blue sunset.

Restoration

I open my eyes in darkness. On my left a luminous dial tells me the time. 3:22. Zero dark thirty. The phrase holds no meaning, yet it popped into my mind. I think I've been dreaming but I can't recall about what. I hear snoring from across the room. A gentle rise and fall that I recognize. The name Stewart drifts into my growing awareness of person, place, and time. I'm not Stewart. I'm Pax and he is my college roommate. We attend Blaze College. The window above his bed frames a solitary star. One I recognize but can't name. I'm supposed to know because I must pass an examination. Astronomy 101, a class at Blaze College requires that. Stewart sits next to me there. I have known him since the first day of college.

I awake more fully, and all manner of facts rush through my mind, so fast I can't catalog them, but I know I can recall them now if the need arises. The star in the window is in fact the planet Jupiter. The date is December 23rd, 1967. The knowledge stirs a memory, but it's without form or attachment. I've just arrived from a warm place. That can't be right. I'm from Pittsburgh.

I rinse my mouth from a glass on the bedside stand. Next to it a pill bottle. The label reads *Paxton Knox. Phenobarbital 100 mg. Take three at bedtime*. I take the pills for seizures. Something else too. Can't put it together at first. One by one, memories return. I'm not like everybody else. Endowed or inflicted with a crazy ability no one would want.

I need to sit and compose myself. I'm in control of my

faculties. A tableau of crazy but connected experiences flashes through my consciousness. Time travel. It's real and I've experienced it. Right now, I can't focus on the details. A manic need to move forward and act consumes me. At the same time, my body can't respond.

I don't want to wake Stewart, so I turn over and try to sleep. My skin feels sunburned. I touch to confirm, and I recoil at the sensation. A persistent ringing, like summer Cicadas, shrieks an alarm in my ears.

Deep sleep returns until Stewart shakes me so hard, I almost tumble out of bed. Jupiter no longer sits in the window. A blue sky replaces the blackness. I don't want to believe my alarm clock. Three o'clock. Afternoon in the blink of an eye.

"Get moving, Pax. Final exam for astronomy in half an hour," says Stewart.

I sit up. "Yeah, I know."

"You made noises all night. I tried waking you once. Didn't help."

"Stewart, is my face sunburned?"

He slips on his glasses and peers in my direction.

"I'd say so. Definitely pink."

I slide into my jeans and see for myself in the mirror. He's right. It's weird.

"I feel out of it today," I say.

"Maybe you should postpone the exam."

"Can I do that?"

"Go to the health service for a doctor's note."

I think about it. Decide not to. I need the semester to end today, catch up with Eve before she leaves for Charleston. A crazy thought rattles my mind. A dream that ended right before Stewart woke me. I hesitate before I share it. It will bug me all day if I don't.

"You're kidding," he says after I tell him.

"It felt real. I slept with a girl named Lauren. I told her I loved her more than anyone."

Stewart pushed his glasses back. "Do not tell Eve. I don't have a girlfriend, but if I did that would never be something I'd talk to her about."

"I don't know a girl named Lauren."

"Doesn't matter. I think the medication is doing things to you."

I take the astronomy exam and regret it right away. I can't retrieve facts without major effort. As if I'd heard the lectures years, not weeks before. A mental fog hangs over everything I do. I walk around the quadrangle, unable to shake my disquiet. Chance, or so it seems, takes me to the Math building where I first met Eve. It's open and for a change without the standard demonstrators. Their handmade picket signs lie scattered like autumn leaves. My vision blurs but nothing happens. A sense of morbid dread surrounds me. Telling me to escape, run now and don't return.

I have no place to run. Eve is at the hospital. Stewart has commandeered our room to study Spanish, the only subject that gives him trouble. I need to find a friend, fast. An idea sprouts. I jog back to my old dorm and knock on David Rono's door. Most of the students have left. Overflowing trash cans sit unattended in the halls. A nasty odor from nearby reminds me of visiting a long-dead aunt who hoarded cats.

David opens the door in his monogrammed bathrobe, always elegant in his choices.

"What's going on?" I say, not wishing to interrupt.

For once he lacks female company. Maybe that explains his

unhappy expression. No matter, he invites me in and brews tea. That stirs a memory of something but like everything else, the trail of recognition remains cold.

"I don't drink tea normally, but for some reason the idea sounds great," I say.

"What's on your mind?"

I lay out the peculiar train of thoughts and feelings that started earlier.

"In some ways, I feel that I'm following an old path," I say.

He laughs. "Déjà vu."

"I know what that's like. This is different. I feel that it should be familiar, but it isn't. Like I took a road trip in the past and am repeating it, but nothing looks familiar." I hesitate to bring David into my confidence. One more person to worry that I'm psycho.

"Oh Pax, you have your whole life in front of you. Don't worry about such things. It's all chemical, or so my friends who take drugs tell me."

"Speaking of chemicals, are there cats living here?"

The question amuses him. "No, but I know what you're talking about. Like urine. The smell appears to be coming from next door. Your old room."

"I can't imagine Bear taking care of an animal. He's so self-centered."

"Perhaps his girlfriend?"

"Maybe. I know she has off-campus friends living on a farm. I think they call it the Collective."

I feel a chill after saying that.

"Help me, David. Is that right? Why should I even know about it? Funny things are flying in my mind."

"I never heard it called a collective. Just the farm. I'm sure a lot of cats live in the barn. Strays and feral animals. She has a kind heart, unlike Bear," he says.

"You've been there? I say.

"One time with Missy. She met with a person who knew how to get the abortion."

"Did she go through with it?"

He smiles, shakes his head. "We had a long talk, after you and I talked. What you said made sense to me. Why restrict our choices to what others tell us we must do?

Maybe it's the tea or maybe being around David, but things are beginning to click in my brain. I think of actions without clear purpose. Measures that an inner force commands me to do.

"David, do you have a car?"

He owns a retired cop car, a Crown Victoria, complete with black and white panels. He doesn't question my request that he drive me to the farm. I believe a step toward my destiny waits there, but I don't dare to share the thought. I'm self-conscious about talking crazy. I don't know how far the urge will carry me, only that I must obey it. Sunset is past, twilight retreats into darkness. Despite that I recognize landmarks I know I've never seen. This isn't the route in from Pittsburgh or the way to Washington. A church with a peculiar steeple, an amusement park whose roller coaster stands just off the road, a truck stop with a fifty-foot-tall T. Rex in the parking lot. All look familiar even if they shouldn't.

David swerves on a narrow two-lane highway to avoid a white panel truck crossing the center line. I swivel around and watch the taillights vanish around a bend. I want to tell him to turn around and chase the van. I know a connection exists. At the same time, I can't take shortcuts. I need to follow the path of my memories.

We follow a pair of tire tracks through a field. David keeps the pace up to where he risks breaking an axle. He must be caught up in the journey's drama. Before I have the chance to tell him to slow, we arrive. There stands the barn, next to a rundown farmhouse, unlit, doors open, cats darting out of our way.

"I've been here before. I came with Bear," I say.

"When?"

"Tonight, but years ago."

"I don't understand," says David.

It's time to tell my story. I remember everything and spill out the high points for David. I jump out of the car and run inside the barn. I know what I will find. The stink of ammonia and diesel fuel in the straw spread across the floor. Bear must have gotten it on his clothing preparing for tonight.

"It's an explosive. Fertilizer called ammonium nitrate and fuel oil form a mixture capable of tremendous power. It sounds crazy, David. I've traveled through time. I'm re-living an event I thought remained in my past. Irretrievably lost. Bear and his radical friends are going to park a van in front of the math building to blow it up as a war protest. They don't know or don't care that my girlfriend Eve will be standing on the steps."

Now I've put it out there. David's normally cheerful face looks drawn.

"I don't know what's going on, Pax. You aren't one that tells fables. I trust you. Whatever is causing this, we'll get to the bottom of it."

We climb back in his car, get turned around and head back out the tire track trail only to encounter a pair of blinding headlights blocking us. David turns to evade them, and our front end drops into ditch from which he can't escape. He kills the engine, and we wait for Bear to make the next move.

Bear taps David's window with the Cobra's barrel, short but

full of menace.

We exit, hands held high. Henry opens the rear doors and Bear motions with the Cobra for us to lie down on the stinking pile of ammonium nitrate. A tangle of red and black wires runs to detonators buried in the explosive from a controller next to the front seat. We lie face down as he binds our hands behind us. David and I are shoulder to shoulder. I want to talk to him, but I don't want Bear to realize I'm able to.

Henry drives and Bear talks over his shoulder.

"Something weird last night. I had a dream. You and I were on a boat. Bluest water I've ever seen. You were so old I didn't recognize you. You pointed the Cobra at me. I had friends coming to help. You dropped the gun into the water, and the boat exploded. Can you explain that?"

"It wasn't a dream. I blew you to hell for what you did—what you are going to do—tonight. If I must live another lifetime, I'll come back and do it again."

"Didn't know you dropped acid, Pax." Bear laughs and waves the gun around. "The human brain is a crazy organ. As far as getting blown to hell, you can send me a postcard when you arrive."

Henry drives the lurching van across the field to the county road and accelerates. I whisper in David's ear, knowing the road noise will muffle our voices. Bear turns on the radio, then switches to an eight-track tape.

It's Buffalo Springfield singing *For What it's Worth*. Perfect. I'd sing if my mouth weren't so dry. It's hard to see landmarks from where I'm lying but I need to be ready for David's circus act. I hope his supple body can pull it off.

We reach a stoplight and I know it's the first of three before the campus. Where are the cops when you need them? No reason to stop an ancient van on a day when most of the students have either left or are studying for finals.

Henry turns right and momentum rolls David on his side. I start my role in the effort by rolling him on his back. I fear that Bear will look around and see us, but he's focused on other things. We hit the second light. Probably going over the arming sequence for the bomb. David flexes his hips and drags his bound wrists behind his knees, inching toward his ankles. I can't help him at all. It's a question of natural flexibility and mental endurance. His wrists pass under his feet and rise in front of him. I flip over and he unties me. I do the same for him. The van stoops at the final light and turns. We're a hundred yards from the math building.

The van stops and Henry puts it in park, engine running. I figure they need juice from the battery to detonate the bomb. I nod at David, who throws his arm around Henry's neck and yanks his forearm high and tight under Henry's chin. At the same instant I push Bear's head hard into the dashboard and hold it there. The impact creates a satisfying clunk. I snatch the Cobra from his slack hand and jam the muzzle into his ear. In a few seconds he starts moving around.

"Hold still or your brains will go out the windshield," I say.

The van stands directly in front of the math building. I look for a white bike and see one leaning against the stairs. Perfect timing. Henry remains unconscious from the choke. He's not going to be a threat. I keep the Cobra on Bear until David exits from the side and pulls Henry out. He starts waking and crying like a baby. David puts a foot on Henry's neck.

I motion Bear to get out.

"Keep your hands up, move slow or I'll put all six into you."

He obeys and lies face down next to Henry. David ties them

both and turns to me with a huge grin. I give him the gun, saying, "If either one tries to get up, shoot him."

I bound up the stairs and enter the building. In the background the janitor's radio plays Marvin and Tammi.

When I burst into the computer center Eve pirouettes to face me, angelic in all white. We slow dance in time as the music ends. I kiss her for as long as she'll let me. She is laughing now.

"Baby, you act like you haven't seen me in years."

"I haven't, darling," I say, picking up the phone to call the cops. Eve and I walk to where David guards the prisoners.

I roll Bear over. I need to see his face. It's twisted into a malevolent leer.

"I lived in a different reality before today. One that's beyond my powers of reason to explain or understand. I turned into a caricature of you, full of hatred and violence until the power that possessed me gave me the ability to change back to myself. Life doesn't give second chances to many. I'm lucky in that regard. You'll spend a lot of years trying to figure out where you went wrong. I hope you find the answer."

Sirens approach. The sky lights up with red and blue strobes. Dawn lies hours away. I pray that we will find our way in the darkness.